Robert Crais is the author of seventeen novels, including the international bestsellers *The Watchman*, *The Last Detective*, *Demolition Angel* and the Edgar-nominated *L.A. Requiem*. He has two additional Edgar nominations as well as Anthony and Macavity awards for his series of Elvis Cole and Joe Pike crime novels. His thriller, *Hostage*, was made into a major motion picture featuring Bruce Willis. To learn more about RC, join him on Facebook at www. facebook.com/TheRealRobertCrais, or visit his website at www.robertcrais.com.

By Robert Crais

The Monkey's Raincoat
Stalking the Angel
Lullaby Town
Free Fall
Voodoo River
Sunset Express
Indigo Slam
L.A. Requiem
Demolition Angel
Hostage
The Last Detective
The Forgotten Man
The Two Minute Rule
The Watchman
Chasing Darkness
The First Rule
The Sentry

the
sentry

ROBERT CRAIS

An Orion paperback

First published in Great Britain in 2011
by Orion
This paperback edition published in 2011
by Orion Books Ltd,
Orion House, 5 Upper St Martin's Lane,
London WC2H 9EA

An Hachette UK company

A CIP catalogue record for this book
is available from the British Library.

Printed and bound in Great Britain
by Clays Ltd, St Ives plc

The Orion Publishing Group's policy is to use papers that
are natural, renewable and recyclable products and
made from wood grown in sustainable forests. The logging
and manufacturing processes are expected to conform to
the environmental regulations of the country of origin.

www.orionbooks.co.uk

For

Clay Fourrier

*From River Road to
the top of the Hollywood Sign,
my wingman chasing
the dreams.*

*With love, admiration,
and more than a few feverish beads.*

Acknowledgments

Writing is solitary, but bringing a book to life requires a team. The author would like to thank Patricia Crais for her hard work and long hours improving the manuscript, and Lauren Crais for legal research and information.

Additional thanks go to Steve Brown for sharing his knowledge of the Venice Canals, as well as for providing guided tours and contributions to the story.

Marilyn Ducksworth, Michael Barson, and Matthew Venzon proved themselves to be the best in the business. Their efforts and innovative ideas were not only outstanding, but inspirational. Thank you.

Dittos to Kate Stark and Lydia Hirt for pushing the author and his work into emerging realms, and to Ivan Held and Neil Nyren for their belief and commitment.

In the UK, thanks go to Tim Hely Hutchinson,

Jon Wood, Juliet Ewers, Helen Richardson, Susan Lamb, and Malcolm Edwards.

Also, thanks and respect to Aaron Priest and his team at the Aaron Priest Literary Agency—Lucy Childs, Nicole James, John Richmond, and Lisa Vance—for building it bigger and making it happen.

And for my friend, David Thompson, a book and a margarita.

New Orleans
2005

MONDAY, 4:28 A.M., the narrow French Quarter room was smoky with cheap candles that smelled of honey. Daniel stared through broken shutters and shivering glass up the length of the alley, catching a thin slice of Jackson Square through curtains of gale-force rain that swirled through New Orleans like mad bats riding the storm. Daniel had never seen rain fall up before.

Daniel loved these damned hurricanes. He folded back the shutters, then opened the window. Rain hit him good. It tasted of salt and smelled of dead fish and weeds. The cat-five wind clawed through New Orleans at better than a hundred miles an hour, but back here in the alley—in a cheap one-room apartment over a po'boy shop—the wind was no stronger than an arrogant breeze.

The power in this part of the Quarter had gone out almost an hour ago; hence, the candles Daniel found in the manager's office. Emergency lighting fed by battery packs lit a few nearby buildings, giving a

3

creepy blue glow to the shimmering walls. Most everyone in the surrounding buildings had gone. Not everyone, but most. The stubborn, the helpless, and the stupid had stayed.

Like Daniel's friend, Tolley.

Tolley had stayed.

Stupid.

And now here they were in an empty building surrounded by empty buildings in an outrageous storm that had forced more than a million people out of the city, but Daniel kinda dug it. All this noise and all this emptiness, no one to hear Tolley scream.

Daniel turned from the window, arching his eyebrows.

"You smell that? That's what zombies smell like, brought up from the dead with an unnatural life. You get to see a zombie?"

Tolley was between answers right now, being tied to the bed with thirty feet of nylon cord. His head just kinda hung there, all swollen and broken, though he was still breathing. Every once in a while he would lurch and shiver. Daniel didn't let Tolley's lack of responsiveness stop him.

Daniel sauntered over to the bed. Cleo and Tobey shuffled out of the way, letting him pass.

Daniel had a syringe pack in his bag, along with some poppers, meth, and other choice pharmaceuticals. He took out the kit, shot up Tolley with some crystal, then waited for it to take effect. Outside, something exploded with a muffled *whump* that wasn't quite lost in the wind. Power

4

transformer, probably, giving up the ghost, or maybe a wall falling over.

Tolley's eyes flickered amid a sudden fury of blinks, then dialed into focus. He tried to pull away when he saw Daniel, but, really, where could he go?

Daniel said, all serious, "I asked you, you seen a zombie? They got'm here in this place, I know for a fact."

Tolley shook his head, which kinda pissed Daniel off. On his way to New Orleans six days earlier, having been sent to find Tolley based upon an absolutely spot-on lead, Daniel decided this was his one pure and good chance to see a zombie. Daniel could not abide a zombie, and found their existence offensive. The dead should stay dead, and not rise to walk again, all shamblin' and vile and slack. He didn't care for vampires, either, but zombies just rubbed him the wrong way. Daniel had it on good authority that New Orleans held quite a few zombies, and maybe a vampire or two.

"Don't be like that, Tolliver. New Orleans is supposed to have zombies, don't it, what with all this hoodoo and shit you got here, them zombies from Haiti? You musta seen something?"

Tolley's eyes were bright with meth, the one eye, the left, a glossy red ball what with the burst veins.

Daniel wiped the rain from his face, and felt all tired.

"Where is she?"

"I swear I doan know."

"You kill her? That what you been tryin' to say?"

"No!"

"She tell you where they goin'?"

"I don't know nuthin' about—"

Daniel hammered his fist straight down on Tolley's chest, and scooped up the Asp. The Asp was a collapsible steel rod almost two feet long. Daniel brought it down hard, lashing Tolley's chest, belly, thighs, and shins with a furious beating. Tolley screamed and jerked at his binds, but no one was left to hear. Daniel let him have it for a long time, then tossed aside the Asp and returned to the window. Tobey and Cleo scrambled out of his way.

"I wanna see a goddamned zombie. A zombie, vampire, *something* to make this fuckin' trip worthwhile."

The rain blew in hard, hot and salty as blood. Daniel didn't care. Here he was, come all this way, and not a zombie to be found. Anything was good, Daniel missed out. A life of miserable disappointments.

He looked at Tobey and Cleo. They were difficult to see in the flickery light, all blurry and smudged, but he could make them out well enough.

"Bet I could kill me a zombie, one on one, straight up, and I'd like to try. You think I could kill me a zombie?"

Neither Tobey nor Cleo answered.

"I ain't shittin', I could take me a zombie. Take me a vampire, too, only here we are and I gotta waste my time with this lame shit. I'd rather be huntin' zombies."

He pointed at Tolley.

"Hey, boy."

Daniel returned to the bed and shook Tolley awake.

"You think I could take me a zombie, head up, one on one?"

The red eye rolled, and blood leaked from the shattered mouth. A mushy hiss escaped, so Daniel leaned closer. Sounded like the fucker was finally openin' up.

"Say what?"

Tolley's mouth worked as he tried to speak.

Daniel smiled encouragingly.

"You hear that wind? I was a bat, I'd spread my wings and ride that sumbitch for all she was worth. Where'd they go, boy? I know she tol' ya. You tell me where they went so I can get outta here. Just say it. You're almost there. Give me a hand, and I'm out your hair."

Tolley's lips worked, and Daniel knew he was about to give it, but then what little air he had left hissed out.

"You say west? They was headed west? Over to Texas?"

Tolley was dead.

Daniel stared at the body for a moment, then drew his gun and put five bullets into Tolliver James's chest. Nasty explosions that anyone staying behind would have heard even with the lion wind. Daniel didn't give a damn. If someone came running, Daniel figured to shoot them, too, but nobody came—no police, no neighbors, no nobody. Everyone with two squirts of brain juice was hunkered down tight, trying to survive.

Daniel reloaded, tucked away his gun, then took out the satellite phone. The cell stations were out all over the city, but the sat phone worked great. He checked the time, hit the speed dial, then waited for a link. It always took a few seconds.

In that time, he stood taller, straightened himself, and resumed his normal manner.

When the connection was made, Daniel reported.

"Tolliver James is dead. He didn't provide anything useful."

Daniel listened for a moment before responding.

"No, sir, they're gone. That much is confirmed. James was a good bet, but I don't believe she told him anything."

He listened again, this time for quite a while.

"No, sir, that is not altogether true. There are three or four people here I'd still like to talk to, but the storm has turned this place to shit. They've almost certainly evacuated. I just don't know. It will take me a while to locate them."

More chatter from the other side, but then they were finished.

"Yes, sir, I understand. You get yours, I get mine. I won't let you down."

A last word from the master.

"Yes, sir. Thank you. I'll keep you informed."

Daniel shut the phone and put it away.

"Asshole."

He returned to the window, and let the rain lash

him. Everything was wet now: shirt, pants, shoes, hair, all the way down to his bones. He leaned out, better to see the Square. A fifty-five-gallon oil drum tumbled past the alley's mouth, end over end, followed by a bicycle, swept along on its side, and then a shattered sheet of plywood flipping and soaring like a playing card tossed out like trash.

Daniel shouted into the wind as loud as he could.

"C'mon and get me, you fuckin' zombies! Show your true and unnatural colors."

Daniel threw back his head and howled. He barked like a dog, then howled again before turning back to the room to pack up his gear. Tobey and Cleo were gone.

Tolliver had hidden eight thousand dollars under the mattress, still vacu-packed in plastic, which Daniel found when he first searched the room. Probably a gift from the girl. Daniel stashed the money in his bag, checked to make sure Tolliver had no pulse, then went to the little bathroom where he'd left Tolliver's lady friend after he strangled her, nice and neat in the tub. A little black stream of ants had already found her, not even a day.

Cleo said, "Gotta get going, Daniel. Stop fuckin' around."

Tobey said, "Go where, a storm like this? Makes sense to stay."

Daniel decided Tobey was right. Tobey was the smart one, and usually right, even if Daniel couldn't always see him.

"Okay, I guess I should wait till the worst is over."

Tobey said, "Wait."

Cleo said, "Wait, wait."

Like echoes fading away.

Daniel returned to the window. He leaned out into the rain again, watching the mouth of the alley in case a zombie rattled past.

"C'mon, goddamnit, lemme see one. One freaky-ass zombie is all I ask."

If a zombie appeared, Daniel planned to jump out the window after it and rip its putrid, unnatural flesh to pieces with his teeth. He was, after all, a werewolf, which was why he was such a good hunter and killer. Werewolves feared nothing.

Daniel tipped back his head and howled to match the wind, then doused the candles and sat with the bodies, waiting for the storm to pass.

When it ended, Daniel would find their trail, and track them, and he would not quit until they were his. No matter how long it took or how far they ran. This was why the men down south used him for these jobs and paid him so well.

Werewolves caught their prey.

Los Angeles
Now

THE WIND DID NOT WAKE HIM. It was the dream. He heard the buffeting wind before he opened his eyes, but the dream was what woke him on that dark early morning. A cat was his witness. Hunkered at the end of the bed, ears down, a low growl in its chest, a ragged black cat was staring at him when Elvis Cole opened his eyes. Its warrior face was angry, and, in that moment, Cole knew they had shared the nightmare.

Cole woke on the bed in his loft bathed in soft moonlight, feeling his A-frame shudder as the wind tried to push it from its perch high in the Hollywood Hills. A freak weather system in the Midwest was pulling fifty- to seventy-knot winds from the sea that had hammered Los Angeles for days.

Cole sat up, awake now and wanting to shake off the dream—an ugly nightmare that left him feeling unsettled and depressed. The cat's ears stayed down. Cole held out his hand, but the cat poured off the bed like a pool of black ink.

Cole said, "Me, too."

He checked the time. Habit. Three-twelve in the A.M. He reached toward the nightstand to check his gun—habit—but stopped himself when he realized what he was doing.

"C'mon, what's the point?"

The gun was there because it was always there, sometimes needed but most times not. Living alone with only an angry cat for company, there seemed no reason to move it. Now, at three-twelve in the middle of a wind-torched night, it was a reminder of what he had lost.

Cole realized he was trembling, and pushed out of bed. The dream scared him. Muzzle flash so bright it sparkled his eyes; the charcoal smell of smokeless powder; a glittery red mist that dappled his skin; shattered sunglasses that arced through the air— images so vivid they shocked him awake.

Now he shook as his body burned off the fear.

The back of Cole's house was an A-shaped glass steeple, giving him a view of the canyon behind his house and a diamond-dust glimpse of the city beyond. Now, the canyon was blue with bright moonlight. The sleeping houses below were surrounded by blue-and-gray trees that shivered and danced in the St. Vitus wind. Cole wondered if someone down there had awakened like him. He wondered if they had suffered a similar nightmare—seeing their best friend shot to death in the dark.

Violence was part of him.

Elvis Cole did not want it, seek it, or enjoy it, but

maybe these were only things he told himself in cold moments like now. The nature of his life had cost him the woman he loved and the little boy he had grown to love, and left him alone in this house with nothing but an angry cat for company and a pistol that did not need to be put away.

Now here was this dream that left his skin crawling—so real it felt like a premonition. He looked at the phone and told himself no—no, that's silly, it's stupid, it's three in the morning.

Cole made the call.

One ring, and his call was answered. At three in the morning.

"Pike."

"Hey, man."

Cole didn't know what to say after that, feeling so stupid.

"You good?"

Pike said, "Good. You?"

"Yeah. Sorry, man, it's late."

"You okay?"

"Yeah. Just a bad feeling is all."

They lapsed into a silence Cole found embarrassing, but it was Pike who spoke first.

"You need me, I'm there."

"It's the wind. This wind is crazy."

"Uh-huh."

"Watch yourself."

He told Pike he would call again soon, then put down the phone.

Cole felt no relief after the call. He told himself he

15

should, but he didn't. The dream should have faded, but it did not. Talking to Pike now made it feel even more real.

You need me, I'm there.

How many times had Joe Pike placed himself in harm's way to save him?

They had fought the good fight together, and won, and sometimes lost. They had shot people who had harmed or were doing harm, and been shot, and Joe Pike had saved Cole's life more than a few times like an archangel from Heaven.

Yet here was the dream and the dream did not fade—

Muzzle flashes in a dingy room. A woman's shadow cast on the wall. Dark glasses spinning into space. Joe Pike falling through a terrible red mist.

Cole crept downstairs through the dark house and stepped out onto his deck. Leaves and debris stung his face like sand on a windswept beach. Lights from the houses below glittered like fallen stars.

In low moments on nights like this when Elvis Cole thought of the woman and the boy, he told himself the violence in his life had cost him everything, but he knew that was not true. As lonely as he sometimes felt, he still had more to lose.

He could lose his best friend.

Or himself.

Part One
The Fishmonger

1

SIX MINUTES BEFORE HE SAW the two men, Joe Pike stopped at a Mobil station for air. Pike sensed they were going to commit a crime the moment he saw them. Venice, California, ten thirty-five that morning, warm sunny day, not far from the sea. He had checked his tire pressure before heading to the gym, and found the right front tire three pounds low. If he had not needed air, he would not have seen the two men and gotten involved, but the tire was low. He stopped for the air.

Pike added the three pounds, then topped off his gas. While the pump ran, he inspected his red Jeep Cherokee for dings, scratches, and road tar, then checked the fluid levels.

Brake fluid—good.

Power steering—good.

Transmission—good.

Coolant—good.

The Jeep, though not a new vehicle, was spotless. Pike maintained it meticulously. Taking care of himself and his gear had been impressed upon a then-seventeen-year-old Pike by men he respected when he was a young Marine, and the lesson had served him well in his various occupations.

As Pike closed the hood, three women biked past on the opposite side of the street, fine legs churning, sleek backs arched over handlebars. Pike watched them pass, the women bringing his eye to two men walking in the opposite direction—*blink*—and Pike read them for trouble, two men in their twenties, necklaced with gang ink, walking with what Pike during his police officer days had called a down-low walk. Bangers were common in Venice, but these two weren't relaxed like a couple of homies with nothing on their minds; they rolled with a stony, side-to-side swagger showing they were tensed up and tight, the one nearest the curb glancing into parked cars, which, Pike knew, suggested they were looking for something to steal.

Pike had spent three years as an LAPD patrol officer, where he learned how to read people pretty well. Then he had changed jobs, and worked in high-conflict, dangerous environments all over the world where he learned to read the subtle clues of body language and expression even better. His life had depended on it.

Now, Pike felt a tug of curiosity. If they had kept walking, Pike would have let it go, but they stopped outside a secondhand women's clothing shop directly across the street. Pike was no longer a police officer. He did not cruise the streets looking for criminals and had other things to do, but everything about their posture and expressions triggered a dull red warning vibe. The women's shop was an ideal place from which to snatch a purse.

Pike finished filling his tank, but did not get into his vehicle. A BMW pulled into the Mobil station behind Pike's Jeep. The driver waited for a moment, then beeped her horn and called from her car.

"Are you going to move?"

Pike concentrated on the two men, squinting against the bright morning light even behind his dark glasses.

She tapped her horn again.

"Are you going to move or what? I need some gas."

Pike stayed with the men.

"Jerk."

She backed up and moved to another pump.

Pike watched the two men have a brief conversation, then continue past the clothing store to a sandwich shop. A hand-painted sign on the front window read: *Wilson's TakeOut—po'boys & sandwiches.*

The two men started to enter, but immediately backed away. A middle-aged woman carrying a white bag and a large purse came out. When she emerged, one of the men quickly turned to the street and the other brought his hand to his eyes, clearly trying to hide. The tell was so obvious the corner of Pike's mouth twitched, which was as close to a smile as Pike ever came.

When the woman was gone, the two men entered the sandwich shop.

Pike knew they were likely two guys looking to surprise a friend or buy a couple of sandwiches, but he wanted to see how it played out.

Pike crossed the street between passing cars. The sandwich shop was small, with two tiny tables up front by the window and a short counter in the rear where you ordered your food. A chalkboard menu and a New Orleans Saints Super Bowl Champions poster were on the walls behind the counter, along with a door that probably led to a storage room or pantry.

The events unfolding inside the takeout shop had happened quickly. When Pike reached the door, the two men had an older man on the floor, one punching the man's head, the other kicking his back. The man had rolled into a ball, trying to protect himself.

The two hitters hesitated when Pike opened the door, both of them sucking air like surfacing whales. Pike saw their hands were empty, though someone else might have been behind the counter or in the back room. Then the guy throwing punches went back to pounding, and the kicker turned toward Pike, his face mottled and threatening. Pike thought of nature films he'd seen with silverback gorillas puffing themselves to look fierce.

"You wan' this, bitch? Get outta here."

Pike didn't get out. He stepped inside and closed the door.

Pike saw a flick of surprise in the kicker's eyes, and the puncher hesitated again. They had expected him to run, one man against two, but Pike did not run.

The victim—the man on the floor—still curled into a ball, mumbled—

"I'm okay. Jesus—"

—even as the kicker puffed himself larger. He raised his fists and stomped toward Pike, a street brawler high on his own violence, trying to frighten Pike away.

Pike moved forward fast, and the surprised kicker pulled up short, caught off guard by Pike's advance. Then Pike dropped low and accelerated, as smoothly as water flows over rocks. He trapped the man's arm, rolled it backward, and brought the man down hard, snapping the radius bone and dislocating the ulna. He hit the man one time in the Adam's apple with the edge of his hand, the water now swirling off rocks as he rose to face the puncher, only the puncher had seen enough. He scrambled backward across the counter, and bounced off the wall as he ran out a back door.

The kicker gakked like a cat with a hair ball as he tried to breathe and scream at the same time. Pike dropped to a knee, watching the back door as he checked the man for a weapon. He found a nine-millimeter pistol, then left the downed man long enough to make sure no one was behind the counter or in the back room. He returned to the kicker, rolled him onto his belly, then stripped the man's belt to bind his wrists. The man shrieked when Pike twisted the injured arm behind his back, and tried to get up, but Pike racked his face into the floor.

Pike said, "Stop."

Pike had neutralized the assailant and secured the premises in less than six seconds.

The older man tried to sit up as Pike worked.

Pike said, "You good?"

"It's okay. I'm fine."

He didn't look fine. Blood veiled his face and spattered the floor. The man saw the red spots, touched his face, then examined the red on his fingers.

"Shit. I'm bleeding."

The man rose to a knee, but tipped sideways and ended up on his butt.

Pike took out his phone and thumbed in 911.

"Stay down. I'm getting the paramedics."

The man squinted at Pike, and Pike could tell he had trouble focusing.

"You a cop?"

"No."

"I don't need the paramedics. Catch my breath, I'll be fine."

The kicker twisted his head to see Pike.

"You ain't a cop, an' you broke my arm? You bitch, you better lemme up."

Pike pinned him with a knee, making the kicker gasp.

When the 911 operator came on the line, Pike described the situation and the victim's injury, told her he had a suspect in hand, and asked her to send the police.

The man made a feeble attempt to rise again.

"Fuck all that. Just throw the asshole out."

Pike had seen pretty much every violent injury

that could happen to a human being, so he knew wounds pretty well. Scalp wounds produced a lot of blood and weren't generally serious, but it had taken a hard blow to split the man's forehead.

"Stay down. You have a concussion."

"Fuck that. I'm fine."

The man pulled his legs under himself, pushed to his feet, then passed out and fell.

Pike wanted to go to him, but the kicker was bunching to rise.

"Better get off me, *ese*. You gonna be sorry."

Pike dug his thumb into the side of the man's neck where the C3 nerve root emerged from the third vertebra, crushing the root into the bone. This caused the man's shoulder and chest to go numb with a sharp flash of pain. His diaphragm locked and his breathing stopped mid-breath. The C3 nerve controlled the diaphragm.

"If you get up, I'll do this again. It will hurt worse."

Pike released the pressure, and knew the man's shoulder and arm now burned as if they had been flushed with napalm.

"We good?"

The man gave a breathless grunt, eyes rolling toward Pike like a Chihuahua watching a pit bull.

"Yuh."

Pike straightened the victim so he could breathe more easily, then checked his pulse. His pulse was strong, but his pupils were different sizes, which indicated a concussion. Pike pressed a wad of napkins to the man's wound to stop the bleeding.

The kicker said, "Who the fuck are you, man?"

"Don't speak again."

If Pike had not stopped for air, he would not have seen the men or crossed the street. He would not have met the woman he was about to meet. Nothing that was about to happen would have happened. But Pike had stopped. And now the worst was coming.

The paramedics arrived six minutes later.

2

THE PARAMEDICS WERE TWO sturdy, forty-something women who pulled on vinyl gloves when they saw the blood. They went to work on the victim while Pike filled them in.

The banger, facedown on the floor with Pike's knee in his back, said, "Dude broke my arm. He attacked me, yo? I need somethin' for the pain."

The lead paramedic glanced at Pike. Her name was Stiles.

"He the guy who did this?"

"Him and a friend."

"His arm really broken?"

"Uh-huh."

She told Pike to let the man sit up, then nodded at her partner.

"Check out the lovely. I have this one."

Stiles managed to rouse the victim, whose speech was muddy and slurred, but grew more focused as she checked his pulse and blood pressure. He identified himself as Wilson Smith, a transplant from New

27

Orleans who relocated after the storm. Pike found it interesting Smith did not refer to Hurricane Katrina by name; he called it "the storm." Pike also found it interesting that Mr. Smith did not have what Pike would have called a Southern accent. He sounded like he was from New York.

When Stiles flashed a penlight in his eyes, Smith tried to push her away.

"I'm okay."

"No, sir, you're not. You have a scalp wound with an open flap, and a concussion. My guess, you're looking at ten or twelve stitches here. We're bringing you in."

"I'm fine."

Smith tried to push her away again, but abruptly threw up. He settled down after that and closed his eyes. Pike watched the paramedics work as he waited for the officers to arrive. He was in it now, so he had to stay. There was nothing else to do.

The first responding officers showed up within minutes. The lead officer was a middle-aged Latina with calm eyes and P-3 stripes who introduced herself as Officer Hydeck, the Anglo name probably coming from a marriage. Her partner was a big, tough-looking rookie named Paul McIntosh who stood with his thumbs hooked in his Sam Browne like he wanted something to happen.

Hydeck spoke quietly with Stiles for a few minutes, asked both the victim and the suspect how they were doing, then came over to Pike.

"You the one called it in?"

"Yes, ma'am."

The emergency services operator would have relayed the information Pike provided.

"Uh-huh. And your name would be?"

"Pike."

The banger, who was being fitted with an air splint, said, "Dude broke my arm, yo? I want him arrested. I wanna press charges."

Hydeck asked for their identification. Pike handed over his driver's license, which McIntosh copied onto a Field Interview card along with Pike's phone number. The suspect had none. Pike wasn't surprised. Ninety-five percent of the people he had arrested while a police officer did not have a valid DL. The suspect identified himself as Reuben Mendoza, and claimed he had never been arrested.

McIntosh towered over him.

"You ganged up?"

"No way, bro. I roll clean."

McIntosh pointed at the initials on his neck. VT, which Pike, the paramedics, and the officers all knew meant Venice *Trece*—Venice Thirteen, a Latin gang.

"That why you're inked Venice Thirteen?"

"Them's my initials."

Hydeck said, "How you get VT out of Reuben Mendoza?"

"That's how you spell it in European."

Pike told them what he knew to be true, in short, declarative sentences just as he had been taught when he was a boot patrol officer, and gave Hydeck the pistol he had taken from Mendoza.

"Had this in his pocket."

Mendoza said, "That ain't mine, man, don't put that on me. I never seen that gun before."

"Was he hitting Mr. Smith with it?"

"Not that I saw. It was in his pocket."

Mendoza said, "I'm gonna sue you, bro, way you attacked me. He did something to my neck like Mr. Spock, yo? Gonna get pain and suffering."

McIntosh told him to shut up, then turned back to Pike.

"What about the other one? He have a gun?"

"Didn't see it if he did. When I entered, Mr. Smith was on the floor. The other man was punching him in the head. This one was kicking him. When I took this one down, his buddy ran out the back. I didn't see a weapon."

McIntosh grinned at Mendoza.

"Homie had your back, bro. Right out the door."

Hydeck passed the gun to McIntosh, told him to secure it in their vehicle and call in a second EMS wagon. The victim and suspect would not be transported in the same vehicle.

Another patrol car and the second EMS ambulance arrived a few minutes later. The new officers took Mendoza out while Stiles and her partner brought in their gurney. Hydeck questioned Smith while the paramedics worked on him. Smith told her the two men asked for a sandwich, but he wanted to close so he could go to the bank, and told them to leave. He claimed the two men refused, and that's how the fight started.

30

Hydeck appeared doubtful.

"So they didn't try to rob you or anything like that? You got in a fight 'cause they wanted a po'boy and you wanted to leave."

"I mighta said something. It got out of hand."

The paramedics were lifting him onto the gurney when Pike saw her enter through the rear door. She hadn't seen the ambulances and police vehicles out front, and now the uniforms crowding the small room stopped her as if she had slammed into an invisible wall. Pike watched her eyes snap from the paramedics to the gurney to the police—snap, snap, snap—sucking up the scene until—*snap*—her eyes came to him, and that's where they stayed. She looked at him as if she had never seen anything like him. Pike guessed she was in her early thirties, with olive skin and lines around her eyes. She had smart eyes, and the lines made them better. She wore a sleeveless linen dress, flat sandals, and short dark hair. The dress was wrinkled. Pike liked smart eyes.

Then Hydeck and McIntosh turned, and her eyes left him for them.

Hydeck said, "May I help you?"

"What happened? Wilson, are you all right? Wilson's my uncle."

Smith shifted to see past the paramedics.

"That's Dru. She's my niece."

Her name was Dru Rayne, and she moved between Smith and the police as they told her what happened.

"You were assaulted right here? Right here in the shop? They attacked you?"

"I was doing okay, then this guy here stopped it."

Dru Rayne studied Pike again, and this time she mouthed two words, as if the officers and paramedics and her uncle could not see or were not there, creating a moment between the two of them that included no one else.

"Thank you."

Pike nodded once.

Then she turned to the paramedics.

"Is he going to be all right?"

"They'll keep him for observation. With head injuries like this, they like to keep them overnight."

"I'm not staying. They stitch me up, I'm outta there."

Dru Rayne moved to the gurney and looked down at him.

"Wilson. Please don't be like that."

Hydeck gave her card to Ms. Rayne and informed her that detectives would likely interview her uncle at the hospital. The paramedics finished strapping Smith to the cart, and Pike watched his niece follow them out. She did not look back at Pike as she left.

Hydeck waited until they were gone, then turned back to Pike. She still held his driver's license.

"You think what happened here was a dispute over a sandwich?"

Pike shook his head, and Hydeck glanced at his license again.

"You look familiar. Do I know you?"

"No."

"Those tattoos ring a bell."

A bright red arrow was inked onto the outside of each of Pike's deltoids. She could see them because Pike wore a gray sweatshirt with the sleeves cut off. Government-issue sunglasses shiny and black as a beetle's shell hid his eyes, but the arrows hung on his arms like neon signs. They pointed forward. Pike was six feet one, weighed just over two hundred pounds, and his arms were ropy with muscle. His hair was a quarter-inch short, his skin was cooked dark, and his knuckles were scarred and coarse.

Hydeck thumbed the edge of his license.

"Most people walk into a beat-down like this, they run. But looking at you, I guess you can handle yourself. What do you do, Mr. Pike?"

"Businessman."

"Of course."

Pike expected her to ask what kind of business, but she returned his license. If she noticed a bulge where one of the two pistols he carried was hidden, she ignored it.

"Guess Mr. Smith is lucky it was you who happened by."

She gave him a business card.

"The detectives will probably call you, but this is my card. You think of anything in the meantime, call."

Pike took the card, and Hydeck left to join McIntosh at their radio car. Dru Rayne was with her uncle as the paramedics opened their vehicle. She clutched his hand as she spoke to him, and seemed very intent. Then she stepped away and the paramedics slid the gurney into their truck. Hydeck and McIntosh climbed into the radio car, flipped on their lights, and stopped traffic to let the ambulance leave. The paramedics headed toward the hospital. Hydeck and McIntosh turned in the opposite direction, already rolling to another call.

Dru Rayne watched the ambulance. She stared after it until the ambulance was gone, then hurried back to the shop. Pike didn't like the way she hurried. It looked like she was running for cover.

Pike said, "Why is he lying?"

She startled, making a little jump.

"You scared me."

Pike nodded, then thought he should probably apologize.

"Sorry."

She gave him another grateful smile, then went behind the counter.

"It's me. I'm jumpy, I guess. I have to go to the hospital."

"Why is he lying?"

"Why do you think? He's scared they'll come back."

"They've been here before?"

She turned off the deep fryers and put lids on metal condiment containers, speaking as she worked. Wilson sounded like a New Yorker, but her accent was softer, maybe because she was a woman.

"They live here, we live here, so we have to think about these things. People like that, they always come back."

34

"If you think they'll come back, you should tell the police. Hydeck knows what she's doing."

She cocked her head.

"I thought you were the police."

"No."

"You look like a policeman. Kinda."

"Just passing by."

She smiled again, then offered her hand across the counter.

"Dru Rayne. You can call me Dru."

"Joe Pike."

"Then that was extra nice, what you did, helping like that, Mr. Pike. Thank you."

They shook, then Dru Rayne turned back to her work, speaking over her shoulder.

"Now, I don't want to be rude or anything, but I have to get this place locked up so I can get to the hospital."

Pike nodded, thinking there was no reason he shouldn't leave, but he didn't. He clocked her hand. No wedding ring.

"Would you like me to take you?"

"That's all right, no. But thank you for offering."

Pike tried to think of something else to say.

"Talk to the police."

"We'll be fine. You don't know my uncle. He probably called them names."

She flashed a warm smile, but Pike knew she wasn't going to tell the police any more than her uncle.

She stacked the metal containers, then carried the

stack into the back room. When she disappeared, Pike wrote his name and cell number on an order pad he found by the cash register. He wrote his personal cell number, not the business number he gave the police.

"I'm leaving my number. You need me, call."

She was still in the back.

"Okay. Thanks again."

Pike returned to his Jeep, but did not leave the scene. He found the service alley that ran behind Wilson's sandwich shop, and waited at the far end. A few minutes later, Dru Rayne came out, locked the door, and hurried to a silver Tercel. It was an older model with paint scraped from the rear bumper, and it needed a wash. Pike thought she looked worried.

He sat in the Jeep for a while, then got out and walked the length of the block, first in the alley, then on the sidewalk. He took in the people on the sidewalks and in the stores, and the rooflines of the surrounding buildings. He studied the people behind the wheels of the passing cars, thinking about what she had said: *They always come back.*

Pike was across from the gas station when a maroon Monte Carlo slow-rolled past with the windows down. Two young men were in front, with a third in back, all three showing gang ink and jailhouse faces. They stared at Pike as they passed, so Pike stared back.

The man in the back seat made a gun of his hand, aimed, and pulled the trigger.

Pike watched them go, thinking how Dru Rayne had run for cover.

They always come back.

No, Pike thought. Not if they fear you.

3

WAY IT WORKED FOR anyone else, Officer Hydeck would inform her watch commander that the victim and suspect were en route to the hospital. Her watch commander would relay this information to the Detective Bureau duty officer, who would dispatch detectives to the hospital, where they would speak with Smith and Mendoza, and likely the paramedics. If Mendoza ID'd his accomplice, their case would be made. If Mendoza refused to cooperate, the detectives would call Pike to arrange an interview. They would ask to drop by his home or place of employment, or arrange to meet at a mutually agreeable location, everything low-key and friendly. This was the way it would work if Pike were anyone else, but Pike knew it would work differently for him. Someone would recognize his name, and what the investigators did and how they approached the case would be different.

Pike was correct.

Eight hours, twenty-seven minutes after Pike

eyeballed the maroon Monte Carlo, he returned home to find two detectives in his parking lot. Pike lived in a gated condominium complex in Culver City, not far from the scene of the assault. The condos were bunched in four-unit quads, and laid out so two or three quads shared their own parking lot. Entry to the complex required a magnetic key card to open the drive-through gate, but here they were, a male and a female detective waiting in a predictable tan Crown Victoria.

They climbed out of their car as Pike pulled in, and were waiting with their badges when he stepped from the Jeep. The man was in his fifties, with a fleshy face, thinning red hair, and a blue summer-weight sport coat. The woman was fifteen years younger, with raven hair, black eyes, and a navy pants suit that hung as if she had recently lost weight. Her gun dimpled the coat at her waist, and she stood with her hand floating close as if she might have to draw. Nervous. Pike wondered what she had heard about him that left her so afraid.

The older detective nudged the woman, showing her an exhibit at the zoo.

"Joe Pike."

Then, louder, to Pike, as if Pike was an animal who had been oblivious to the nudge.

"When they said it was you, I thought, well now, if he doesn't shoot me, this one will make my day."

The way he said it made Pike look closer. He now seemed familiar, but Pike did not recognize him.

The man held his badge higher, making sure Pike saw.

"What, Pike, you don't remember me? Jerry Button, from Rampart. Out of Pacific Station now. This is Detective Futardo. We're here on the Smith assault, so no shooting, okay? Don't shoot us."

Rampart brought back the name, but this Jerry Button looked almost nothing like the sharp young officer Pike remembered. This Button was thirty pounds heavier, with blotchy skin and puffy eyes. That Jerry Button had gone through the Academy a couple of years ahead of Pike, and was a fast-track patrol officer in Rampart Division when Pike was a boot. They had been friendly, but not friends. Button had shunned him when Pike resigned, but most of his fellow officers had. Pike couldn't blame them.

Pike read their ID cards, more than a car-length away. Futardo was a D-1, which told Pike she was new to the Detective Bureau and fresh out of a car. Button was now a Detective-3, which was a senior grade usually held by supervisors. A D-3 was too much horsepower for a simple assault.

Pike said, "How's Mr. Smith?"

Button ignored him as he put away his badge.

"You carrying a weapon?"

"Two. And the permits."

Button nudged Futardo again.

"Told you. He's always gunned up."

Futardo's face was a dark little bunker.

"Should we check the permits?"

"Nah. You can't get away with dropping as many bodies as this guy without having your paperwork in order. Your paperwork's in order, isn't it, Pike? You good on the paper?"

Pike stared at Button until Button finally laughed, and held up his hands.

"Just kidding. Let's go inside, talk about what happened."

"Out here is good."

"C'mon, let's go inside. Inside is better."

"The courtesy of a call gets you inside. No call, out here. The rudeness, out here is fine."

Button darkened.

"Are you going to cooperate or not?"

"Ask your questions."

"Here in the parking lot?"

"Here."

Button cued Futardo to take out a pad.

"All right then, here. You know what we need. Tell us what happened."

Pike related the sequence of events just as he had described them to Hydeck, including a description of the second assailant and the arrival and actions of the paramedics and police. Futardo scribbled fast to keep up, but Button looked bored, as if he had heard it all before and didn't much care one way or another.

"According to Officer Hydeck, you produced a nine-millimeter pistol and told her you took it from Mendoza. Is that correct?"

"Yes."

"Mendoza claims you planted it on him."

"What does Mr. Smith say?"

"Says he never saw the gun. Is he lying?"

Pike thought back over searching Mendoza.

"No. He was facedown when I took the gun. If he didn't see the gun before I arrived, he wouldn't have seen it after. The gun was in Mendoza's pocket."

Button glanced over at Futardo.

"Okay, let's see the pictures."

Futardo slipped a manila envelope from her jacket, and shook out several sheets.

"We'd like you to look at some booking photos. Each sheet—"

Button interrupted her.

"He knows what they are. He used to be one of us. Don't forget that."

Each sheet contained six color booking photos of adult males in their twenties and thirties, all of approximately the same size and weight. Because each sheet held six pictures, the sheets were called six-packs. Pike could tell by the tattoos that most were or had been members of Mendoza's gang.

Pike identified Mendoza's partner on the second sheet, middle of the bottom row.

"This one."

Futardo cocked her head to see.

"Figures. Alberto Gomer."

Button spiked her with a nasty glance that made her pale. She had made a rookie mistake by identifying a suspect by name to a witness, and Button would chew her out for it later. She wet her lips nervously before continuing.

"Will you sign a sworn affidavit so stating, and

testify to that effect under oath in open court?"

"Yes."

Futardo took a pen from her jacket, and held out the sheet and the pen. Her fingers shook.

"Circle the image you are now identifying as the man you saw assault Mr. Wilson Smith on this date and sign it."

Pike circled and signed. Button hadn't been a bad guy when Pike knew him, but now he came across as angry and mean. Pike thought he was probably an asshole to work with.

"Did Mr. Smith recognize him?"

Button snorted.

"None of these people looked familiar to Mr. Smith. Isn't it funny how that works? Mr. Smith was not what we call a helpful witness."

Futardo softened for the first time as she took back the pictures.

"He's afraid."

Button snorted again, and cued Futardo.

"Anything you want to ask, Detective?"

Futardo finished whatever she was writing, and looked back at Pike.

"Let's back up to when you first saw Mendoza and his friend. What were you doing when you saw them?"

"Buying gas."

"Uh-huh. And what were you doing in Venice?"

"Buying gas."

"So you just happened to be there?"

"Where should I be?"

43

"Had you met Mr. Mendoza before this morning?"

Futardo was watching him closely, and Pike realized Button was watching him, too. As if they had been trying to get here from the beginning, and were intent on reading his reaction. They should have been asking about Wilson Smith and Reuben Mendoza, but they were asking Pike about Pike.

"Where are you going with this?"

"Wherever. Of all the people in L.A., it's you over there kicking the shit out of this turd."

"Ask Mr. Smith."

"I'm asking you. You're what makes this interesting."

"This isn't about me."

"It's about whatever I say."

Pike nodded, and now he understood why a D-3 was running a simple assault investigation. Pike's voice was quiet as a leaf floating on a pond.

"We're finished."

"We're finished when I say we're finished."

Futardo looked scared, and suddenly interrupted to defuse the situation.

"What happens next is we'll type up your statement and call about getting together so you can sign it. You'll have to sign it."

Button snapped at her.

"He knows that. Saddle up. I'll be along in a minute."

Futardo took her pad and the pictures and looked relieved to be going.

Pike kept his voice soft.

"What did you tell her about me, make her so scared?"

"The truth."

"You didn't come here to make a case against Mendoza."

"We see a hundred assaults a day. A chickenshit assault case is nothing."

"What happened to you? You used to be better than this."

Button watched Futardo get into their car, then studied Pike for a moment as he worked out an answer.

"I am a police officer. I believe in the law, and I have devoted my life to upholding it, but you, Pike, the law is nothing to you. These young cops, they talk about you like you're some kind of gunfighting legend, but I know you're shit. I don't like what happened when you were an officer, or how you've gotten away with putting so many people in the dirt since we ran you off the department. You're dangerous, Pike. There's something wrong with you, and sooner or later we'll put you away."

Button went to his car, calling over his shoulder.

"Thank you for your cooperation. We'll be in touch."

Way it worked for anyone else, Button and Futardo would be trying to find out what really happened in Wilson Smith's shop, and making sure Mendoza and his accomplice couldn't hurt Wilson and Dru again. This was the way it would work if Pike were anyone else, but Pike knew it worked differently for him. Button didn't care about the assault or whether Wilson Smith would be assaulted or robbed again. Button was in it to grind Pike, which meant Wilson and his niece were alone.

Pike was glad he had given his number to Dru Rayne.

4

HE HADN'T EXPECTED HER to call so soon.

Twenty-two minutes after eight the next morning, Pike was driving to his gun shop when his cell phone rang. He did not recognize the incoming number, but answered anyway.

"Pike."

"They came back. You said to call, and, well, I didn't know if I should—"

Dru Rayne.

Pike glanced at his watch to note the time, then turned toward the sandwich shop, thinking he could make it to her in less than six minutes.

"Are they at your shop now?"

He heard voices behind her and pressed the accelerator harder.

"Ms. Rayne? Are you safe?"

"They broke the window, and— Yes, I'm all right. I guess it happened last night. Oh, man, I'm sorry, I shouldn't have called. Wilson is—I'm sorry, I have to go."

Pike eased off the accelerator, but continued to their shop, and once more pulled into the gas station across the street. He left his Jeep, and went to the curb for a better view. The front window was mostly missing, and the front door was now propped open with a black garbage can. A young man with a two-by-four was calmly breaking what was left of the glass from the frame. A woman wearing a bright aqua dress stood nearby, pointing out the remaining glass teeth as if directing him which to knock out next. Shadows moved inside, but Pike couldn't tell whether Dru Rayne was one of them.

Pike studied the surrounding area, but saw no one who looked suspicious. Mendoza would still be in jail awaiting arraignment, so Gomer or Mendoza's banger friends had probably been behind it. Offering up a little payback for his arrest.

Pike walked along the sidewalk for a better view of the surrounding buildings. No one drew his attention, but an inner radar slowly pinged with the weight of watching eyes. The young troops Pike knew, fresh back from the desert, called it spider-sense, taking the term from the Spider-Man movies. They told him if you humped the desert long enough you developed a sixth sense that tingled like angry ants when the crosshairs found your skin. Pike had humped jungles, deserts, and pretty much everywhere a man could hump for most of his life, and now he felt the tingle. He turned in a slow three-sixty to clock the storefronts and rooflines and passing cars, but saw nothing.

Then the feeling ebbed like a receding tide until it was gone.

The station manager came out of his office when Pike returned to his Jeep. He looked worried.

"You aren't going to leave it here again, are you? You tied up my pump for more than an hour yesterday."

"Not today."

The manager looked relieved.

Pike drove along the alley behind Wilson's shop, parked beside the Tercel, and let himself in.

Wilson and Dru were in the front room, along with a second young man and the woman in aqua. The tables normally by the window were pushed to the side. Dru stood near them, speaking into her phone as Wilson swept glass onto a piece of cardboard the second kid was using as a dustpan. Wilson had been good as his word when he told the paramedics he wasn't going to stay at the hospital. A square yellow bandage now covered half of his forehead.

The aqua woman was pleading with Wilson.

"Would you please listen to Dru? You shouldn't be doing this. Your brain will fall out."

"Let it. I'll be out of my misery."

Pike saw the vandals had done more than shatter the window. A large splash of green paint cut across the floor, and another green smear made a freak rainbow on the wall behind the counter.

Dru saw Pike first. The smile flickered in her eyes, then she held up a finger, telling him she had to finish the call.

49

Wilson saw him next, and pushed angrily to force the glass onto the cardboard.

"Look at this mess. You see this? I told you, just throw the bastard out, but no—now I've got these asshats on a vendetta."

The aqua woman fluttered at the boy holding the cardboard.

"Ethan, be careful of that glass. Watch you don't get cut."

Dru quickly finished the call and came over, gesturing with the phone.

"The glass people. They'll be here as soon as they can."

Wilson swept even harder.

"They coming for free?"

Pike was focused on Dru. She had thrown on shorts and a faded T-shirt in her rush to the shop, and now her hair was mussed and her feet were smudged with green. Pike thought the smart eyes seemed worried this morning, but he couldn't stop looking at her—as if she were a book he wanted to read.

"You okay?"

The smile again, quick and calming, and she moved a step closer.

"I'm fine. Thank you so much for coming. I didn't mean to waste your time."

"You should call the police."

Dru glanced at the aqua woman.

"They've already been here. Betsy saw the glass when she got in this morning. She called the police even before she called us."

The aqua woman introduced herself.

"Betsy Harmon. I have the shop next door. That was quite something, the way you saved Wilson."

Wilson said, "Nobody saved me. I had it under control."

Betsy rolled her eyes.

"Just be glad he saved your scrawny butt and you should thank me for calling the police this morning. You'll need their report for your insurance."

Wilson made a disgusted snort as he helped Ethan carry the pile of shattered glass on the cardboard to the garbage can.

"There's no insurance here, lady. We pay as we go, one oyster at a time. I'm not made of money."

He cocked an eye at Pike.

"You know what that emergency room is gonna cost?"

Wilson appeared to be breathing hard. Pike thought he had probably left the hospital against the doctor's advice, but here he was, making his place right. Pike liked him for that, and knew he would play it the same way. He turned back to Dru.

"Anything missing?"

"No, the police had us look. They just broke the window and threw in the paint. I don't think they came inside."

Wilson said, "It was the same two cops as yesterday, the Mexican gal, what's her name?"

Dru frowned.

"Officer Hydeck probably wouldn't appreciate being called a Mexican. Or a gal."

"She's supposed to tell the detectives, for all the good that's gonna do. I said, you know what, do me a favor, don't. You shoulda seen those idiots who came to the hospital."

Wilson stopped sweeping to squint at Pike.

"What's with all the questions about you? They were more interested in you than me. They're not gonna find the asshat who did this."

Dru glanced up at Pike.

"It has to be the man they arrested, doesn't it? Him and his friend?"

Pike explained about Mendoza being still in custody, which left Wilson thoroughly disgusted.

"Doesn't matter if it was him or his friends or his goddamned relatives. You watch. When he gets out, he's gonna come back and break it himself."

Wilson lifted the broom to continue sweeping, but hesitated as if he had lost his train of thought. Then he pivoted in a slow circle and staggered into the tables.

Dru screamed, "Wilson!"

Ethan caught him first, sagging with the older man's weight as Pike grabbed Wilson's arms.

Wilson clutched a table for support and eased onto a stool.

"I'm okay. Just lemme sit—"

Dru's face had paled.

"You take it easy now. Breathe. You calm down, and I'm taking you home."

He pushed at her hands, but Pike caught his wrists and put himself between them. Wilson tried to pull away, but couldn't. Pike made his voice gentle.

"You're going to hurt yourself. You see?"

Wilson glared up at him, but Pike did not move, and didn't let go. Pike held him until Wilson relaxed. Then Pike let go, and Wilson averted his eyes.

"We got the glass man coming. We have to get this mess cleaned up. We get this mess squared away, I'll go home, but, Jesus, give it a rest."

Pike looked at Dru, then gave them some space.

He walked out the front door and stood on the sidewalk. He thought about the police. Hydeck was a good officer, but this wasn't the crime of the century. Button and Futardo would have issued paper on Alberto Gomer yesterday. They might or might not have visited his last known address, but if Gomer didn't answer the door, they weren't going to spend a lot of time on a simple assault case. They would kick it back to the patrol officers like Hydeck and McIntosh. Gomer's picture would have been distributed at roll call along with the pictures and warrants of the rapists, murderers, pedophiles, and other dangerous criminals believed to be in the area. Hydeck and McIntosh would probably drop a word with the Venice bangers they knew, asking about the vandalism, and telling them it better not happen again, but that was as far as their investigation would go. They were too busy cleaning up after the rapists and murderers.

Pike scanned the buildings and cars and roof-lines again. He waited for the feeling that he was being watched, but now he felt nothing and went back inside.

He looked at Wilson first, then Dru.

"This won't happen again."

Wilson scowled.

"What are you, a swami? How do you know it won't happen again?"

"I'll talk to them."

Wilson leaned back on the stool as if Pike was no smarter than the asshats who came to the hospital.

"You know what? It's over, all right? It's done with, and we don't know who did it, so let's not make it worse."

He waved toward Betsy.

"Between you and this one, I'm gonna wake up murdered."

Betsy said, "Don't be a jackass."

Dru stared at Wilson with worried eyes, then turned away and went into the storage room. Pike followed her, and found her crying. She closed her eyes hard, then opened them, but the wet didn't go away.

"He's impossible. It's been so hard, trying to make a go of this place, and now we have these people on top of everything else."

She closed her eyes again, and raised a hand, stopping herself.

"I'm sorry."

Pike touched her arm. One touch, then he lowered his hand.

"It will be fine."

"I've been telling myself that for years."

"This time is different."

Pike went back to his Jeep and once more checked the time. Gomer was in the wind, but Pike knew where to find Mendoza. He would have been transported to the Pacific Community Police Station to await his arraignment after he was released from the hospital. The District Attorney's Office had forty-eight hours to arraign him from the time of his arrest, but Pike knew they would likely bump him to the head of the line because of his injury. This meant he would probably be arraigned sometime today. If he made bail or posted bond, he would be released.

Pike phoned his gun shop. He had five employees, two who were full-time and three who were former police officers. A man named Ronnie ran the shop, and had been with Pike a long time.

Pike said, "You okay without me this morning?"

"Yeah. Why?"

"Something came up. I'm going to be busy for a while."

"Take your time. Do it right."

"Can Liz find out something for me?"

"If she can. Whatcha need?"

Ronnie's youngest daughter was a Hardcore Gang prosecutor for the D.A.'s Office in Compton. Pike explained about Reuben Mendoza waiting at Pacific Station for his court appearance.

"They'll probably arraign him today, but they might hold him until tomorrow. Can she find out?"

"Where are you?"

"Cell."

"Call you right back."

Ronnie got back to him eight minutes later.

"It's today. They took him over this morning. That's gonna be the Airport Courthouse down in Hawthorne. You need some help with this?"

"I'm good."

Pike closed his phone and went hunting for Reuben Mendoza.

5

THE AIRPORT COURTHOUSE WAS one of forty-eight superior courts spread among the four thousand square miles of Los Angeles County. It sat in the southwest corner of the Century Freeway/San Diego Freeway interchange, less than a pistol shot from LAX, and looked like a giant green moth with glass wings, struggling to get into the air.

Pike left the 405, dropped down La Cienega to the courthouse, and found a place to park with an easy, eyes-forward view of the back entrance. The public could enter the building through either a front or a back entrance, but Pike knew from experience that defendants who made bail were released through the back. Pike also knew the arraignment court had no hard-and-fast calendar for seeing defendants. Right now, Mendoza would be in a holding cell with a number of other defendants. Their order of appearance before the judge would change with the changing schedules of public and private defense attorneys, attorney-client meetings, motions, and arguments. Pike was okay with waiting and would wait all day if necessary, but he suspected the court staff would take pity on Mendoza's broken arm.

Pike made himself comfortable. He took a deep breath, exhaled from the bottom of his lungs, then did it again. He felt his body relax and his heart rate slow. He watched the door, and breathed, and thought about nothing. Pike could sit like this for days, and had, in places far less comfortable than a dry, clean vehicle in the shade of a giant moth. He found much peace in waiting, and the waiting was made easier by thinking of nothing.

At seven minutes after eleven that morning, the maroon Monte Carlo drifted into the parking lot. The corner of Pike's mouth twitched. The Monte Carlo suggested Mendoza had made bail, called his friends for a ride, and was now being processed out.

Pike studied the lone occupant. Pike had been hoping for Gomer, but this wasn't Gomer. The driver was a young, thin Latin dude with a bandanna around his head and a pencil mustache. He didn't park in a designated parking place, but eased to the curb near the door. Another good sign.

Ninety seconds later, Reuben Mendoza emerged from the moth with a smile on his face and a cast that extended up his forearm from his right hand to just below his elbow. He wasn't using a sling. Mendoza pointed at his friend with both hands, broke into an exaggerated, shoulder-rolling shuffle to show off his cast, then flipped off the court with both hands and climbed into the car.

58

Pike followed them back onto the 405, letting the Monte Carlo float five or six cars ahead in the light, late-morning traffic. They didn't seem to be in a hurry, so neither was Pike. The Monte Carlo slipped onto the Marina Freeway, then cruised up Lincoln Boulevard into a low-end commercial area off Venice Boulevard. Several blocks later, they pulled into a place called Our Way Body Mods. A six-foot wrought-iron fence guarded the lot, with double-wide gates on the main and side street entrances. The gates were open. A service building with two open bays sat behind a small parking lot where damaged vehicles waited for work, and freshly repaired or customized cars waited to be picked up. Most of the vehicles were hobby cars—Japanese imports sporting elaborate spoilers and nitrous-blown engines, or American classics like Bel Airs and Impalas that had been chopped to ride low and painted as bright as M&M's.

When the Monte Carlo pulled in, several men emerged from the bays to greet Mendoza. Pike counted nine heads, excluding Mendoza and his driver. Businesses like Our Way Body Mods were often owned by multigenerational gang families. They were run as legitimate or semi-legitimate businesses, but their primary purpose was so gang members could claim they were employed when making their appeals to judges and parole officers. Such businesses also served as clubhouses, drop points, and tax dodges to launder illegal gang income.

As the men crowded around Mendoza, Pike

studied their faces. Most sported elaborate gang tats and shaved heads, which had replaced slicked-back hair as the homeboy style of choice. Pike knew that not all of these men would be in the gang. Most were, but a couple would likely be wannabes, and a couple more were probably just friends. Three of the men showed the grease and soil of work, but most of them had just been hanging around. Pike saw the man who had aimed his gun hand from the Monte Carlo's back seat, but Gomer wasn't among them. The man hugged Mendoza and lifted him from the ground. When other men made a joke of grabbing Mendoza's cast, the back-seat man playfully pushed them away. Protecting his friend. Any of these people could have vandalized Wilson's takeout shop, but Pike had no way to know, though he thought he knew someone who could help deal with the problem.

Pike scrolled the directory in his cell phone until he found the number, then dialed. A cheery young woman answered.

"Angel Eyes. May I help you?"

"Artie there?"

"Yes, he is. May I ask who's calling?"

"Tell him Joe Pike is coming by."

Pike drove to a small stucco house in a residential neighborhood east of Abbot Kinney Boulevard. Known by the people who lived there as Ghost Town, the streets were lined by modest homes originally built for African-American laborers during the thirties. Ghost Town had seen a slow gentrification in some of its neighborhoods, but

60

not all, leaving a sad reminder of days gone past and dreams unrealized. But men like Father Arturo Alvarez were trying to change that.

Father Art was not a priest, though the women and kids in his care called him Father and blessed him with the love and respect of a man of God. Artie Alvarez was a murderer. He murdered his first and only victim when he was eleven years old—a thirteen-year-old Shoreline Crip named Lucious T. Jefferson, whose only mistake was pedaling a blue Schwinn bike past Artie's house. Artie was brutally honest when he told the story of how and why he killed the boy, which he told often to elementary-school children, civic leaders, and business groups throughout the Southland. He spoke to kids because he hoped to change their lives for the better. He spoke to civic leaders and business groups to raise money to fund his programs.

The heat was merciless on an August afternoon the day Artie committed homicide. Artie, his two younger brothers, and baby sister were on their front steps, waiting for their mother to return from work as a housekeeper in Cheviot Hills. Their father was away, which meant he was doing time in Soledad Prison. Artie recalls that he and his siblings were bored, and making up lies about their father, entertaining themselves by pretending he was a larger-than-life outlaw instead of a drunken bully with mild retardation from huffing too much paint thinner and glue. Artie and his siblings had reached a lull in the stories when Lucious Jefferson pedaled past. Artie's baby sister, Tina, was on his knee when Artie saw Jefferson on the shiny blue bike. Jefferson wasn't even looking at them. He was pedaling past, taking his time, and for no other reason than the rage in his heart, Artie called out—

"Get off our street, you Crip nigger!"

Jefferson, who, until this time, had paid no attention to the four children on the steps, flashed a gang sign and shouted back.

"Spic beaner! Fuck yo' pussy ass!"

As Arturo told the story, he flew into a blinding rage that left him alone in the world. His two brothers and sister vanished. Thoughts of his mother, now only moments from home, vanished, and reason as civilized men know reason ceased to exist. He has no memory of pushing his sister from his knee, nor of her screaming when her head split so deeply on the step she would require eight stitches.

Artie ran into his house, snatched his father's .22-caliber rifle from beneath his mother's bed, frantically checked to see it was loaded, then crashed out of the house. He caught Lucious Jefferson a block and a half later where Lucious was waiting to cross a busy street, whereupon he pushed the rifle's muzzle into the older boy's back and pulled the trigger. Killed him. Murdered him. 187'd his ass.

Lucious Jefferson did not even see Artie coming. He was watching the traffic for a break in the onrushing river of cars when Artie ran up behind him and shot him between the T5 and T6 thoracic vertebrae, destroying his spinal cord and sending a bone chip from the T6 transverse process into Jefferson's pulmonary artery. Artie would later say, in that moment, the real world and the reality of what he had done crashed into him like a freak wave, waking him from the mindless place of his rage by crushing him with the horror of what he had done. Lucious collapsed onto his bike, fell, and landed on his back. His eyes were wide as saucers, so wide they were balloons bulging out of his head. Artie saw the terror and pain in the dying boy's eyes, a horrible pain that flowed from his eyes like a spirit leaving his body and flowed into Artie, forever changing his life.

Following that terrible event, Artie Alvarez spent three years at a special facility for boys, where he kept to himself, took part in regular counseling, and was visited by Lucious Jefferson's eyes every night in his sleep. The arrogance of his youth was replaced by guilt and a thoughtful shame. He eventually obtained his bachelor's and master's degrees in psychology at Cal State Northridge, and became a counselor to youth groups, nonprofit organizations, and outreach programs throughout the city, with the goal of ending hate and violence through education. He created Angel Eyes as a nonprofit outreach program for at-risk children, and worked with gangs throughout the city. At-risk meant at risk of joining a gang, at risk of going back to drugs, at risk of becoming a prostitute, at risk of turning to crime. The Angel Eyes message was simple—act as if someone is watching, which was the Angel Eyes motto: *Someone is Watching*. His audiences thought this was a reference to God until Artie explained that not a night had passed without his seeing Lucious Jefferson's tortured eyes in his dreams. Lucious Jefferson was watching.

Angel Eyes HQ occupied a small stucco home on a residential street with mixed zoning ordinances. When Pike rolled up, the house was surrounded by a couple of dozen older children and younger teenagers of both sexes, along with two counselors in their early twenties. Most of the kids were Latin, but African-American, Anglo, and Asian kids were among them. Armed with brushes and rollers, they were painting the house a peaceful beige color under Artie's direction.

When Artie saw Pike, he came to the street and opened the gate. He was wearing shorts, sandals, and a T-shirt with the Angel Eyes logo.

"Marisol told me you'd be dropping by. Good to see you, my friend."

"Got a minute?"

"Hang on—"

Artie called out to his army of painters.

"Ladies and gentlemen, here is my friend, Mr. Joe Pike. Please welcome him."

The kids answered back.

"Hello, Mr. Pike. Welcome to Angel Eyes."

Artie beamed, and Pike nodded.

"How many you have here?"

"Twenty-three here today. Another twenty at the South L.A. facility. Eighteen up in Van Nuys."

Though Artie employed counselors who resided at the various houses, his kids weren't allowed to live on-site except for short-term cases where they risked at-home physical abuse or assault from neighborhood gangs. The sites existed to give them a place to go, counselors they could talk to, tutors to help with their studies, and a peaceful harbor from the stormy waters of their lives. Artie Alvarez charged nothing for these services, and covered his costs by fund-raising and donations. Though the grounds were neat and orderly and the house was being painted, Pike noticed missing roof tiles, torn window screens, and other indications that Artie was running low on funds. When Pike mentioned it, Artie shrugged.

"It's the economy. The state's broke. Rich people aren't feeling as rich as they used to, so they give less."

He smiled at the kids as if he admired their courage to change.

"We'll get by. Now c'mon in, and let's talk this out."

Pike followed Artie into the house. The living room was set up like an office and waiting room with two desks, two couches, and two chairs. A pretty young Latina who was probably Marisol was at the front desk, speaking on the phone while typing at a computer.

As they passed, Artie said, "Joe, Marisol, Marisol, Joe."

Marisol raised a hand in greeting without interrupting her conversation. She was trying to convince a local restaurant to donate their leftover food to a shelter for abused children. Pike noticed a pearl of sweat running down the side of her face before she brushed it away. The house was not air-conditioned.

Artie led him to what was once the master bedroom, though it now served as Artie's office. Every window was open and a couple of fans moved the air, but it was still hot. The cool ocean breezes rarely ventured this far from the sea.

Artie dropped into a secondhand chair behind a cast-off teacher's desk.

"Sit. What can I do for you?"

"Venice *Trece*?"

"All right. They've owned the Westside for years. Which clique are we talking about?"

"*Malevos Pacíficos*."

"Pacific Gangsters. They're at the end of the boulevard, right by the water."

"I want to speak with the *jefe*."

Each clique had its own boss, known as the *jefe*.

Artie arched his eyebrows and leaned back.

"Speak as in talk, or speak as in someone won't be speaking again?"

"As in talk. If I wanted the other thing, I would not have involved you."

Pike explained the situation about Mendoza and Gomer, and the vandalism that had occurred. Pike understood bangers from his days as an officer. He could make them dead, but he could not make them listen. Only their *jefe* had that power. If their boss told them to leave Smith alone, they would leave Smith alone. A reasonable request. Made in the spirit of cooperation.

Artie said, "Mm. So you want to make a personal appeal."

Pike nodded, and Arturo leaned back again.

"I don't see why not. They have a new kid over there. Miguel Azzara. Goes by Mikie. This kid will surprise you."

Pike nodded again. Mikie.

"You have a relationship?"

"I talk to all these cats, man. V-Thirteen sets, the Culver City and Santa Monica gangs, the Shoreline Crips. They don't all like me, but they know I'm trying to do right. They all have little brothers and sisters."

Artie tapped the desk for a moment, thoughtful, then studied Pike.

"You want him to know who he's dealing with?"

"Whatever you think is best."

"He won't respond to a threat."

"This isn't a threat."

Artie thought about it for another moment, then shrugged.

"I can reach out, ask as a favor to me. He's a bright guy. Not what you expect."

Pike said, "Good."

Art laughed as he picked up his phone.

"Give me a minute, okay? I'll see what I can do."

Pike took the hint and stepped out to let Art

speak in private. A few minutes later, Art emerged with the answer. Miguel Azzara agreed to meet Pike at three o'clock that afternoon.

6

MIKIE AZZARA MET PIKE at a coffee shop on Abbot Kinney Boulevard, not far from the Venice Canals. The afternoon sky there near the beach was clear and blue, and the temperature was in the mid-seventies. Pike was surprised when Artie told him where Azzara wanted to meet. Abbot Kinney was an upscale area of restaurants, designer shops, art galleries, and bars, and now here at the coffee shop, seated outdoors, he was surrounded by attractive affluent women who went well with the surroundings. Most were tanned, and most were between their twenties and forties, and most were fit. Most wore light summery dresses or shorts and sandals, and none of them smoked. It wasn't a place a V13 *veterano* would frequent.

Pike arrived early, and sat outside as had been agreed, sipping black coffee. The coffee was weak, but he didn't care.

At three-oh-five, a black Prius pulled to the curb on the opposite side of the street. A man in his late twenties got out, checked for oncoming traffic, then strolled across to the coffee shop. He wore a lightweight Hugo Boss sport coat over an AC/DC T-shirt, tailored jeans, and huaraches. He was fit, clean-shaven, and handsome enough to be an *Esquire* model. The women seated around Pike watched him approach.

The man searched the crowd when he reached the curb, saw Pike, and came to the table. He smiled as he offered his hand, flashing perfect teeth and dimples.

"Mr. Pike? Michael Azzara. Father Art told me I'd spot the arrows. May I sit?"

Pike nodded, noting he had introduced himself as Michael, not Mikie or Miguel. He was slick, clean, and as different in appearance from the street-dog *veteranos* at the body shop as the Prius was from a candy-red '56 Bel Air. Miguel Azzara looked like a frat boy from USC, built strong, though, as if he had been a pretty good high-school wrestler.

Azzara sat, laced his fingers, and looked at Pike with an innocent curiosity.

"I love Father Art. He does so much for our community."

Pike nodded, and waited for Azzara to continue.

"How can I help you?"

Now, seated, Pike noticed the skin on the side of Azzara's neck was mottled with faint blemishes. When he was fourteen or fifteen, he had the ink, but sometime between then and now, he'd seen the laser. Small scars laced the knuckles of his left hand and split the line of his left eyebrow. Maybe

70

he hadn't always looked so different from the men at the body shop.

Pike lifted his cup.

"Want something?"

"That's all right, thank you. How can I help?"

"You speak for *Malevos*?"

Azzara checked to see if the nearby women were listening. A woman in her late thirties saw him glance over, and smiled. Azzara smiled back, and looked like a movie star.

"Hey, how're you doing?"

She blushed and turned back to her friends, pretending she wasn't drooling. Azzara turned back to Pike.

"That's why I'm here, yes. How can I help?"

Third time he'd said it—how can I help?

"Reuben Mendoza and Alberto Gomer."

"Those guys are idiots. Mendoza was just arrested."

"You know why?"

"I know I had to cover his bond. Is this about that?"

"I'm the man who put him down. Is that going to be a problem with us?"

Azzara looked surprised.

"Depends on what you want. If you want money for some reason—say, a payoff so you'll refuse to testify—then, yes, it's going to be a problem."

"Nothing like that."

"I didn't think so. Not with Father Art vouching for you."

Pike went through the events exactly as he had with Hydeck, Button, and Artie Alvarez. He told Azzara that Wilson Smith was a friend, and that now, early that morning, someone had vandalized his shop.

Azzara listened with a thoughtful frown, nodding occasionally in the way people do, and did not speak until Pike finished.

"Uh-huh, okay. I get it. These people are your friends. You don't want them hassled."

"That's right."

"Done."

Pike waited, thinking there would be more, but there wasn't. After a few moments, Azzara realized Pike wasn't going to say anything, so he explained to fill the silence.

"This nickel-and-dime stuff is bullshit. It draws heat, pisses off the CRASH units, and for what? So an idiot like Mendoza can bag a free sandwich or shake down some dude for twenty bucks? Is it worth twenty dollars, that kind of trouble, me sitting here with you? Please."

"*Trece* will leave Mr. Smith's shop alone. No more vandalism. No trouble."

Azzara shifted, irritated he had to deal with small-time stuff like this.

"It's done. This nonsense with the paint? What are they, in the sixth grade? Look, I don't know if it was Gomer or whoever—this is the first I've heard of it—but I'll find out, and this will stop. I don't want these *vatos* out doing things like this. I mean, this is

72

the lesson right here—me and you, right here right now, wasting our time. This is absurd."

Pike said, "Thank you."

Azzara checked the time, sighed, then studied Pike for a moment. Pike wondered why he hadn't left. They were finished. Miguel Azzara could leave.

Then Azzara leaned forward and lowered his voice.

"The Father told me you're a dangerous man. I said, Art, what are you, crazy? Is this guy trying to front me off?"

Pike shook his head.

"I'm not fronting you."

Azzara raised his palm.

"Art covered that. He specifically said you told him this wasn't a threat, and you told him to make sure I understood. I'm cool with that. These matters of respect are important."

Pike knew more was coming, and waited it out.

"He says to me, listen, I just think you should know, and then he tells me some things. I don't know if he's making these things up, but he tells me these crazy things about you, and I don't know if he wants me to be scared or what, so I tell him to stop."

Azzara made a big show of holding up both palms this time, reliving his conversation with Art.

"I say, what are you saying here, Art, this man will go to war with me? I don't give what he wants, he'll come for me, me and my homes, all of the *Trece*?"

Pike waited for it to pass.

"And Art, he says no, no, no, nothing like that, he

just felt obligated because he was putting us together, so this wasn't coming from you. The Father wanted me to know who I was getting involved with. Can you imagine that guy?"

Azzara paused for a response, but Pike didn't respond.

"You don't say much."

"What do you want me to say?"

"You don't have to say anything. But if there are things I must understand, then there are things you must understand, too."

Azzara leaned forward, and now he stared.

"You look dangerous. You look like everything Art said, but looking is different from being. I know what I *look* like, too."

"Is there a problem?"

"I want things clear between us. I understand you're not threatening me. You're coming to me like a man, asking me to help your friends."

"Yes."

"I'm not going along with this because of an implied threat."

"I understand."

"You know *La Eme*?"

"Of course."

"Then you understand why I have no fear."

La Eme was the Mexican Mafia, so strong in numbers they controlled the drug trade in the southwestern United States and virtually owned the prisons in California and Arizona. They were an existing criminal army within the borders of the U.S.

"I understand."

Azzara flashed the dimples and stood.

"Man to man, you ask. Man to man, I answer. It's done. Tell your friends to relax. I'll talk to my homes. This will never happen again."

Pike glanced across the street.

"You like the Prius?"

"Love it. It's important to be environmentally conscious. What do you drive?"

"Jeep."

"Go green, Mr. Pike. The planet needs love."

Azzara flashed the dimples, once more offered his hand, then made his way to his car.

One call. Simple. It's done.

It should have been finished, but wasn't.

7

WHEN PIKE RETURNED TO the sandwich shop, the air was warm with a silky inland breeze. The glass people had finished their job, and now a new glass window was in place. A CLOSED sign sat in the door, but Pike saw someone moving inside.

Pike went around to the back entrance. A large fan sat in the door, blowing out. Dru was on her knees by the counter, scrubbing the floor with what looked like a large towel. The two little tables were against the far wall with their chairs upended on top and their legs thrust up like antlers. The shop was heavy with the smell of turpentine. She had probably spent the morning cleaning the floor, and now was trying to scrub away the turpentine.

Pike watched her. She was faced away from him with her butt in the air, bearing down on the towel with both hands. She was barefoot even though the ___r had been covered with broken glass that ___ Pike watched the play of her back as she ___ pulled on the towel, coming up and down on her heels. Her tan was deep. Even the soles of her feet were tanned.

Pike stepped around the fan, then rapped on the wall—knock, knock.

She casually glanced over her shoulder, then went on with the scrubbing. She smiled as if she had expected him, and liked it that he had returned.

"Hey. How's it look?"

"Looks better."

"The wall is okay, but this floor is ruined. See how the paint worked down in the cracks? Those creeps ruined it."

Pike saw she was right. The paint had seeped into the seams between the Marmoleum squares and would be there until the floor was replaced.

Pike said, "They won't be back."

She paused again, then stood, pushing a rope of hair from her face. Her eyebrows arched, and Pike saw humor in her eyes, as if she already knew how his story would end and wanted to have fun with him.

"And you know this how?"

"These people in a gang, they have a leader like in any other organization. I spoke with the person they answer to."

She studied him for a moment, then deepened her voice, trying to sound like Marlon Brando.

"You made him an offer he couldn't refuse?"

Pike wasn't sure what to say, so he drifted past her to peer out the new window. The street appeared normal.

77

"You got your uncle to go home?"

"He's not going to stay in bed. He gets dizzy when he stands, but he won't listen. That's just how he is."

Pike glanced at the tables, waiting to return to their places.

"Help with the tables?"

"That's okay. I've got it."

Pike nodded. He had done what he could, let her know she wouldn't have any more trouble, and now there was nothing to do except see if Azzara was good as his word. They were finished, but, like the day before, Pike didn't want to leave.

"You did a good job."

"We won't win any beauty prizes."

Pike drifted past her to the counter, and saw that his phone number was tacked to the order board.

"Okay. You need anything, call."

She said, "Ring."

He turned back, and saw her smiling.

"That was me calling."

She dropped the towel into the bucket, and appraised herself.

"I'm wet, hungry, and I smell like turpentine. I want a beer. How about we go have a beer? There's a great little place right over here, the Sidewalk Cafe. How about it? My treat."

Pike said, "Okay."

The Sidewalk Cafe was everything Wilson's tiny takeout shop wasn't, with a large bar, indoor and outdoor seating, and a spectacular location on Ocean Front Walk. The outside area was already crowded with regulars come to enjoy the sunset, but the waitress recognized Dru and smiled them to a table. Joggers, skaters, tourists, and beach people flowed past on the sidewalk between the café and a row of vendors and performers. A manicured grass park, swaying palms, and a deep expanse of sand lay beyond. Directly across from their table, two street performers painted silver pretended to be mechanical men, locking and popping in unison. An open briefcase at their feet held a cardboard sign: CONTRIBUTIONS WELCOME.

Dru knew what she wanted and waved off the menu.

"I'll have a hamburger and a Blue Moon. They have the greatest hamburgers here, really thick and juicy. You want a hamburger?"

"Don't eat meat."

The waitress flashed a sparkling grin.

"Me, neither. The veggie nachos are killer, and I *love* the Corita salad."

"Beer's fine. Corona."

As the waitress left, Dru slumped back in her chair and grinned.

"Dude. You totally look like a carnivore."

Pike checked the vendors and the people strolling past. Checked the beach and the people beyond the palms. Habit. He checked Dru Rayne. Round face, one front tooth overlapping the other, a scar on the bridge of her nose that matched the lines beginning to cut the corners of her mouth. Not a kid, but still in her early thirties. Ten feet away, bikini-clad skater chicks, hard-bodied swimsuit models, and beach bunnies out for the sun flowed past, but Dru Rayne held him like a magnet.

She touched his arm.

"Thanks. For helping Wilson, and the rest. Really, thank you."

Pike nodded. When he offered no conversation, she filled in the gap.

"I'm curious—what is it you do? For a living, I mean?"

"Businessman."

Dru burst out laughing, then held up a hand, apologizing as she laughed, and covered her mouth with her free hand.

"I'm sorry. Laughing is bad. I shouldn't be laughing."

Pike liked her laughing. It was strong and confident, as if she was completely at ease. Pike liked her familiarity. He had spent most of his life seeking and maintaining control.

Her eyes grew shy, as if something had been on her mind and now she was going to mention it.

"May I ask you something?"

Pike nodded, watching her.

"The detectives who came to the hospital, remember how Wilson said they asked about you?"

Pike stared past her, now watching the water because he knew where this would go.

She touched his arm again, and Pike was pulled back to her.

"They told us you used to be a police officer, but you left because you were dangerous. That detective we saw, the one with the big belly—"

"Button."

"He said he can't count the number of people you've killed. He said you like killing people so much you even went off to be a mercenary, and we shouldn't have anything to do with you."

Her saying these things reminded Pike of his conversation with Miguel Azzara, only this conversation left him feeling open in a way he did not like. Pike had killed men. He had placed himself in situations where death was inevitable, but knew most people would not understand his motives or reasons. He rarely spoke of these things.

She said, "Is that true?"

"I used to be a police officer. I was a professional military contractor after I resigned. The part about the killing, that's what people like Button want to believe."

She nodded, and he wondered what she was thinking.

"Are you dangerous?"

"Mendoza thinks so."

She smiled again.

"Is that a joke? You made a joke."

Pike once more clocked their surroundings. He hadn't been making a joke, but if she wanted to laugh, he was pleased.

"What Button said, does it bother you?"

"No. I like being with you. I feel safe. Is that weird?"

Pike changed the subject when her hamburger came.

"What about you? Will you go back to New Orleans?"

Dru stared at the ocean for a moment, and seemed thoughtful. She had some of the burger and sipped the beer.

"Pretty here. I've moved around so much since the storm, but nowhere like this. I was in Jackson, then Little Rock with my sister and her husband. My mom went to Atlanta. Everyone was everywhere—Wilson was in Houston for a while, then Dallas, then he went back to New Orleans, but, I don't know, it was just too hard."

She trailed off and shrugged.

"Did you go back?"

"For a while, but I had no one to go back to. I didn't have a boyfriend, and my family was scattered. I didn't own anything, so I left again—stayed with my mom for a while, then my sister. Then Wilson came here, and he liked it, so I thought I'd give it a try. I like it here. I'd like to stay."

Pike enjoyed the play of thought on her face as she spoke.

The robot men called it quits. The smaller man gathered their earnings, closed the briefcase, then lined up behind the larger, both taking the same exaggerated pose. They marched away in lock-jointed unison. No one watched them go except maybe for Dru. Pike couldn't tell if she was watching the robot men or something behind them—maybe the lowering sun.

She said, "It's beautiful here."

She stretched, and spread her hands to the sky, as she smiled again.

"I love the breeze we get. Everyone makes fun of the smog, but most of the time it's clear. Don't you love it? Don't you love that fabulous ocean breeze?"

Pike said, "Yes."

That's when Pike saw a man outside the surf shop a few doors down from the restaurant. A life-sized statue of a surfer with a shark's head stood outside the shop. The man was behind the statue. He moved when Pike turned. A small move like a buoy rocking on a wave, just enough to disappear behind the shark's surfboard.

The man was lean, dark, and probably Latin, though Pike couldn't see him well enough with the bad angle to tell. With the quick glimpse, Pike made the man for his early forties, with a shaved scalp and furry arms.

Dru smiled lazily.

"This is nice, being here like this."

Pike said, "Yes."

She couldn't see Pike's eyes behind the dark glasses, and didn't know he was watching the man.

The man sauntered out from behind the statue and fell in with a group of passing tourists. He wore an unbuttoned pale orange short-sleeved shirt over a white T-shirt, dark jeans, and sunglasses. The shirt and the bald head keyed a memory, and Pike realized the man had passed them before. Pike had not seen him double back, which made Pike suspicious because Pike had outstanding situational awareness, which meant he noticed everything in his environment. In Pike's world, the things you didn't notice could and would hurt you.

As the man drew closer, Pike saw a tattoo on the side of his neck. The ink suggested a gang affiliation, but Pike couldn't see it clearly enough to tell. He wondered if Azzara had lied, and now Mendoza's friends were upping their game, or maybe Azzara had not had time to call off the dogs.

The man left the crowd to take a position behind a street vendor selling hats and T-shirts. Now he was on a cell phone, and Pike wondered whether he was talking or only pretending.

Pike said, "We'd better go."

Dru's face drooped in exaggerated disappointment.

"Wow. This is a short date."

"Is this a date?"

"It could be."

Dru made an effort to pay, but Pike put down cash and told her they didn't need to wait for change. When he glanced over again, the man in the orange shirt was gone.

Pike was trying to spot the man when Dru noticed, and turned to see.

"What are you looking at?"

Pike stepped in front of her, hoping the man hadn't seen.

"Don't look."

She stepped to the side, trying to see—

"Is it one of those guys?"

Pike slid in front of her again.

"It's nothing to worry about."

She was frightened, and now Pike felt irritated with himself. He took her hand. It was soft, but firm beneath the softness.

"We're fine. Come on. I'll walk you home."

Pike squeezed her hand once, then let go, but he could feel her tension as they walked back to the shop.

On the way, he touched her back to stop her twice, pretending to window shop so he could check for shadows, but the man in the orange shirt was gone and no one else was following.

When they reached the corner, Pike paused again. He checked the cars lining the curbs, the rooflines, the nearby shops, and the gas station across the street. Wilson's sandwich shop was quiet and undisturbed, but now Dru walked as if she were brittle. Her confidence and ease were gone, and Pike felt a sense of failure. He had lost control of the moment, and Pike did not like losing control.

She said, "Are we okay?"

"We're fine. I overreacted."

She shook her head.

"You don't look like the overreacting type."

He followed her to her car, the silver Tercel parked directly behind the sandwich shop.

"Want me to come in with you?"

"I've done all I can with this place, believe me. I have to see about Wilson."

Pike nodded, the two of them facing each other, neither of them moving to leave.

"Listen. Thanks. I mean it. I know I keep saying it, but thanks."

"Can I see you again?"

Her smile returned.

He said, "A date."

She smiled wider, but the smile vanished in what Pike read as a wave of uncertainty.

He said, "What?"

She pulled a slim billfold from her pocket, flipped through a card carrier, and showed him a picture of a little girl. The girl wore a fluffy dress and stood beside a green couch.

"This is Amy. My sister's taking care of her until we know whether or not I can make it out here."

Pike said, "Pretty."

"Love of my life. She's three now."

Dru stared at the picture a moment, then slipped the billfold back into her pocket. She looked at Pike, then glanced away with a shrug.

"I dunno—I guess I just wanted you to know."

Pike nodded, sensing she was afraid he would not want to get involved with a woman who had a child. He asked her again.

"Are you going out with me or not?"

Her white smile flashed again. She dug out her cell phone and asked for his number. Pike told her, and watched as she sent him a text.

"This is my number. Call me. I'd love to go out with you. On a real date."

She put her cell phone away, then went up on her toes, and kissed his cheek. Pike cupped the small of her back as her body pressed into his. Pike was moved. She had given him a secret piece of herself when she told him about the child, and now, when she stepped back, he felt compelled to do the same.

"What Button said—Button doesn't know anything about me."

Pike fell silent, thinking how best to explain about the way he had lived his life and the choices he had made. Rescuing a businessman's family from Nicaraguan narco-terrorists. Stopping the bandits who looted farms and villages in Central Africa. Pike had chosen his jobs as a military contractor carefully, and speaking about them now seemed pretentious and self-serving. He finally gave up.

"I tried to help people. I'm good at it."

Pike couldn't think of anything else to say. He let it go at that, and felt embarrassed for bringing it up.

Then Dru laid her palm on his chest, and it felt like she touched his heart.

"I'll bet you are."

She climbed into her car, then looked up at him.

"Do you ever take off those sunglasses?"

Pike took off his sunglasses. The light made him squint, but he fought it to let her see.

She studied his eyes for a moment.

"Good. Very good."

She started her car and gave him a parting smile.

"If you're going to be dangerous, you might as well be dangerous for me."

Pike watched her drive away, then scanned the length of the alley. Nothing.

He put on the sunglasses, then walked around the end of the building and returned to his Jeep. Reaching the door, he saw what looked like a flyer wedged under the windshield wiper. Closer, he saw it was not a flyer, but a folded piece of paper. Pike clocked the surroundings again, and now his inner radar pinged with the weight of eyes.

He lifted out the paper and unfolded it.

GREEN MALIBU
FOUR SPOTS AHEAD

Pike saw the green Malibu parked four spots ahead just as the man in the orange shirt stepped from the secondhand clothing store. The man pointed a thumb at the Malibu. Jerry Button pushed out of the passenger door. A second man got out of the driver's door. He was all hard angles and edges, like a mirror that had been broken and taped back together. He looked impatient, and studied Pike with thoughtful eyes as they walked over.

Button said, "This is Joe Pike. Pike, this is Jack Straw. He's with the FBI."

Straw said, "You're screwing me up, brother. That has to stop."

8

THE MAN IN THE ORANGE shirt walked away when Button and Straw got out of the car. He did not look at them or Pike again.

Button said, "Let's take a ride. Better if we're not seen."

The Malibu was a brand-new rental, but smelled of cigarettes. Pike sat in back, with Straw behind the wheel and Button in the shotgun seat. Button twisted to see Pike as they pulled from the curb. He looked as if he had hoped never to see Pike again, but here they were, and now he was irritated.

"That business between you and me, we have to forget that now, okay? Special Agent Straw is out of the Houston Field Office. Turns out he has an investigation running, and we've stepped into the middle of it, thanks to you."

Pike looked into the mirror and found Straw watching him.

"The man in the orange shirt."

"I'm going to tell you some things I'd rather not,

but I can't divulge where I have people placed. You understand why?"

"We'll see."

"Okay. Hang on, and let me get pulled over. Easier to talk."

Straw drove three short blocks inland and parked behind a row of upscale beachwear shops. The moment they stopped, he rolled down his window and lit a Marlboro. Pike and Button rolled down their windows, too.

Straw turned to face Pike, and showed his credentials. Special Agent R. Jack Straw. Federal Bureau of Investigation.

"Okay?"

Pike nodded, wondering what this was about.

Straw tucked away his badge case and considered Pike through the smoke.

"What did you think of Mikie Azzara?"

Pike was surprised, though he showed no expression.

Straw read his silence anyway, and smiled.

"Not your traditional Mexican Mafioso, is he, all sleeved-out and nasty? He's the new generation, and we're all over him—"

Straw checked his watch.

"—which is how I know you met with him two hours ago at the Starbucks on Abbot Kinney. After which you hooked up with Ms. Rayne and went to the Sidewalk Cafe. They make a good pizza. My favorite meal since I've been here."

Straw craned his head to geyser more smoke out

the window, then glanced at Button.

"My new best friend here, Detective Button, he thinks this conversation is a mistake."

Button stared out the window.

"It is. You're going to regret it."

"I don't think so, but either way I need your help, Mr. Pike, so here we are. Ms. Rayne tell you what's going on?"

"What would she have told me?"

"The two *carnales* you bounced, Mendoza and Gomer? This wasn't the first time they've been to see her uncle, and they didn't kick the shit out of him over a sandwich—they were sending a message."

Button nodded along.

"It's what you and I talked about, Pike. Smith lied. Those pricks were shaking him down."

Straw had more of the cigarette. He looked fit enough, but Pike thought the man probably couldn't run twenty feet.

"Mikie's spooling up a protection racket—pay the man or get your ass kicked, we'll break your window, steal your truck, whatever. It's a street-level thing, small-time, but it's only one of a number of new scams he's running. Underline new. These guys are making it up as they go."

Button shifted in his seat, glancing at Pike but talking to Straw.

"The girl may not know. Smith probably doesn't want her worried about it. He'd be up shit creek if she walked out on him."

Pike said, "What does this have to do with me?"

91

Straw had more of the cigarette.

"You just scared Mikie off, and that's bad. We're clocking his business."

Pike cocked his head.

"The FBI rolled out for a neighborhood protection scam?"

Straw smiled again.

"I wouldn't give two shits and a cup of coffee about this, but the new *jefes* like Azzara, they aren't content to deal tar like their daddies. *La Eme* is entering the modern age, Mr. Pike. They're trying new business models, and this shakedown thing is just one piece. They're also developing international ties with several cartels, and that interests me very much. Hence, my operation and this conversation."

Pike glanced at Button.

"You didn't know?"

"Not until this morning."

Straw finished his cigarette, and flicked it over his shoulder.

"With apologies to Detective Button, we didn't have boots on the ground two weeks ago. When we learned about Mikie's new venture, we decided this was our way into *La Eme*'s new food chain. It's happening fast."

Pike said, "Through a neighborhood shakedown."

Straw shrugged.

"It's down at the street level, we can reach it, and it's easy. Easy means fast. New boys like Azzara are popping up in *Eme* sets from Brownsville to Phoenix to San Diego, and we don't even know who they are. If we can get inside Mikie's set, we can find out, which is what we were doing until you got in the way."

Straw shifted again, and looked apologetic.

"Brother, listen, you did the right thing. If I saw those two clowns stomping some poor guy, I'd weigh in, too. I respect that. But now it's over, and I need things to go back to the way they were."

Pike said, "Meaning what?"

Button shifted angrily.

"He wants you to mind your own fucking business. What don't you get about that?"

Straw raised a hand, telling Button to take it easy.

"I'm asking you to cool it. Stay away from Smith and let him go back to being Smith. Don't be his personal sentry. Let Azzara be Azzara."

Pike saw what Straw wanted, and didn't like it.

"Azzara being Azzara means he puts the pressure on Smith. Mendoza and Gomer will be free to lean on him."

"I need the little men, so I can trade for the big men. This means I need the little men out doing crime so I can jam them. If I jam them up bad, I can use them as informants."

Button nodded along, still scowling at Pike.

"Smith isn't the only guy these turds are trying to milk, Pike. It's not like he's in this alone. Straw and his people are watching five or six shops—"

Pike leaned toward Straw.

"You were watching his place and let him get a concussion. You watched a brick go through his window."

93

Straw hit Button with a glance so hard it could have knocked him out of the car.

"We didn't *allow* those things. They just happened, and now we'll cover him better."

"I won't leave these people hanging."

"You're not. I have it covered."

"You had it covered when he got a concussion."

"We'll cover him *better*."

Straw suddenly opened his door.

"Pike, step out for a moment. Excuse us, Detective."

Pike pushed out, leaving Button alone. Straw came around the car to meet Pike on the sidewalk. Straw's lips were pursed tight, but he lit another cigarette, and lighting it seemed to relax him. He fanned at the smoke.

"We fucked up, okay? We're still learning how these guys do things, but we're learning. Just back away. That's what I'm asking."

Pike studied the man. Straw had serious eyes, but he also looked nervous. Like he had a lot riding on this, and might lose it all.

Pike said, "If I tell Wilson and Dru, you're done."

"You won't tell."

"You have no idea what I'll do."

"Maybe not. But I did some checking. You worked for top-flight PMCs. Even did some work for the government, time to time, though no one's supposed to know. They don't give those clearances to people who can't keep it wrapped."

Straw looked at Pike, out from under his eyebrows, and now the smile was back.

"Surprising what a guy like me can find out, isn't it?"

Pike didn't respond, so Straw shrugged again.

"Listen, you want these people safe? Brother, so do I, and I guarantee you my way is best. Wilson Smith could've sunk these guys right in the ER, but he didn't. He's scared. He's just some poor bastard who wants to fry oysters. You let me get what I need from Azzara, I can help him for real."

Pike didn't like any of it, and he didn't like Straw or the Malibu stinking of smoke.

"How long?"

"Two or three weeks. Maybe less."

Pike scanned both sides of the street, wondering if the man in the orange shirt was watching.

Straw said, "You think about it. In the meantime, don't say anything to Smith or his niece. They need to act natural. If you tell them we're watching, you know what will happen. I might as well head back to Texas."

Pike said, "Man in the orange shirt, he's good."

Straw squinted at Pike through more smoke.

"What man in the orange shirt?"

Straw turned back to his car.

"C'mon. I'll give you a lift back."

"I'm good."

Pike walked.

9

LATER THAT NIGHT, just after ten, the air was cool as Pike jogged toward home through Santa Monica, wearing the forty-pound pack. Pike was a runner. He had been a runner since he was a boy, and ran every day. He sometimes ran twice a day, once in the morning and again at night, and three or four times every week he carried a pack bearing four ten-pound bags of flour. Not nearly so much as the ninety pounds he rucked as a young Force Recon Marine, but it got his heart going.

That night, he ran the Fourth Street steps. One hundred eighty-nine concrete steps climbing the steep bluff from the bottom of Santa Monica Canyon to San Vicente Boulevard. One hundred eighty-nine steps was as tall as a nine-story building, and Pike ran them twenty times, taking them two to a stride. He preferred running at night.

During the day, the steps were clotted with hard-core fitness zealots, marathoners, aerobics instructors, and ordinary trudgers who were trying to get into shape. But at night in the dark when the footing was dangerous, the steps were deserted, and Pike could run at his peak. He liked being alone with his effort and his thoughts.

Now, finished with the steps and jogging for home, Pike chose a route past Wilson's takeout shop. The hour was still early enough that people were out, but the little shop was deserted. Pike wondered if the man in orange was watching, but Pike didn't care. Pike had decided he would not tell Wilson and Dru the FBI was watching their shop, but his silence was as far as he would go. If Mikie was good as his word, the matter was settled. If not, Pike's loyalty lay with the victims, not with a case Straw might or might not be able to make. Pike would not back away. His arrows pointed forward, not back.

When Pike reached home, he stretched in the parking lot to cool, then peeled off his sweatshirt, deactivated the alarms, and let himself in. His condo was austere and functional with little in the way of decoration. Dining room set off the kitchen; couch, chair, and coffee table in the living room; a flat-screen television for sports and news. A black stone meditation fountain burbled in the corner. Pike found peace in the natural sound, as if he were alone in the forest.

Pike stood for a moment, listening, not to the water, but beyond the water—checking to make sure he was alone. He did this every time he came home. Habit.

Pike drank a half-liter of bottled water, then placed

the bottle with others waiting to be recycled. His condo was quiet and empty, but sometimes felt more empty than others. He thought about Dru Rayne and the little girl in the picture, and why Dru had felt the need to show him. Pike liked it that she had shown him the picture. He thought it spoke well of her, and suggested she thought more of him than a beer at the beach.

Pike ate a meal of leftover polenta, black beans, and broccoli sprinkled with a minced serrano pepper. He ate standing up in the kitchen.

Pike had not been in a serious relationship for a long while. Dates, yes, and sex, and he enjoyed close friendships with several women, but nothing he would call a romantic relationship. Maybe for the same reason he didn't have pets. He often disappeared for long periods, and often left without warning.

Pike finished eating, drank more water, then stripped out of his remaining clothes. He spread a foam mat on the living room floor and proceeded through a series of yoga *asanas*. After a lifetime of strength training and martial arts, he could lay his chest on his thighs and face on his knees; he could spread his legs one hundred eighty degrees and become one with the floor.

Pike worked slowly, allowing his body to melt into the postures. The only sounds in his life were the gurgling water, his heart, and the brush of his skin on the towel. After a while he assumed the position of resolve, and meditated. His body calmed, his breathing slowed, and all he knew was the singular sound of his heart. Forty-two slow-motion beats per minute, like thunder alive in his chest.

Pike meditated for exactly fifteen minutes. He did not check his watch, but he had been meditating for most of his life. When fifteen minutes had passed, his consciousness floated to the surface, and Joe Pike was back.

Inhale. Exhale.

At eleven-fifteen that night, Pike brought his things up to his bedroom. His house was orderly and neat. His equipment was clean and squared away. He showered, dried himself, then pulled on a pair of white briefs. He went downstairs for another bottle of water, and noticed his cell phone on the kitchen counter. The screen showed a missed call. He studied the number until he realized it was Dru. She phoned while he was in the shower, but had not left a message.

Pike called her and got her voice mail.

"Hi, this is Dru. You know what to do, so do it."

Her message line beeped.

"It's Joe."

He was still thinking what else to say when the phone cut him off. He called back, and this time finished his message.

"Call whenever. Doesn't matter how late."

He brought the phone upstairs, turned off the lights, and climbed into bed. His mattress was hard. The sheets were crisp and tight as the skin of a drum. He listened to the water, softly bubbling downstairs in his empty home. He wondered what it would be like to have another person's sounds in his house.

Pike waited for her to return his call, but the phone remained silent.

Part Two
Princess of
the Angels

10

HYDECK CALLED AT 10:08 the next morning, identifying herself as if they had never met.

"This is Officer Hydeck with the Los Angeles Police Department. Sorry to bother you, but do you know how to reach Ms. Rayne?"

The professional lack of expression in her voice told Pike something was wrong.

"Why?"

Hydeck hesitated long enough for Pike to hear radio calls in the background.

"Someone trashed their place again. I have a number for Smith, but he isn't answering. I thought you might have a number for his niece."

Pike wondered why she thought he would have Dru's phone, but dropped the thought quickly. He was picturing Miguel Azzara at the coffee shop. Smiling. *It's done.*

"Are you there now?"

"Yes, Pike, I'm here now, and I'm trying to get them here, too. The place is a mess. Do you have her number or not?"

"Yeah, hang on."

Pike gave her Dru's cell, hung up, then immediately dialed the number. Like the night before, his call went to her voice mail. Pike left another message, then decided to see the damage for himself. Gomer had almost certainly broken the window on the first night, but Mendoza had probably wanted some payback of his own after he was released. After Pike saw it, he thought he might encourage Azzara to make Gomer and Mendoza clean it up.

When Pike arrived, he expected to find the new glass shattered, but Wilson's shop appeared undisturbed. The new window was bright, shiny, and intact, and the CLOSED sign hung in the door. An LAPD radio car was at the curb, but Hydeck and McIntosh weren't out front, so Pike rounded the corner to the service alley. He found them clustered at the back door along with Betsy Harmon and her son, Ethan. All four of them turned as Pike rolled up, and Hydeck walked over to meet him.

Pike said, "Did you reach them?"

Meaning Wilson and Dru.

"Left more messages. Those poor people will be walking into a nightmare when they see this place. The pricks really did a job."

McIntosh tried to make a joke.

"But the good news is, we can add B&E and illegal disposal of animal parts to the tab."

Betsy Harmon said, "You should see what they did. Disgusting."

She wore a bright lemon dress today. She stood

with her arms tightly crossed, looking strained and rigid.

Pike saw that the metal security door was bent at the knob where the door had been levered open. The jamb above the lock was dimpled where the lever buckled the frame. It had taken a strong man or more than one man working hard to bend the metal.

"Ms. Harmon called when she saw the door."

"No, I called when I saw *inside*. Degenerates. What kind of people would do this?"

McIntosh widened his eyes at Pike.

"This shit is sick, dude. Check it out."

Pike stepped past the officers and opened the door.

The dank odor of blood and raw meat enveloped him. Pike moved through the storage room, but stopped by the counter as soon as he entered the dining room. Lumbering bottle flies had already homed on the scent and buzzed in slow loops past his head. The counter was red with a viscous pool of drying blood that traced darker red paths to the floor. Long thick pieces of what was probably beef liver, kidneys, and intestines floated in the blood like blue islands. More pieces were draped over the cash register and prep area, and what appeared to be a large gray beef heart was nailed to the New Orleans Saints poster. The skinless heads of three goats hung from the ceiling lights, their lidless eyes dull and bulging. Bottle flies fed on their eyes.

Behind him, McIntosh whispered.

"What if it's people?"

"It's not."

"I know these are animal heads, but this could be human blood. These organs could be from people."

"They aren't. Butchered people smell different."

McIntosh studied Pike as if wondering how Pike knew that, then pointed out the wall behind the counter.

"Check it. Your boys left a message."

Three words were written in blood on the wall above the prep counter.

I AM HERE.

I, not *We.* Singular. Pike wondered what it meant.

Hydeck came up beside them.

"C'mon, it's time to go. I got some snaps for the report. All we're doing is letting in flies."

Pike said, "Have you called Button?"

Hydeck's irritation turned to annoyance.

"Yes, Pike, I put in a call. I'm waiting to hear back from him, too. Right now I'm more interested in getting the owners out here so they can get this place cleaned up and secure."

Pike stepped around the goat heads to the front door. He studied the gas station and buildings across the street, and wondered if Straw's people had seen anything, and whether they had stood by and watched this happen.

Hydeck said, "Let's go, Pike. I mean it. You shouldn't even be in here."

Pike followed them out.

Betsy Harmon still had her arms locked across her chest.

"Are we going to have the CSIs out here and all of that?"

McIntosh said, "That's on TV. Our people are SIDs."

Hydeck pushed the door closed. The bent frame made it difficult, so McIntosh leaned in to help. It still didn't close all the way.

"Those are animal parts, Ms. Harmon. The people who did this probably robbed a Latin market. Latin butchers sell a lot of goat meat. What time does Mr. Smith usually get here?"

"Wilson is always here by nine, every day but Sunday. If they get a food delivery, he'll come in earlier, but one of them should have been here. They're always here by now."

Pike checked his watch and saw it was almost ten-thirty. Hydeck glanced at her watch at exactly the same time, then frowned with impatience.

"Maybe they're not coming in, him with the concussion. He should be in bed, anyway."

Betsy Harmon held herself even tighter.

"In bed doesn't mean you turn off your phones. Someone has to clean up that mess."

"We've left messages. There isn't anything else we can do."

"What if they don't check their messages? That mess in there is going to rot. I can't have my customers smelling it. People can see it from the street."

Hydeck's cell phone buzzed. She glanced at the incoming number, then turned away to take the call.

Pike said, "Is it them?"

"It's Button. Let me see what he wants to do."

As Hydeck walked away, Betsy Harmon turned to Pike.

"They can't just leave it like this, can they? Aren't they supposed to do something?"

Pike had nothing to say. He didn't like it that Dru and her uncle weren't answering their phones. The blood and heads and the message on the wall felt like more than an act of malicious vandalism. There was a darkness to what had been done that left him feeling as if a shadow had passed beneath him out on the open sea.

Hydeck glanced over as she spoke with Button, and Pike could see something was wrong in the way she held herself. Her agitation grew as their conversation went on, then she put away the phone and returned.

"Mr. Smith and Ms. Rayne won't be coming in today. They're leaving for Oregon."

Betsy Harmon stepped back as if she had been kicked.

"Oregon? Who said they're going to Oregon?"

"Mr. Smith. Apparently, he came by earlier and decided enough was enough. He phoned Detective Button about it this morning."

"He's going to leave it like this?"

"I don't know."

"But who's going to clean up the mess?"

"I'm sorry, but that's all I know. I'm sure he'll take care of it before they go."

Pike was surprised, and wondered why Dru hadn't called him.

"Were they threatened?"

"Pike, look inside again and open your eyes. I'd say that's a threat. The guy's scared. He wants to get out of town until these idiots cool down, and he says he won't cooperate with any further investigation. I don't know any more than that, and frankly, if he doesn't give a shit, neither do I."

She glanced at McIntosh.

"We're done here. Let's roll."

Pike said, "Is Button coming out?"

"Don't hold your breath. He was pretty pissed off."

Betsy Harmon's face pulled tight with anxiety.

"But Wilson isn't answering his phone. What if he leaves it like this?"

"If it's determined to be a health hazard, Mr. Smith will be cited. If Mr. Smith doesn't take care of it, I suggest you call the landlord or leasing agency."

"That's it? That's all you're going to do?"

"That's all we can do. I'm sorry."

Pike watched Hydeck and McIntosh head back to their radio car, then took out his phone and tried Dru again. His call went to voice mail, but this time he did not leave a message.

Beside him, Betsy Harmon said, "I don't think they would leave it like this. I just don't believe it."

Pike didn't believe it, either, thinking that anyone who would dump goat heads and blood in the man's shop might not stop with vandalism. He put away his cell.

"You know where they live?"

Betsy Harmon brightened for the first time that morning.

"Yes, I do. They're only a few blocks away."

She had once helped Wilson and Dru bring home perishable food when the shop's refrigerator failed. She didn't remember the street address, but gave Pike directions and described a house on the Venice Canals. She also gave him the cell phone number she had for Wilson Smith.

When Pike turned to his Jeep, Betsy Harmon called after him.

"I saw you."

Pike glanced back, and saw her smiling.

"You and Dru. I saw you kissing yesterday. She looked very happy."

Pike nodded once, such a small nod she might not have seen, then climbed into his Jeep. Dru would have called. He didn't understand why Dru hadn't called.

11

THE VENICE CANALS WERE the dream of a man named Abbot Kinney, a tobacco millionaire from back East who developed the area as a beachside resort. The canals were originally dug to drain marshy land, but Kinney reasoned that one Venice was as good as another, so he decided to re-create Venice, Italy, complete with gondola rides. Sixteen miles of canals were dug, but over time they were filled or shortened. The remaining six were laid out in a perfect square with four canals running side by side and the fifth and sixth canals laid across their tops and bottoms, cutting the land between the canals into three identical, rectangular islands. What began as an amusement park became weekend getaway housing in 1905 that eventually devolved into run-down bungalows on tiny lots in the fifties and sixties occupied by hippies, beachside denizens, and artists. But proximity to the beach and rising property values eventually elevated the area, and the shabby bungalows were replaced by expensive homes.

Pike followed Betsy Harmon's directions into the grid of narrow alleys that lined the canals. He crossed an even more narrow arched bridge, then turned onto an alley lined by houses. According to Betsy Harmon, Wilson and Dru lived in the third house from the end on the left side, a redwood home hidden behind an ivy-covered fence. Pike found the house easily, and parked.

The lots along the canals were small, so the houses all had two or three stories and were built shoulder-to-shoulder out to the street, with their front yards facing the canals and their garages flush on the alleys. A carport was carved into Wilson's house next to a wood gate, but the house and its entrance were hidden by the fence. The carport was empty. Pike was surprised by the house. This was an expensive address.

Pike went to the gate, but found it locked. He pressed a buzzer. A chime sounded inside the house, but no one answered. As he pushed the buzzer again, he noticed a thin young man with straggly black hair watching him from a second-story window at the house next door. The watcher turned away when Pike saw him.

Pike still got no answer, so he went into the carport and banged on the wall. If Wilson and Dru were going to leave, one of them might be inside packing while the other was shopping for last-minute necessities. Hence the missing car.

Pike pounded hard on the wall three times, got no response, and was pounding again when a woman came out of the house next door and called out to him.

"Excuse me!"

She was in her mid-forties with leathery skin, tight jeans, and a tighter T-shirt that highlighted her breasts. She had large breasts, and wanted them seen.

"Are you trying to knock down that house? I can hear you all the way over here."

"Is this Wilson Smith's house?"

"Hardly. They're house-sitting. The owner is in London. He goes there a lot."

She rubbed her thumb and fingers together.

"Made a load in television."

This explained how they could live at such an expensive address. House-sitting.

"But Wilson and Dru live here now?"

"That's right. Is something the matter?"

"There's been some damage to his place of business. I need to speak with him about it."

The woman came out into the alley far enough to peer into the empty carport.

"Well, their car isn't here, so I don't know what to tell you. I'll let them know if I see them."

The thin man came to the door. Close up, he looked like a teenager. He was eating a banana, and squinted as if the sun was overly bright. Pike read them for mother and son.

"S'up?"

"He's looking for Wilson."

He headed back into the house.

"I'm gonna lay out."

"How about looking for a job instead?"

She made a big show of acting disgusted as her son slouched away.

"Three years at Berkeley, and all he does is lay out. My fault, I guess. No man around to set an example."

Her eyes lingered on Pike a beat too long, then she sighed as if realizing she'd just had another bad idea.

"It's a single-mom thing."

She put out her hand.

"I'm Lily Palmer. Who are you?"

"Pike."

"Well, *Pike*, you want me to give them a message when I see them?"

"Tell them to call. They have the number."

Pike returned to his Jeep, but didn't start the engine. Dru and Wilson might very well be leaving, but Pike felt they would not have had time to leave yet. They would have to make arrangements, pack, and do all the things people do to prepare for a trip. Pike told himself they were doing those things now, which is why they weren't home, so he decided to wait.

A few minutes later, Pike called Dru again, then the number Betsy Harmon gave him for Wilson. Both calls went immediately to voice mail as they had every time before, which implied their phones were turned off or being used. Pike didn't like it. The odds both of them were talking on their phones at the same time were slim, and no one turned off their phones when they were getting ready for a trip.

Pike climbed out of the Jeep and returned to the gate. He checked to make sure Lily's son wasn't watching, then hoisted himself over the gate into a tiny courtyard. The front door was locked, and showed no sign of forced entry.

Pike moved along the side of the house, looking into each window he passed, and checking for signs of tampering. The first room appeared to be a guest bedroom, and the next was the kitchen. The bedroom appeared undisturbed, but Pike's view was limited. He saw dirty dishes, three empty beer bottles, and a cutting board on the kitchen counter. Pike told himself the dishes indicated Wilson and Dru planned to return home, but the goat heads and flies hung over him like battlefield smoke.

After checking the last window on the far side of the house, he returned to the backyard. It was small, with a low wood fence bordering the sidewalk that ran along the canal. A latched gate opened to the sidewalk, and a blue fiberglass kayak hung on a small wooden dock across from the gate. Pike studied the houses lining the bank. Even with all the walls and gates, entering the properties would be easy from the water.

Pike checked his watch. Forty-five minutes had passed since he decided to wait, but now the passing time didn't feel like waiting. It felt more like he was allowing something precious to slip away.

Pike was deciding what to do next when he saw Lily Palmer's son. The kid had returned to his second-floor window, which gave him a view into

Wilson's backyard. This time the kid didn't duck. He made a smirking grin before turning away, and Pike wondered how much time he spent in the window.

Pike made his way back along the side of the house, let himself out, and knocked on Lily's door. Her eyes brightened when she saw him, and she gave him a pleasant smile.

"Oh. Hi. I thought you left."

"No. I've been looking around next door. I didn't tell you the whole truth. Wilson has been having trouble with some bad people. I'm concerned those people might have followed them home. Have you seen or heard anything suspicious?"

Her pleasant smile turned into a concerned frown.

"No, I don't think so. Like what?"

"Loud voices. Cars that didn't fit."

She frowned even harder, then shouted into the house.

"Jared! Jared, come here!"

Jared appeared a few seconds later, shirtless and glistening with sunscreen. His thin chest looked like a birdcage.

"I was just going out."

"The gentleman wants to know if you saw or heard anything suspicious over there."

"Next door?"

"Yes, next door. Jesus, what's wrong with you?"

Jared rubbed his birdcage ribs and nodded toward Pike.

"He was in their backyard just now. That's pretty suspicious."

"I *know* he was in their yard. He told me. Would you please answer the man?"

Jared raked the hair from his face, and made the same sneer he'd made in the window.

"He was peeping in their windows. Probably trying to see Dru's tits."

Pike took a step closer, and Jared quickly crossed his arms.

"Dude. It was a joke."

His mother said, "Would you please act like a man? Wilson and Dru are having some kind of trouble. Try to help."

"I didn't see anything suspicious or otherwise. I'm sorry. There's nothing to see."

Pike glanced toward Jared's window.

"Good view from your window. You looking at nothing?"

Jared flushed.

"What should I do, stare at the walls? Bro, it's another day on the Venice Canals—sunshine and water."

"When was the last time you saw them?"

"Wilson or Dru?"

"Either."

"Last night, I guess. That would be Dru. She pulled in when I was coming back from my walk. Gave her a wave. You know. Said whassup. She said whassup back."

Pike edged closer, and Jared held himself tighter.

"What time?"

"Around six, I guess. Something like that."

Pike decided this fit. She drove directly home after leaving him at the takeout shop.

"What about this morning?"

"Didn't see'm this morning, either one."

Jared waved toward the carport.

"Saw the car, though. Went out to score some brown moo, saw the car."

"When?"

"Oh, dude, early."

His mother helped with the answer.

"The *Today* show was beginning its second hour when he left, so that was just after eight. He got back during the second half-hour, so that was about eight forty-five."

Pike tried to fine-tune the window.

"Was the car there when you got back?"

"Yep. For sure."

"See it leave?"

"Nope. Saw it when I got back with the moo, but I couldn't say when it left."

"How many cars do they have?"

"Just the one."

Lily nodded.

"They have one car."

"The silver Tercel."

"Yeah."

The silver Tercel was something Jared saw every day. Something a person sees every day becomes invisible, but something out of the ordinary stands out. He had asked these same questions or questions like them a thousand times when he was a cop.

"Forget the Tercel. When you were coming back with the moo, did you see anyone you didn't recognize? Maybe a car that wasn't familiar?"

Jared shook his head.

"Nobody like you mean. A couple of ladies with dogs walked by. Some gardeners were working next door."

Pike hesitated.

"At Wilson's?"

"Yeah. A couple of Latin dudes."

Almost every house along the canals would employ professional gardeners, and most would be Latin.

"You know they were gardeners because you've seen them before, or do you assume they were gardeners because they were Latin?"

Jared turned dark red, as if he had been accused of racial profiling.

"Dude! Hey, here are these dudes, they have the work clothes, not exactly dressed for success, I see'm going in through the gate, who else would they be?"

Lily Palmer said, "Did they have blowers, honey? A mower?"

"It's not like I studied them. I wasn't paying attention."

Pike touched the side of his neck.

"Ink?"

Jared pressed his lips together as he tracked through his memory, then he suddenly brightened.

"Yeah, I think, but the one dude, I remember this, he had a cast on his arm."

Pike felt very still, and heard only the soft whisper of his breath and the heavy, slow-motion thump of his heart.

"Which arm?"

Jared touched his right forearm.

"This one. He had one of those wrist casts, goes from the thumb up to about right here."

Mendoza was wearing exactly that cast when he was released from the Airport Courthouse.

"And the car was still there when you saw them?"

"Yeah. It was there."

"And later it was gone."

"Yeah. Gone."

Pike turned toward Smith's house. His slow-beating heart grew louder until each beat boomed like thunder on the horizon. He had seen the outside of the house, but very little of the inside. A nightmare worse than goat heads could be waiting inside.

Lily Palmer touched his arm.

"Are they the people you were talking about?"

Pike nodded, still staring at the house.

"Should we call the police?"

Pike shook his head.

"I'll take care of it."

Then he gave Lily something to help ease her concerns.

"When you see Wilson or Dru, ask them to call me. They have the number."

"Of course. As soon as I see them."

Pike returned to his Jeep and backed out the narrow

street. He turned the corner, then immediately pulled over and parked.

He trotted back fast, checked again to see if anyone was looking, then hoisted himself over a fence on the side of Wilson's house away from the Palmers. Having seen the property once, he knew where he wanted to go and carried the things he needed to enter.

On this side of the house, Pike had found a window used for ventilation for a laundry room. He pulled on a pair of vinyl gloves, then set to work. It had not been tampered with before, but now he levered it open with a small pry bar and shimmied through the opening.

Once inside, Pike pulled a pair of paper booties over his running shoes, then quickly moved through the house. His sole mission was to search for bodies. He would take the time for nothing else because nothing else was as important.

Pike slipped through the laundry room into a hall, then swept through the kitchen, a large family room, a small bedroom with an adjoining bath. He did not touch or examine anything, though he quickly scanned each floor for blood. He found no obvious drops or splatters, no signs of a violent struggle, and no bodies.

He took the stairs three at a time to the second floor, flowing through a large office, an enormous master bedroom, and the master bath as smoothly as if he were liquid.

He went through the entire house in less than

sixty seconds, and never once stopped moving until he knew there were no bodies. Wilson and Dru had not been murdered here. Their dead bodies were not waiting here.

Pike came out of the master bedroom and paused for the first time on the second-floor landing. Only now, for the first time, the outside world slowly found its way in. Pike felt himself sway, just a little, as if from a tiny temblor. A helicopter passed nearby. He caught the scent of lilacs, and knew the scent was Dru's.

Pike left the house as he entered, and moved quickly back to his Jeep. He saw Reuben Mendoza, and the heads in Wilson Smith's shop. He saw two men opening Wilson's gate, one with a cast on his arm. He saw Miguel Azzara with his brilliant male-model smile, saying it would never happen again.

Hello, Reuben.

Hello, Miguel.

I am here.

12

PIKE CRUISED PAST THE Our Way Body Mods shop, turned at the next block, then circled the block and pulled into a loading zone on the opposite side of the street. Their corner location on the busy street made reconnoitering easy.

Pike wanted Gomer or Mendoza, but they were not around. Neither was Michael Azzara or his shiny new Prius, but the maroon Monte Carlo was parked at the curb outside the fence.

Pike studied the number and locations of the people, the position of the vehicles in the parking lot, and everything surrounding the building. Something about the body shop bothered him.

Pike counted one man in the service bays and two in the parking lot by a 1969 candy-gold SS396. The man in the service bay was fitting a fender onto a car, but having a difficult time. None of them were familiar, but the men by the 396 drew Pike's attention. One was a younger man in grease-stained work clothes who was showing the other man something under the hood. The other man was duded up in lizard-skin cowboy boots, an immaculate white Stetson, and a pink-and-white cowboy shirt under a suede sport coat. A Western belt with an enormous brass buckle held up jeans sporting a razor crease. A few minutes later, the cowboy had seen enough. He walked over to the service bays, said something to the man with the fender, and that's when a man Pike recognized from the Monte Carlo appeared. He was the man who had pointed his gun hand at Pike; the man who lifted Mendoza off his feet to welcome him home. The two men shook hands, then the cowboy walked through the main gate to an anonymous Buick and drove away.

Watching the cowboy leave, Pike understood what had been troubling him. Yesterday, a dozen men were present and the yard was busy. Today, only three men remained, leaving the body shop deserted. Pike found this curious, but it would also make his job easier.

Pike circled the block again, but this time he parked on a residential street behind the body shop. He stripped off his sweatshirt, then strapped into a lightweight ballistic vest. He cinched the Velcro tight, pulled the sweatshirt back on, and reset his holster. When he was good to go, he let himself out of the Jeep and approached the body shop from the rear.

The man from the Monte Carlo had disappeared, but Pike saw the yard man helping his co-worker with the fender in the far bay. Pike did not care about them. He wanted Mendoza's friend.

Pike stepped into the first bay and spotted the man from the Monte Carlo in an office at the rear of the building. He was in front of a television with his back to the door. The Dodgers were playing a day game. Pike checked to see that the other two men were still struggling with the fender, then slipped toward the office as silently as a fish gliding through water.

On TV, Vin Scully called the play as the Dodgers took a 2–0 lead in the first off a two-run homer by David Snell. The man watching pumped his fist and shouted to himself.

"Thass what I'm talking about! Show them bitches how we do it out here!"

Pike hooked an arm around the man's neck, lifted his feet from the floor, and closed his carotid artery. This shut off the blood to his brain. The man struggled hard for the first few seconds, but sagged as he lost consciousness. Pike held him until the man went limp, then lowered him and tied his wrists behind his back with a plasticuff. Pike had made dozens of high-speed entries in different parts of the world, usually into tear-gassed rooms where armed hostiles hid behind hostages, desperate to kill him. His moves now were practiced and efficient.

Out in the far service bay, the two men were still busy with the fender when Pike left the office. They were fitting the driver's side front fender in place, one man bolting the front, the other the back. Pike angled to their midpoint blind spot, and drew his .357 as he closed. Behind him, Vin Scully filled the silence, saying what a fine acquisition Snell had been from the Kansas City Royals.

Pike hit the first man with the pistol above the right ear, then pivoted to meet the second man, thumbing the hammer to let the man hear the pistol cock.

The man stared, mouth open but soundless.

Pike tipped the muzzle toward the floor.

"Down. Hands behind your head."

The man did it immediately.

Pike tied off both men at their ankles and wrists, then whispered to the man who was still awake.

"Man in the office. What's his name?"

"Hector Perra."

"Close your eyes. Make a sound, I'll kill you."

He closed his eyes.

Hector was on his feet when Pike returned to the office. He was spinning in a circle like a dog chasing its tail, trying to see his wrists. Then he saw Pike, lowered his head, and charged.

Pike guided him headfirst into the door frame, jerked him upright, then snapped a backfist onto the bridge of his nose. Hector's eyes fogged, but Pike held him up.

"Look at me. Focus."

Hector's eyes cleared.

Pike made his hand like a gun with his thumb up and index finger out, and pointed at Hector.

"Remember?"

Pike hit him again, moving so fast Hector did not see it coming. His head snapped back, but Pike had not hit him hard. Pike wanted him awake.

"Where are they?"

"Whachu talking about?"

"The people who own the sandwich shop."

"I don't know, bro. Whachu talking about?"

Pike studied the dark eyes. They were angry and fearful, but also confused. Father Art told him the *Malevos* had over sixty known members spread throughout Venice. Not all of them would be part of every crime committed, nor even know what the other members were doing. Pike decided Hector was telling the truth.

"Where's Mendoza?"

"How the fuck I'm supposed to know? Off doing his thing."

"You see him this morning?"

"Man, we ain't married. I got my own life."

Pike hit him again, harder than before, then shook him to help clear his head.

"When's the last time you saw him?"

"Yesterday. After his release."

"Where?"

Pike wanted to see if Hector was playing it straight.

"Here, bro. Homes made bail, he hung out for a while, then split. You know how it is."

"Where'd he go when he left here?"

"Home to his old lady, I guess. I dunno. We was gonna get together, but I never heard back."

"Was Gomer with him?"

"I dunno."

Pike searched Hector for weapons, but found only keys, a cell phone, and a wallet. He held up the keys.

"The Monte Carlo?"

Hector nodded, and Pike jerked him to the door.

"Let's go. Outside."

"You takin' my car?"

"I'm taking you."

13

PIKE SHOVED HECTOR INTO the passenger seat, then slid in behind the wheel and powered away. Hector shriveled from Pike like a deflating balloon, his eyes snapping like shutters.

"Where you takin' me? Where we goin', homes?"

Pike didn't answer. He drove five blocks into the residential neighborhood to put distance between himself and the body shop before he pulled to the curb. Hector shrank even farther away, inching up the door.

Pike went through Hector's wallet. He found thirty-two dollars, pictures of people who were probably Hector's family, some discount coupons, and two California driver's licenses. Both showed Hector's picture, but with different names, addresses, and DOBs. One identified Hector as Hector Francis Perra with a Ghost Town address, the other as Juan Rico with a Van Nuys address. Pike returned everything to the wallet, then looked at Hector.

"Mendoza."

"I don't know where he is. I tol' you. How the fuck I'm supposed to know?"

Pike drew the Python and pressed it into Hector's thigh.

"Show me where he lives."

Hector directed him to a small flat-roofed bungalow at the edge of Ghost Town near Inglewood. The stucco siding flowered with water damage, but the yard was surprisingly neat. Two stringy palms cast Marks-A-Lot shadows across a Honda Maxima in the drive. Pike cruised past, then parked on the next block with an eyes-forward view of the house.

Pike said, "That his car?"

"His girlfriend. This is her place. He lives with her."

"What's her name?"

"Carla Fuentes."

"Kids?"

"No, but that bitch is tryin'. I tell him he better watch out."

The house showed no life, but the same was true for most of the surrounding houses. An older woman pruned dusty roses in a yard farther down the street, and a mongrel dog that had probably dug its way to freedom sniffed at a street sign, then burst away at a sprint. Pike would have preferred to watch the house until Mendoza emerged or returned, but felt he didn't have time. Pike's nature was to drive the play, and driving the play meant moving forward.

Pike holstered his gun, took the keys from the ignition, then reached under the dash at the base of the steering column. He disconnected the wires that controlled the turn signals and horn, then got out of the car. When he pulled Hector across the seat, Hector looked hopeful.

"You lettin' me go?"

"No."

Pike clipped the plasticuffs off Hector's wrists, but immediately tied his right wrist to the top of the steering wheel and his left to the bottom. He pulled the plasticuffs tight.

"Damn, bro, that cuts."

Pike closed the door.

"Start screaming, you won't like how it ends."

Pike walked directly to Mendoza's house, then cut down the drive and picked up his pace. The drive led to a detached one-car garage, but Pike broke hard to the side of the house. He stayed low, rising only long enough to glance in each window as he circled the house. He slipped past a screenless back door, then across a small patio. The next two windows were blocked by drawn shades, but he could see into a bathroom and bedroom on the opposite side of the house. Both were empty, but the bathroom allowed a narrow view across a hall into the living room. He saw a TV playing, but not who was watching. There were at least three rooms that Pike could not see into. Mendoza and Gomer could be in any of them, but Pike would not know this until he entered the home.

Pike was still watching the living room when a young woman carried a large bundle past the bathroom. Mendoza's girlfriend, Carla. She went into the living room, then disappeared as she turned toward the kitchen.

Pike ran to the backyard and reached the corner of the house as the screen door kicked open. Carla Fuentes came out, carrying her bundle to the garage. She wore a thin tank top that was too tight for her bulges, bright purple shorts, and was barefoot. She elbowed open a door on the side of the garage, and went in. Laundry.

Pike waited a five-count to see if anyone would follow her out, then crossed the yard fast. He slipped in behind her as she pushed sheets into a top-loading washer. She didn't know he was there until he wrapped his arms around her, one hand over her mouth, the other pinning her arms. Her body went stiff with an electric jolt of fear. She was strong. She arched her back, trying to twist away, kicking and stomping his legs. Pike held her close, trapping her, and made his voice calm.

"You're safe. I want Mendoza."

She tried to bite him.

"Is Mendoza inside?"

She finally stopped fighting, but her body was rigid. He took his hand from her mouth, but stayed ready to clamp down if she screamed. She didn't.

"You motherfucker. Who the fuck are you?"

"Is Mendoza inside?"

"Lemme go, you bastard. You the police? Who are you?"

"Yeah, I'm the police. Is Mendoza inside?"

"Ain't nobody here. I don't know where that bastard is."

"Let's see."

Pike walked her to the house, keeping her in front of him as he drew his weapon. He let her open the door, but listened hard before they entered. The kitchen smelled of bacon and marijuana. Pike heard the television, but no living voices or movement. He whispered in her ear.

"Slow."

As they stepped inside, the girl suddenly called out.

"Loo-cee, I hoannn!"

Pike gripped her tighter, but she barked out a laugh.

"Homes, he ain't here. You gotta relax."

Pike walked her into the living room first. A large glass hash pipe sat on a coffee table opposite the television as if it were watching. He pushed her through the living room to the hall, then through the rest of the house. He checked the closets, the bathtub, and under the beds. He didn't release her until they were back in the kitchen, where he pulled a chair from the table and told her to sit.

"Fuck you, you bitch. I ain't gotta sit in my own fuckin' house."

"Sit, or I'll make you."

Pike saw a fading bruise high on her left cheek as Carla Fuentes looked him over. Her eyes held on his tattoos as if seeing something familiar, and then she sat.

"You ain't five-oh. You're the dude broke his arm."

"Where is he?"

"You find him, you tell me. I hope you kicked his ass good."

Pike circled the kitchen, looking for something that would give him leverage over the girlfriend or help him find Mendoza.

"If you know about me, it means you've seen him."

"Bullshit it does. Means he called when they were processing him. Said he would be home last night, but that bitch never showed. I got stress in my life."

Pike found a pink cell phone on the counter by a pack of cigarettes. He opened it, and scrolled through the directory.

"Was he here this morning?"

"You listenin' to me? I got no call, no nothing, so fuck him and fuck you. I signed off this house to guarantee that bond. That bitch runs off, I'm losing my home."

Pike glanced over. Azzara had told him he covered Mendoza's bond, but now the girlfriend was telling a different story. Pike believed the girl. Her eyes were red and the corners of her mouth were dimpled with tension. The bond on Mendoza's assault wouldn't have been more than fifty thousand dollars, and would likely be less. The bondsman was ripping her off.

Pike returned to the phone and found a speed-dial listing for REUBEN. He memorized the number, then held out the phone.

"Call him. Let's see where he is."

"He ain't gonna answer. I been callin' all day."

Pike checked the outgoing call list, and saw she was telling the truth. Mendoza's number had been dialed fourteen consecutive times. Pike dialed the number again. Mendoza's phone immediately went to voice mail, so Pike killed the call.

"He tell you what he was doing when I broke his arm?"

"Said you were fighting. Said he was gonna fuck you up real good, he catch you again."

"Is he looking for me?"

"Said he was, but seein' you now, that was just him spinnin' shit."

Pike wondered if this meant the harassment toward Wilson was directed at him. Hurting Wilson and Dru to get back at Pike. He put the phone with the cigarettes, then stood in front of her.

"Is that why he wasn't going to be home until last night, he was looking for me?"

"That was just mouth. He said he had business."

"Business like what?"

"He hadda go help some friends. Thass what he says when it's *Trece*."

"Gang business?"

"Thass what it means, helpin' some friends. He was callin' from jail, homes, the Sheriff's right there, you can't just say what you're sayin'. He said he hadda help some friends, and tol' me he would be home, only he never showed up and he ain't callin' back, and now I got you in my house. I signed off my *home* for that fuckin' bitch, and for all I know he jumped bail and left."

Pike believed she didn't know anything more, but he still didn't have anything that would help him find Mendoza.

"Where else does he stay when he's not here with you?"

"This is his *home*. I let him move *in* here. We're gonna get *married*."

"What kind of car does he drive?"

"An eighty-six El Camino. It's brown. Like a turd."

"Where does he keep his paperwork? Car registration, bills, things like that."

Pike followed her back to the bedroom where she pulled a cardboard shoe box from the top drawer of a scarred and faded cabinet. It contained a few family photos, birth information, and miscellaneous warranties and receipts. Pike found the bill of sale and registration information for the El Camino along with the tag and VIN numbers. He didn't waste time copying the numbers. He tucked the box under his arm.

"What you doin', man, thass his things!"

Pike noticed a large blue purse on the dresser. He went through it and found Carla's wallet.

"I ain't got no money in there."

Pike wasn't looking for money. Seeing Mendoza's family photos gave him an idea. Her wallet held a vinyl picture holder, and the first picture was Reuben Mendoza. Mendoza was smiling so wide he looked like a pumpkin. Pike took the picture, then placed the purse back on the dresser.

"You fuckin' thief. I'm callin' five-oh."

Pike decided there was nothing more to be had, and walked out of the room. Carla Fuentes trailed after him, anxiously pulling his arm.

"Let me ask you somethin'. If he skips on the bond, they really gonna take my house?"

"Yes."

"But it's not my fault if he runs."

"You signed the bond."

"Waitaminute. Wait, now, what about this? If he gets himself killed, will I still lose the house? If he's dead, they can't blame me for that, can they? They won't take the house?"

Pike stopped when he reached the door.

"No. You'll lose the bond fee and application, but the court will release the bond back to the bondsman."

"What does that mean?"

"You won't lose the house."

She thought it through, and some of the terror left her eyes.

"What you gonna do if you find him?"

"What would you like me to do?"

"Break his other damned arm. Break it real good, then beat him to death."

Pike stepped into the sun and headed back to the Monte Carlo.

137

14

PIKE CLIMBED INTO THE Monte Carlo, but this time into the passenger seat, leaving Hector tied to the wheel. Hector once more scrunched as far from Pike as possible.

"Look at my hands, homes. Look at'm! They're turnin' blue!"

Pike fingered through the papers in the box, wanting to see what he had.

"You gonna let me go? You gotta let me go, bro, this shit here is kidnappin'. That's a federal offense."

"Shut up."

Hector fell silent, but grumbled under his breath.

Pike found cash receipts and instructions for three disposable phones Mendoza purchased from Best Buy. Pike wondered if his friend Elvis Cole could use the information to locate Mendoza or identify who he was calling. Cole was a private investigator, and had relationships with most of the cell service providers. He might also be able to help find Alberto Gomer.

Pike studied Reuben Mendoza's picture last, then dropped it into the box. A plan to flush Mendoza out of the weeds was forming, and the picture would help.

Pike said, "Hold still."

Hector's eyes bulged when Pike drew his knife. Pike clipped the ties, cutting him free.

"Get out."

"What get out? This is my car."

"Out."

"Bro, what, you takin' my car?"

"I won't tell you again."

Hector shoved open the door, and got out in a sullen funk. He slammed the door as Pike slid behind the wheel.

"This ain't right, stealin' my car. You takin' my wallet, too? You takin' my phone?"

Pike drove back to his Jeep. He left Hector's wallet in the Monte Carlo, but added his phone to Mendoza's box. Pike didn't take time to examine these things because he wanted to keep pressing.

Pike drove directly to Lily Palmer's house, parked in Wilson's carport, and rang the bell. She answered the second ring.

"I knew you'd be back. Did you find Wilson and Dru?"

"Not yet. Is Jared here?"

She sighed.

"Jared's always here."

She called into the house, and Jared's flip-flops announced his approach. He was freshly slathered with sunblock and carried a bottle of beer. He frowned when he saw Pike and tugged the iPod buds from his ears.

"Dude, you got it all. I don't know anything else."

"The man with the cast—"

Pike showed him the picture of Reuben Mendoza. "Was this him?"

Jared glanced at the picture, then brightened with a surprised smile that made him look proud of himself.

"Dude! That's him! The Cast Man!"

"You're sure?"

"Fuckin' A."

Jared beamed, and continued to vomit up memories.

"Dude had khaki baggies and a gray plaid shirt, but it was open. Shirt was huge, dude, like fifty sizes too big, and a white T-shirt underneath. And he was bald."

Pike had seen witnesses have similar explosions of memories when he was an officer. If a witness was given a visual trigger, a memory that had been vague would often snap into focus. Psychologists called these memory cues, and the resulting cascade of recollections were memory chains.

"You remember anything about the second man?"

Jared thought for a moment, but his lips peeled from his teeth in frustrated effort.

"Not really getting him. He was in front, kinda already through the gate. The Cast Man was behind him. I remember black hair. And shades. He might've been wearing shades."

Jared finally ran out of gas.

"Sorry, bro. That's all I got."

Pike could now tie Mendoza to the scene with a picture ID. The second man was almost certainly Gomer, but Mendoza would be enough.

Pike went back to his Jeep to decide on his next play, but knew he would ultimately have to return to Button. Button was the last person to have contact with Smith. Pike wanted to know exactly what Smith said, how he had said it, and when. These things could be crucial, and so could having Button back in the game. The police would increase the pressure on Mendoza, but timing their entry was a trade-off. Once the police reinserted themselves they would block Pike's moves and kill his momentum. He had to cover the primary plays before they came in, and keep himself ahead of the curve.

Pike fished Hector's phone from the box, spent a few seconds figuring it out, then scrolled through the directory. He found Mendoza's number under R MENDOZA, but nothing for GOMER or ALBERTO. No numbers were listed for AZZARA, but he found a number for MIGUEL.

Pike pressed the send button, heard two rings, and Mikie Azzara answered.

"Don't bother me with crap at that body shop."

Answering this way because the caller ID told him it was Hector.

Pike said, "I am here."

Mikie hesitated.

"Who is this?"

"One of your boys wrote it on their wall."

Azzara hesitated again, but this time he recognized Pike's voice.

"How'd you get this phone?"

"I want Mendoza and Gomer."

Azzara lowered his voice, as if he was someplace where he didn't want to be overheard.

"What are you talking about?"

"Mendoza was at their home this morning. Now they're missing."

Azzara cleared his throat. Pike heard something in the background, but couldn't make out what it was. Then Azzara tried to sound reassuring, which left Pike wondering why Azzara wanted to reassure him.

"Listen, I don't know anything about this, but I will find out. I promise you—you don't have to worry. I'm sure these people are fine."

"You're a liar, Miguel. You told me you covered Mendoza's bond. You didn't. What else are you lying about?"

"Would you listen? I'm in the middle of something now, but I will help you here, homes. Just relax. Kick back, give me a few hours, and—"

"Time's up."

Azzara fell silent. It was several seconds before he spoke again. Then his voice was softer, but not reassuring.

"You are making a mistake. You think you're talking to some pretty-boy Mexican, but you are talking to *La Eme*. We are two hundred thousand strong. You should wait like I say. You don't want to go to war with us."

Pike waited him out, letting the pressure of his silence build. When Azzara finally spoke again his voice showed a strain Pike found curious.

"Are we clear on this? Do you get it?"

Pike said nothing.

"Do. You. Get. It?"

"You don't understand."

"What? What don't I understand?"

"War is what I do."

Pike hung up, then called a friend named Elvis Cole.

15

EXPERIENCED INVESTIGATORS REFERRED to the site where an abduction took place as ground zero. It was the intersection where the paths of the victim and perpetrator converged, and merged into one. It was an ambush zone of abrupt furious violence or quiet threat where two paths led in and only one path led out, but these paths weren't made in a vacuum. The physical world was disturbed—a fish rippled the water; a gliding bird cast a shadow. Pike knew this better than most because he spent most of his life trying to move without being heard or seen, or leaving a trail that others could follow. It was difficult. Jared Palmer had seen Reuben Mendoza. This was the first ripple, but Pike knew there would be others. The problem was time. Pike was building a pressure wave and riding it like a surfer shooting the green tunnel. But returning to Smith's house to develop the trail could take hours and would diminish the pressure. The wave would collapse. Pike needed help to maintain the pressure, and believed no one was better at finding and recovering missing persons than his partner, Elvis Cole.

Cole was a licensed private investigator Pike met back in the day when Pike still wore the badge. Not the likeliest of pairings, Pike being so quiet and remote, Cole being one of those people who thought he was funny, but they were more alike than most people knew. Cole was an apprentice then, working for an old-school L.A. dick named George Feider to pile up the three thousand hours of experience the state required for a license. When Cole clocked the three-thousandth hour, Feider was ready to retire and Cole wanted to buy his agency. Pike had resigned from LAPD by then, and was making fat cash on military and security contracts. They bought the agency together, though Pike stayed in the background. He preferred it that way. Unheard and unseen.

While Pike waited for Cole to arrive, he phoned Hydeck and Betsy Harmon, hoping he was wrong about their disappearance and that Wilson or Dru had returned their calls or finally showed up at their kitchen. They hadn't, and Betsy Harmon once more complained that no one had cleaned up the mess.

Twenty-five minutes after Pike called Elvis Cole, Cole slid into Pike's Jeep outside a bar on Abbot Kinney, a few short blocks from the canals. Cole had made good time. If he was in the middle of something when Pike called, he had not mentioned it.

Cole said, "What's going on?"

Pike began with Mendoza's arrest two days earlier, and sketched the sequence of events up to and including his search for Mendoza and his call to Miguel Azzara. When he finished, Cole studied the snapshot of Mendoza before looking up.

"So you don't believe they went to Oregon."

"No. If Mendoza hadn't been seen at the house, then maybe, but Mendoza changes the game."

"So you think, what, he followed them home to threaten them, but it turned into an abduction? He forced Smith to make the call?"

Pike nodded, but did not voice his darker fear—that the abduction had become a body drop.

"Have you tried calling them again?"

"You call, you get voice mail. They don't call back."

Cole nodded, his face vacant as he thought the scene through.

"Which is what would happen if their phones were taken away from them."

"Yes."

Cole glanced over.

"Forgetting Mendoza for a minute—maybe they were so freaked out, they figured enough with the bad news and turned off their phones."

"Wilson, maybe, but not Dru. Dru would call if she could."

"She would?"

Pike realized Cole was staring.

"I know her."

"Ah."

Pike thought he probably should have phrased it another way.

"We had a beer."

"I see."

"We made a date. She asked me to call."

"I understand."

Cole asked for their numbers, saying he would try to learn about their account activity from the service provider. Pike recited the numbers, then gave him Mendoza's shoe box and Hector's phone. Cole fingered through the contents.

"Okay, good—I can work with this. What about the police? Are they treating it as an abduction?"

"They don't know about Mendoza."

Cole glanced up from the box.

"Why not?"

"I want you to see the house first. You have fresh eyes, you're faster, and you'll see things they miss."

Cole tried to look modest.

"That goes without saying."

"But you won't have much time. We get you set up, I'm going to Button. He'll move on Smith's house, so we have to move on it first."

Cole glanced at Mendoza's picture again, then handed it back.

"Let's get busy."

Pike led the way with Cole following in his own car. Because of the narrow lanes and difficult parking, they left their vehicles on Venice Boulevard and approached Smith's house on foot. Pike didn't want another conversation with the Palmers, so he stopped well out of their view to point out Smith's house. Pike had already warned Cole about Jared.

When Cole saw the house, he glanced at Pike.

"A dude trying to make a go of a sandwich shop owns this place?"

"They're house-sitting. It's owned by a retired TV writer."

"Were you inside?"

"Only to check for bodies. I entered through the side window at the laundry room, but I didn't disturb the scene."

Pike described finding no signs of forced entry outside the house, and no blood evidence or signs of struggle in the carport or courtyard inside the front gate. He wanted Cole to concentrate on the interior because their time would be limited once he went to the police.

"When I finish with Button, I'll call you, then I'll sit on the girlfriend's house. I put her and Azzara in play to stress Mendoza. When Button comes in he'll jack the pressure even more, and Mendoza might break for home."

Stressing the enemy was a tactic Pike had used in the field. Put enough stress on the target, he would panic and run. They almost always broke for home.

Cole said, "Sounds good. I'll see what I can find out about Mendoza and Gomer, and relieve you later tonight."

They were finished, and Pike knew he should roll out, but he stared at the house. He imagined Dru and Wilson inside after they returned from their shop. He saw Mendoza and the second man moving toward the gate, then put what he saw next out of his head.

Pike realized Cole had said something, but hadn't heard what. Cole was watching him with a curious expression, and when he spoke again, his voice was gentle.

"You okay?"

"I told her I took care of it. That they wouldn't be bothered again."

The sudden sympathy in Cole's eyes left Pike feeling embarrassed. He looked away.

Cole said, "Hey."

Pike looked back.

"Am I not the World's Greatest Detective?"

Pike nodded.

"I'm on it, Joseph. We'll find her."

Cole walked away before Pike could respond.

Pike watched his friend for a moment, then headed back to his Jeep. Time was passing, and time was the enemy.

Pike drove hard for the Pacific Community Police Station.

16

THE PCPS WAS A LOW, modern brick building surrounded by a block wall and wispy pine trees on Culver Boulevard less than a mile from Pike's home. A flagpole bearing the American flag stood proudly out front, across from a billboard advertising a bail bondsman. The middle-class homes across the boulevard were neat and attractive. These neighborhoods—like the police station—made it difficult to believe that wars between rival gangs often filled the streets with blood only a few minutes away.

Pike pulled to the curb by the flagpole at seven minutes after three. The watch would change at four, so any detectives not in court or in the field would be inside finishing up for the day. Pike needed to find out if Button was one of them.

He phoned Information for the PCPS detective desk number, then called.

"Pacific. This is Detective Harrison."

"This is Dale King at the PAB. Is Button still there?"

The Police Administration Building was the

new administrative building that had replaced Parker Center.

Harrison said, "Yeah, hang on. I'll get him."

Pike waited until she put him on hold, then closed his phone. Believing Button would refuse to see him, Pike walked around the side of the station through the civilian parking lot, then hopped a low wall and went to the two-story parking structure where officers kept their cars. He didn't like losing the time, but he didn't have long to wait.

Fourteen minutes later, Button came out the rear of the station in a loose file of other detectives and uniformed officers on their way to their cars. He carried a briefcase with his jacket and tie over his opposite arm, and wore a light blue shirt with sweat rings under the arms. A small revolver was clipped to his belt.

Pike was behind a column when Button passed, angling toward a tan Toyota pickup. Button shifted his jacket from his right arm to his left, and was fishing for his keys when Pike stepped from behind the column.

"Button."

Button lurched sideways at Pike's appearance. He scrambled for his gun, dropping his briefcase and keys as he got hung up in his jacket.

Pike calmly raised his hands, showing his palms.

"We're good."

If Button was embarrassed by his reaction, he didn't show it. He picked up his briefcase and keys, and continued toward his truck.

"This is an off-limits police parking area. Get out."

"They were abducted."

"What the fuck are you talking about?"

"Wilson Smith and Dru Rayne. They're gone."

Button unlocked the truck, and tossed his jacket and briefcase inside.

"They're on their way to Oregon, man. And another thing—Straw is fucking livid, not that it matters a damn. Fucking self-important Fed. He probably hates you more than I do."

"Reuben Mendoza and a second man who might have been Gomer were at their home at eight forty-five this morning. What time did Smith call?"

Button already had one leg in the truck, but now he backed out, squinting at Pike.

"How do you know he called me?"

"Hydeck. I was at Smith's shop when you spoke with her. From there, I went to Smith's house."

"Is this for real?"

"They have a locked front gate you have to go through to enter the property. The kid next door saw Mendoza and another man going through the gate at eight forty-five. Jared Palmer. Talk to him."

Pike saw the strain on Button's face as he weighed his hatred of Pike against what he was hearing, as if he had to climb a wall before he could move forward. He finally walked over, leaving the Toyota's door open.

"How's the kid know Mendoza?"

"He doesn't. I showed him this."

Pike held out the snapshot. Button gave it a glance, but did not touch it.

"One to ten, how confident was he?"

"Ten."

"He's sure about the time?"

"The mother pegged it to the *Today* show. Jared went out for some chocolate milk at the beginning of the eight-o'clock hour and got back a few minutes after the half-hour break. That puts Mendoza there at about eight forty-five. When did you hear from Smith?"

Button glanced at the snapshot again, and this time he took it to examine Mendoza more closely.

"What about the second man? Was it Gomer?"

"I didn't have a picture of Gomer. What time did you talk to Smith?"

"Around nine, right in there, maybe a few minutes after."

Button frowned as he thought about it and what it would mean if it were true, but he still didn't buy it. He shook his head.

"There's no way. He didn't say anything about this."

"Maybe Mendoza had a gun to his head."

"There's no way. The kid was confused."

"He saw the cast. I didn't prompt him, Button. He told me the man was wearing a cast. He saw them going in through the front gate at eight forty-five."

Button glanced at the picture again as if he still couldn't see it clearly.

"I talked to the man. He was fine."

"Not if Mendoza was with him."

Button flushed, and his eyes shrank into dark little bullets.

"Are you saying I missed something?"

"Did you?"

The Academy taught officers that people making statements under duress exhibited telltale cues. They were typically terse and hesitant because they were scared to say the wrong thing. Their sentence structure was often confused or repetitive for the same reason, and their voices would quaver or break due to a constricted trachea brought on by the adrenaline flooding their systems.

"He was *fine*. The guy did not sound like a man with a gun to his head. Even thinking back now, there were none of the cues."

"Then forget the cues. What did he say?"

"That people like us—that would be me and *you*, Pike, who he specifically mentioned—were making things worse, costing him a fortune, and were gonna get him killed. You want more? He told me to shove Mendoza and pretty much the rest of Los Angeles up my ass."

Button grew loud as he went through it, which caused three passing officers to stare. He waited until they were gone before he spoke again, but his eyes remained angry.

"What the hell do you care anyway? This isn't your business."

"Like Smith said, maybe I made it worse."

Button glanced away as if he was suddenly uncomfortable.

"Why do you think they're missing?"

"You're the last person they had contact with. A lot of people have been calling them, but they don't answer and haven't returned the calls."

"That doesn't mean shit. You can come up with a hundred different reasons for that."

"Until Mendoza goes through the gate."

Button stared at the pavement again, then sighed.

"The guy was angry, okay? But he sounded natural. Just pissed off and venting. Told me what they did to his shop with the heads and all that, and that they were going to get out of Dodge for a few weeks to let things cool down."

"Oregon."

"Said they have friends up there. That was it. Even if I accept this business about Mendoza going through the gate, nothing the man said stands out. He wasn't trying to send a hidden message. There weren't any subtle pleas for help. I don't see it."

Pike took Button's read at face value, though his description of Smith's call didn't jibe with Mendoza's presence. Pike had hoped for some hint or clue to what had happened and where they might be.

"Then what was Mendoza doing at his house?"

Button sighed, and Pike knew he was wondering the same thing.

"What's the kid's name?"

"Jared Palmer. He lives in the white modern next door to Smith."

Button took a pad and pen from his pocket and jotted the note.

"Okay. I'll bring along the six-pack with Gomer."

He slipped the pad back into the pocket, but didn't look happy about it.

"He told you about the cast on his own? You didn't tell him about it first?"

Pike shook his head, and Button scowled.

"Fucking douchebags. Mendoza's looking at an assault charge he *knows* the D.A. will dispo down to a battery, and he just can't leave it alone."

Pike knew what Button was saying, but offered nothing in response because his thoughts were too dark. Prisons were filled with convicted murderers who got a drumstick when they wanted a thigh, or who felt dissed when a woman wouldn't speak to them on a bus, or who decided a bartender was ignoring them. When a man felt frustrated or angry enough, any reason would do.

Button started away, then turned back. Pike saw he still had the picture of Mendoza. He held it out, but when Pike took it, Button did not let go.

"I guess you don't remember the rules of the road, you giving up the badge. If we have to make a case on this asshole, you took this kid Jared off the board as a witness. You showing him the one picture like this, his attorney is going to argue you convinced this kid that Mendoza is who he saw, even though he saw someone else. And the judge is going to go with it."

Button released the picture, and went back to his truck.

Pike knew Button was right, but he didn't

care about the case. He cared about saving Dru Rayne.

He was halfway back to his Jeep when Elvis Cole called.

17

ELVIS COLE

Standing in the alley between the canals as Joe Pike left to find Button, Cole knew Pike already thought the worst, and was in full-on Terminator mode. Pike had focused on a goal and would drive forward like a relentless machine. Back in Cole's Ranger days, they had called this mission commitment, and Pike's mission commitment was off the charts. But Cole wasn't convinced the worst was at hand. He wanted to enter the house without preconceived notions, and interpret the facts as he found them. Like Joe said—he wanted to see with fresh eyes.

Cole ambled to Smith's front gate as if he were just another resident out for an afternoon stroll. Pike had warned him about the problem with Jared and explained it was safer to hop the fence on the opposite side of the carport, but Cole wanted to see the gate Mendoza used. Jared's window was clear, so he studied the handle. It was set with a simple key lock that was weathered and scraped. A button on the post could be pushed to let people inside know you were here. There was probably another button inside the house that would unlock the gate. A metal shield covered the gap between the gate and the gatepost where the bolt fit into the post. The shield was designed to prevent someone from slipping the bolt, but Cole knew these were easy to beat. He saw no fresh cuts or scrapes on the surrounding metal, but Cole also knew it was easy to leave no marks.

Cole checked to see if Jared or anyone else was watching, then climbed over.

The front door was a standard wood entry, stained dark to match the house. A Master deadbolt was set in the frame above the knob lock. Cole pulled on a pair of vinyl gloves, selected a pick and a tension wrench from his pick kit, and went to work. Two minutes for the deadbolt, one for the knob. On-the-job training courtesy of the United States Army.

Cole opened the door slowly, and stepped into a small tiled entry. The house was cool. He smelled grease, seafood, and a flowery scent he could not place. Cole listened for several seconds, then announced himself with authority.

"Police department. This is Detective Banning with LAPD. Is anyone in the house?"

Cole gave it a full ten seconds, then closed and locked the door. The entry was the stressful part. Cole had walked into pit bulls, sleepwalkers, three naked men practicing yoga, seven abandoned children under the age of four, and, once, two cranked-up meth addicts with 12-gauge shotguns laying in wait for their dealer. That had not been one of his better days.

Without moving, Cole scanned the entry's floor and walls. He saw no blood, heavy scuff marks, shell casings, upended or out of place furniture, or other evidence of a struggle.

His plan of attack was to search the second floor first in case the police showed up, so he moved to the stairs, checking each step as he climbed. He cleared the landing quickly, then went to the office. Pike had already briefed him on the layout.

The office was nicely furnished, and clearly belonged to someone who had enjoyed a successful career in television. Framed credits from crime shows that were no longer on the air dotted the walls, most of which Cole recognized by the actors. The credits all showed the same name. Produced by Steve Brown. Written by Steve Brown. Directed by Steve Brown.

Though Cole didn't recognize the name, he liked the shows.

"Nice work, Steve. Well done."

Though the room was well furnished, Cole noticed empty places on the walls where pictures were missing and gaps on bookshelves where books had been removed. There was also no computer, typewriter, or other office equipment present except for a phone. These were probably items Brown had placed into storage while away. No sense tempting the guests.

Cole picked up the phone, but found the line dead. Brown had probably turned off the service.

Even though a forced entry on the second floor was unlikely, Cole checked the windows and doors leading out to the deck. He found them undisturbed, and moved to the master bedroom.

The master was large, messy, and disappointing. Cole had hoped to learn whether Smith left voluntarily by seeing if his clothes and toiletries were missing, but it was obvious the owner had left a huge wardrobe behind. The large master closet and bathroom were crowded with many more clothes and toiletries than a temporary house sitter would have brought. Cole had no way of knowing what belonged to Brown and what, if anything, belonged to Smith, so he couldn't tell if any of Smith's things were missing. There were even a few women's clothes, but these could as easily belong to a girlfriend of Brown's as Dru Rayne.

Cole found only one item he knew belonged to Smith. A battered metal file box was on the floor beside the bed. It contained receipts, invoices, and billing statements pertaining to the sandwich shop, a pink slip for a 2002 Tercel, insurance policies, and the other mundane paperwork of day-to-day life. Nothing that couldn't be left behind for a couple of weeks, and nothing anyone would steal.

Finished with the second floor, Cole went downstairs. He began in the laundry room, saw Pike's marks on the window, then quickly moved to the downstairs bedroom. Wilson up in the master, his niece in the lower. Unlike the master, the bed was made and the room was clean, neat, and orderly. The windows had not been tampered with. Cole found a few women's tops, dresses, and jeans in the closet. There weren't many clothes, but Cole had no way to know if this was everything the woman owned or if she had packed a few things for a trip.

Cole moved to the kitchen, which opened into a large family room lined with French doors showing a pleasant view of the canal. Another dead digital phone sat on the counter near a sink stacked with dishes. The dishes bothered him. It was like the goat heads and blood. Nobody would walk away from a mess like that, but Button claimed that was exactly what Wilson had done. Cole had a bad feeling about it, but in and of itself it proved nothing. Except maybe that Smith was a slob.

The fridge was scaled with takeout menus held on by magnets. Cole opened it and found the refrigerator stocked with milk, beer, soda, and what appeared to be fried oysters and shrimp in greasy white cartons. Would two people in the restaurant business leave food they knew would go bad in the refrigerator?

When Cole closed the fridge, he noticed a hand-printed note taped to the door. He hadn't seen it before because it was lost among the takeout menus.

IF EMERGENCY, CALL 911.
PLUMBING PROBLEM, CALL NICKY TATE – 323-555-8402
IF YOU NEED ME WHILE I'M IN LONDON
STEVE – 310-555-3691

London was eight hours ahead. It was late, but Steve Brown might be up. If Smith took the time to call Button, maybe he called his landlord, too. Cole dialed the number.

Brown's phone rang six times before voice mail picked up.

"Mr. Brown, my name is Elvis Cole. I'm in Los Angeles. Would you please give me a call about Wilson Smith and Dru Rayne?"

Cole left his number, hung up, then went to the window over the sink. It was the last thing he would check before leaving. He had found no hard evidence of either an abduction or a trip, and was already deciding which of his LAPD contacts to call about Mendoza and Gomer. The house had been a bust, and his head was out of the game.

He studied the window's latches and interior frame, and that's when he saw a single deep cut on an exterior part of the frame. A thin, bright groove sparkled across the metal near the latch, far shinier than the surrounding metal. Cole touched the handle, and the window slid effortlessly open. Once the window was open, he saw a deep dimple in the frame. Cole closed the window. He stared at it for a few seconds, then called Joe Pike.

"Did you check the kitchen window?"

"Yes. All the windows."

"The window over the sink."

"You found something?"

"Someone forced it open. I'm looking at it. There's a scratch on the frame where the screwdriver slipped, and the frame is bent by the latch. None of this was here this morning?"

"No."

"The latch is broken. The window slides free."

"Not this morning."

"Which means this didn't happen until three or four hours after Jared saw Mendoza."

"Find anything in the house?"

"Nada. No sign they were taken. No sign they went on a trip. Nothing."

"I understand."

"I don't."

"Understand later. I just left Button. You don't have much time."

Cole put away his phone and stared at the window. Maybe he did not find evidence of a crime because someone had already found it. Maybe there had been many signs of a struggle, but someone cleaned the crime scene.

Cole returned to the front entry and was about to let himself out when he noticed the empty bookcase. Steve Brown showed prudence by storing his valuable items. Maybe his books and computers weren't the only things he decided to hide.

Cole ran his fingers along the top of the bookcase and found a weathered key. He tried it in the front door, and found that it fit the deadbolt perfectly. Brown had stashed his spare key inside while he was gone instead of leaving it outside where a passing burglar might find it. A smart move made by someone who knew all the tricks because he had written so many cop shows.

Cole let himself out. He used the key to lock the deadbolt, then hid it behind the fence.

Cole cracked open the front gate, made sure no one was watching, then pulled off the vinyl gloves and let himself out. He took a single deep breath, released it, and let the tension he carried out with it. He had seen with fresh eyes, and now everything was different, and maybe everything Pike feared was true.

Cole crossed the alley for a better view of Smith's house, then looked from one end of the alley to the other. It was crowded by wall-to-wall houses, with only one way in or out for cars. A person could enter or leave by the pedestrian bridges, but for cars there was only one way out. It was a lousy place to do crime, but lousy places for crime were great places for witnesses.

A skinny guy with stringy black hair came to the upper window at the Palmer house. This would be Jared. He stared at Cole with a serious frown, and Cole stared back, thinking if there was one Jared, there might be more.

Cole had decided to knock on doors when a tan Crown Victoria turned into the alley, heading his way. A man was driving, with a woman in the passenger seat. Cole knew they were cops, and wondered if the man was Button.

The outsized Detroit sedan was so wide it filled the street. Cole stepped to the side to let them pass, and gave them a cheery wave.

"Beautiful day, isn't it? Great walking weather."

The man looked at Cole as if Cole was litter.

"Great if you don't have to work for a living."

The woman seemed embarrassed.

Cole continued on his way. Behind him, the Crown Vic stopped in front of the Palmers' house, and the man and the woman got out.

Cole strolled down the center of the street, checking the houses for large facing windows or decks with clear views of the street, but found something better.

A dark green contemporary home sat across the street and two doors down from the Smith house. It had sleek lines, a flat roof, and a large steel door. A security camera that looked like a black bubble clung to a wall beside the door.

Cole checked to see what the police were doing, and saw that the Palmers' front door was now open. Jared and his mother were in the street with the officers.

Cole drifted closer to the camera. Because it was focused on the gate, the camera probably did not have a full-on view of the street, but it might see enough for a glimpse of a passing car.

Cole felt a subtle electric tingle that came when he knew he was in the hunt. Many security systems were hooked to a DVR. Some only recorded when the bell was pressed, but others recorded continuously on a rewritable disk. The camera might give him nothing, but it also might give him everything.

Cole took a last glance back at the Palmer house.

The door was closed, and now the two officers were inside. Talking to Jared.

Cole turned the corner, and then, like Joe Pike, he ran.

18

DARKNESS TOWERED ABOVE Joe Pike like an ominous black cloud. He did not know when or where he was, or how he came to be trapped here with this awful thing. He only knew the giant shadow would smother him with a darkness he could not escape. The shadow fell over him with the delicate grace of fog, but held him with the awful weight of concrete, a rising pool of blackness that would fill his mouth and nose and ears. Pike fought desperately to scramble away, but his arms and legs would not move. He strained to break free, grunting, hissing, spit and tears flying as his head whipped side to side. Pike did not know what it was, this shadow. He did not understand how it held him, or why he could not escape. It rose from the dark as always, and one day it would kill him . . . as he feared it had killed him before.

19

PIKE WOKE WITH DAMP sheets twisted around his legs. He was alert and awake, but had no memory of his nightmare. Pike never remembered. Sometimes in the first moments of consciousness, he saw dim shapes, one shadow over another, but never more than that. Nothing new, and nothing he wasted time worrying about. Pike had suffered night terrors since he was a boy.

Pike checked his watch. The luminous hands told him it was 3:17 in the morning. Cole had relieved him ninety minutes ago, and now sat outside Carla Fuentes's house, waiting for Mendoza. Pike had come home to grab some rest, but his sleep was finished for the night.

Pike untangled the sheets, then swung his feet from the bed. He saw his cell phone on the nightstand and thought of Dru. He checked the phone, but found no messages or missed calls.

Pike pulled on a pair of light blue running shorts, yesterday's sweatshirt, and carried his shoes downstairs before putting them on. He didn't turn on the lights. He didn't need to. He saw well enough in the dark.

Downstairs, he drank half a bottle of water, put on his shoes, then strapped on a nylon fanny pack. He wore the fanny pack to carry his phone, keys, DL, and a .25-caliber Beretta pocket gun.

Pike deactivated his alarm, set it to re-arm in sixty seconds, then let himself out.

He stood very still, taking the measure of his surroundings, then stretched and set off on his run. Pike almost always ran the same four or five routes, heading up along Ocean Boulevard through Santa Monica to the canyons, or around Baldwin Hills on La Cienega past the oil pumps. That night, he ran west on Washington Boulevard straight to the sea, then north to the top of the Venice Canals and an arched pedestrian bridge. He stopped at the crest of the bridge to look down the length of the canal.

A dog barked further inland somewhere in Ghost Town, and Pike heard vehicles on nearby Pacific Boulevard, but here the houses slept. The smell of the sea was strong. The largest canal—Grand Canal—ran to the ocean through Marina del Rey, and fed the five inland canals with life. Small fish swam in the shallow water, and sea plants grew in wavy clumps.

Pike had chosen this bridge because it gave him a view of Dru's house. Many of the homes had exterior security lights, which now shimmered on the water, but the distance and coastal mist made picking out her house difficult. He found Lily Palmer's large white modern first, then Dru's redwood on the far side. Like many of the other homes, it was dotted by bright exterior floodlights which were probably on an automatic timer. Then he noticed the upstairs bedroom was lit. He watched the light, searching for shadows, but nothing moved.

Pike trotted off the bridge and along the narrow alleys to Dru's house. Nothing and no one stirred, and no dogs barked. Pike thought, these people should have dogs.

Streetlamps and security lights blazed hot in the confined lane, giving the mist a purple-blue glow. Pike stopped outside Dru's house. A few windows glowed dull ocher in the surrounding houses, but most were dark and all were quiet. No one was awake. Even Jared's window was dark.

Pike took his cell phone from the fanny pack, and thumbed the speed-dial button for Elvis Cole. Cole answered on the second ring, his voice soft, but completely alert.

"What's up?"

Pike spoke in a whisper.

"You leave a light on in the top bedroom at Dru's?"

"A light?"

"I'm outside the house. The upstairs bedroom is lit."

"I was up there. I don't remember turning on a light, but I don't remember not turning it on, either. I don't know."

"Mm."

"You think someone's in there now?"

"Just wondering about the light."

"You going inside?"

"Yes."

"The spare key I found, it's behind the fence next to the gatepost. Not the one next to the house. The other side."

"Anything on your end?"

"Lights out, game over. She's in a coma."

"Okay."

"Listen. Call me when you leave there, okay? You don't call, I'm gonna come over there expecting to save you, then I'll miss Mendoza."

Pike put away the phone. He breathed in the air and the street and the scent of the sea, listening, but heard only ambient noise. He stepped into the shadows near the gate, then lifted himself over and dropped silently into the courtyard. He paused to listen, then felt for the key.

He used a full minute to ease the key into the lock, another minute to turn the knob, and two full minutes to open the door. The entry was dark, fielding only a dim glow that escaped from above. Pike strained to catch sounds from the house, but heard nothing. Only then did he close the door.

Pike moved through the house without turning on lights, and avoided the windows. The big windows allowed enough ambient light for him to see that nothing was disturbed. Everything was as he remembered and as Cole described.

He reached the top bedroom, but did not enter. A nightstand lamp was on. Pike thought back to his fast trip through the house that morning, but didn't remember the lamp. It was a small lamp. During the day, its light could have been swallowed by the sun, which explained why he and Cole didn't remember it, but Pike didn't like not knowing. The lamp was a problem.

Pike backed away, let himself out, locked the door, and replaced the key by the fence. He stood in the courtyard for another moment, listening, then slipped through the shadows alongside Dru's house until he reached the edge of the canal.

He wondered where Dru and Wilson were, and if they were all right. He wanted to believe they were, but he knew this was unlikely. He heard a distant barking again, and wondered if it was a sea lion out past the locks.

Pike studied the houses across the canal, and the far bridge where he had just been standing. Needle feet crept up his back along with the words in Wilson's shop.

I am here.

Pike stepped backward into the shadows. He slowed his breathing, and silenced his body to listen. He searched the far bank for reflections and movement. The water lapped. Lights bounced on its obsidian surface. Pike wondered if predators swam this far inland. He wondered if they hid beneath the surface.

20

DANIEL

Daniel watched him cross the bridge, tall dude out for a run in the middle of the night, dark glasses tight across his eyes, these L.A. people, what's up with that? Probably used sunblock, too.

Cleo whispered, "Shh. He'll hear you thinking."

Tobey hissed, "Shh. Hear your brain."

Like water snakes in the weeds.

Daniel said, "Please be quiet. Doesn't the water feel good?"

"Cold."

"Cold."

Their voices echoed to silence.

Daniel was submerged to his nose in shallow water, hidden beneath a wooden dock on the opposite side of the canal. Daniel, Cleo, and Tobey, watching.

Tall dude left the bridge, scuffed whisper on the street, passed through a column of blue light, cut hard with muscles and what's that on his arms? Squint. Focus. See. These big red arrows, glowing like embers in the blue-purple light. Daniel thought they were cool.

When the man was gone, Daniel pushed along the muddy bottom, moving to deeper water as he pulled his load with him, so slow the water did not ripple, enjoying the kiss of tiny fish on his skin. Heading toward the bridge.

After a while, he slid beneath the arch, then turned toward the house, keeping the load tucked in close as he floated in the shadows. Daniel had watched the house since midday, and his care had paid off twice. Others had appeared to watch the house, too, and now he knew they had been watching for him. He took this as an excellent sign, and proof that he was close.

"Can you feel it, boys? We are so close I can feel it."

"So close we can touch it, touch it."

"So close we can taste it, taste it."

Their feathery breath caressed his ears.

Daniel bobbed in the darkness, waiting without any real sense of passing time when a flick of black moved at the end of their fence, catching his attention. Another flick, and the black became a shadow at the edge of the water. A glint of light flashed at the top of the shadow, flashed once more, and then the glint and the shadow were gone. Daniel thought about this and decided the glint was light from a house across the canal flashing off the tall dude's glasses. Had to be. The tall dude had gone to their house.

Daniel waited for the shadow to reappear, wondering who the man was and why he was here. This made Daniel smile because the truth was always the same. He was here for the same reason as everyone else. This would be worth a call to his friends, which Daniel would make in the morning.

Daniel waited another twenty minutes, just to be sure, but the shadow and its glint did not return. Like all good hunters, Daniel was patient, but after a while he determined it was safe to move on.

Daniel whispered, soft as a kiss.

"Be seeing you."

Daniel had been holding the body for well over an hour, but now he released it. The body rolled over once, a hand rising to wave good-bye, then slid beneath the cold black surface.

Daniel waited, and watched, and wondered who would come next.

Part Three
The Lord of War and Thunder

21

AT FOUR MINUTES AFTER seven the next morning, Pike received the call that changed everything. One minute earlier, at seven-oh-three, he was watching Carla Fuentes's house from a camellia bush in her backyard, the milky sky overhead promising a hazy day even between the leaves.

Pike had relieved Cole at four that morning, parking a block and a half from Carla's house in a deep pool of shadow beneath a sycamore tree. He slouched low behind the wheel, safe enough while the neighborhood slept, but he knew people would stir with the dawn. A man sitting in a parked vehicle would quickly draw attention, so Pike found a new position behind the camellia bush well before the eastern sky lightened. He could not see the front of the house, but had a good view of the back door, most of the drive, and the interior of the kitchen through the windows.

A light in the master bedroom came on at ten minutes after six. A few minutes later, the kitchen light followed, and Carla Fuentes entered the kitchen. She was alone, and wore a white T-shirt. She spent several minutes at the counter doing something Pike could not see, then returned to the bedroom. Pike guessed she had put on a pot of coffee. This was confirmed a few minutes later when she returned to the kitchen, poured a cup, and took it into the living room. Pike thought she was probably watching TV.

He saw her twice more before seven-oh-three. During this time, the sun rose, finches chirped through the bushes, and a mockingbird took a noisy position on the garage. Pike planned what he would do if Carla left the house or Mendoza appeared, but by seven-oh-three she had made no move to leave and Mendoza had not arrived.

At four minutes after seven, Pike received the call.

His phone made a soft buzz when it vibrated. It was on his thigh, where he had placed it so he could reach it with minimal movement, wrapped in a soft cloth to muffle the sound. He was surprised when the Caller ID showed CTY LOS ANG. This meant the call originated from a phone issued by the city. Pike debated whether or not to answer, but decided to pick up the call.

"Pike."

"You answer fast for this time of the morning."

It was Button, sounding quiet and knowing.

"Did you check out Mendoza?"

"Yeah. I think there's something to what you said. Did you find him?"

"No."

"I can help you with that. Got something here I want you to see. Come take a look."

Button's voice was so flat Pike knew this wasn't a friendly request, and something in the nature of his word choice and the early time of the call cut Pike like a desert wind.

"Is it Wilson and Dru?"

"You want a ride, I'll send a car."

"Did you find them?"

"I'm at Washington Boulevard where it crosses the canal. Can't miss me."

"Tell me if it's them, Button."

Button hung up without answering, and now the desert wind blew through Pike's chest like a cold rail. Pike worked his way out of the bush, slipped over the fence into the neighbor's yard, then ran for his Jeep. He was less than ten minutes from Button's location, and filled Cole in as he drove.

Cole said, "You want me back on Mendoza?"

"Not now. If this is Wilson or Dru, the police will be all over their house as soon as they clear the scene. If there's more to find on their street, we have to find it now."

"I'm on it, Joe, but listen—"

Cole's voice softened.

"Hold a good thought, okay?"

Pike broke the call in silence. Moments later he was bogged down in traffic three blocks from the canal, and knew he was heading for a major crime scene. Westbound traffic was rerouted through the marina by a uniformed officer who forced everyone to turn.

When Pike identified himself, the officer directed him into a parking lot behind a Thai restaurant. Several radio cars were along both sides of the canal, and two more blocked the Washington Boulevard Bridge. A Medical Examiner's van was on the far side of the canal. Even as Pike pulled into the parking lot, he saw that the water level was down. The Venice Canals did not flow freely into the sea. Once or twice a week, locks built into the bridge were opened, allowing the canals to drain with the falling tide, and refill with clean water as the tide rose. Now, the tide was out and the water was down, revealing a low wall of gray concrete stones that firmed the banks and the shallow slope of the bottom.

Pike spotted Futardo as he parked. She was with a small group of detectives and uniforms at the edge of the canal who stared at something in the water. Button was on the other side of the bridge with Straw. The man with the orange shirt was with them, only now he wore blue. He saw Pike first, then Button and Straw turned. Button came across the bridge to Futardo and motioned Pike to join them.

Pike felt his heart rate increase as he got closer. Two men in waders stepped into the water while two other men in knee boots spread a blue plastic sheet on the muddy bottom. All four wore long rubber gloves that reached to their shoulders. A stretcher waited solemnly nearby.

Button's face was blank as Pike approached, but

a deep line cut Futardo's brow. Pike wondered what she was thinking. Button's jacket was already off in anticipation of the coming heat, and his hands were in his pockets. He didn't take them out to shake. Instead, he nodded toward the canal.

"There you go."

Pike looked, and in that moment he realized all his assumptions were wrong.

22

REUBEN MENDOZA'S BODY WAS on its side in the shallow trough of water that remained in the canal. The arm with the cast reached toward the bank as if he had been trying to pull himself out when he died, but Pike knew this had not been the case. Mendoza's neck was cut so deeply the white core of bone was revealed, and the blue-gray pallor of his flesh indicated he had bled out long before he drifted to the bank. He wore baggy khaki shorts, a long-sleeved plaid shirt so big it cloaked him like a shawl, and Keds—the same clothes Jared described. Carla Fuentes would be able to keep her house.

Button clucked his tongue.

"Looks to me like your boy Mendoza here didn't abduct anyone."

Futardo moved closer, watching him the way cops watch a suspect.

"Do you recognize this man?"

Pike nodded.

"When is the last time you saw him?"

Pike glanced at Futardo, and saw Button smile.

"Detective Futardo here wants to work homicide. She thinks you're a person of interest."

Futardo flushed dark and her thin lips grew tighter as Button went on, lecturing her.

"This isn't Pike's style. Pike here, he'd shoot the guy point-blank or beat him to death, but he wouldn't do this. Hey, Eddie—"

A man in waders looked over.

"Roll him and open the shirt, please. We want to see the wound."

Most of the body was still in the water. They rolled it to face Button, then pulled back the plaid shirt. The shirt was unbuttoned as Jared described, but the T-shirt beneath was ripped from the upper left chest down through the center of the shirt to his pants. Washed clean of blood by being in the canal, picket-fence ribs protruded through the chest and internal organs bulged like blue balloons from the abdomen.

"Gutted him. Cut his neck to kill him, then gutted him thinking the body would stay down."

Pike watched the team maneuver the body, then gazed up the canal. Grand Canal was the longest canal of the six, letting the five smaller canals breathe from the sea through the locks built into the bridge. Pike wondered how long it took for the body to work its way down from the upper canals as the water drained.

"How long has he been in the water?"

"Thanks, Eddie. That's good."

The recovery team returned to its work as Button answered Pike's question.

"Cold as the water is, the window is wide open. More than six, but less than twenty-four. They'll tighten it up when they get him on the table, but that's the CI's best guess for now."

"Could have happened after. He took them first, and someone killed him after."

"Whatever you say, Pike. And maybe the one thing doesn't have anything to do with the other, but I wouldn't bet on it."

"You find Gomer?"

"You think Gomer killed him?"

"Did Jared make him as the man with Mendoza?"

"Didn't see him well enough, but I doubt it was Gomer. Gomer's too lightweight for something like this. You kill someone the way this man was killed, you're a heavyweight."

Pike guessed Button probably had several candidates for the kill, and Pike was probably high on the list despite Button's comment to Futardo.

Futardo moved closer again.

"The homicide detectives want to talk to you. You feel like answering a few questions or you want to lawyer up?"

"Now's fine."

Button smiled again.

"I was you, I'd lawyer up."

"I'm good."

Pike wasn't going to tell them anything Button didn't already know. If he told them more, they would promote him from person of interest to suspect.

Button glanced at Futardo.

"Tell'm they can have him when I'm finished. Stay with them so Pike and I can have a word."

Button watched her walk away, then turned back to Pike.

"Let me ask you something, between you and me, and I don't care what you tell the homicide dicks. You know where Smith and his niece are?"

"No."

"You think Smith did this?"

The thought had occurred to Pike, but he hesitated before he answered.

"Open the ribs like that, you have to be strong, and you have to know what you're doing. I don't know that he has the skill or the strength."

Button grunted.

"Maybe not, but cooks know their knives. Mendoza and Gomer go to threaten the man like they did in his shop, only this time they get the big surprise."

"It's still two on one."

"Gomer's a runner. Ran before when you showed up, and this time he beat feet when the knife came out. Then it's one on one, only the girl's there to help her uncle. Once the body is down, they panic and decide to get rid of it. Then Smith calls me with that bullshit about Oregon to buy some getaway time."

"They didn't have to run. If that's how it happened, they killed him in self-defense."

187

Button grunted again.

"People lose their minds when they kill someone, Pike. That's why they call it blood simple."

Pike wondered why Button was sharing his theory, like they were in this together, until he realized Button's true purpose. He was trying to read whether Pike was involved in the murder or subsequent cover-up with Wilson and Dru.

Pike shrugged, willing to let Button think what he wanted, when Futardo reappeared. She looked excited.

"Boss, they need you over here. It's important."

Button told Pike not to leave, and went over to see what the detectives wanted.

The men in the waders had the body on the plastic sheet. Working together, they lifted the body, but their footing in the mud was bad. One of the men slipped, and the body went down.

Pike took out his phone. He was going to let Cole know what was happening when he saw Straw approaching. The man in blue remained on the bridge.

Straw didn't hurry. He strolled over like a man rehearsing what he wanted to say. When he arrived, he nodded at Pike.

"This time yesterday, I had a serious hard-on for you. Today, not so much."

Straw paused. Pike knew he was now supposed to ask why Straw no longer had a hard-on, but Pike didn't ask. He didn't care. Straw finally nodded toward the homicide crew. The homicide detectives were talking as if they were excited about something, and two were on phones. One trotted to a waiting radio car, and jumped into the back seat as it left.

"Our detective friends are split down the middle whether you or Smith did this. They're even running a pool."

"How'd you bet?"

"I don't think you or Smith had anything to do with this. That mess with the heads in Smith's shop, I don't think these bangers had anything to do with it. Something more complicated is in play."

Pike studied Straw for a moment, and thought he was probably right. Straw's shakedown operation was finished, so now he was digging for a replacement.

"Like what?"

"No idea."

"Weren't you guys watching the shop?"

Straw showed his first sign of irritation.

"We were watching the entire street, Pike. We had the front of his shop. Whoever made that mess broke through the back and got away clean. But you know that. You were there the next morning."

"Too bad you didn't see something helpful."

Straw's jaw flexed one time, then he studied the ground for several seconds before he looked up.

"You have any idea where these people are?"

Pike nodded toward Mendoza's body.

"I thought he had them."

"If he did, someone else has them now."

"Who?"

"Whoever. I'm seeing Smith and his niece

jammed up by something a helluva lot worse than a shakedown."

Straw handed Pike a card.

"You learn anything or need any help, let me know. I'd like to find these people before whoever did that to Mendoza finds them."

Button and Futardo returned from their group. Pike thought they were coming to get him for the homicide dicks, but Button had news, and the news made him smile.

"Alberto Gomer is no longer missing in action. Homeless dude found him an hour ago in a parked car up at the north end of the canal. His throat was cut ear to ear. That makes your boy Smith two for two."

Futardo gestured toward the homicide detectives.

"They'd like to speak with you now. You ready to talk?"

23

ELVIS COLE

When Pike phoned Cole that morning to tell him about Button's call, Cole heard the strain in his friend's voice. Pike was a man who showed nothing, projecting a zen-like detachment that Cole sometimes found amusing, but also admired. Cole often wondered what such calm cost his friend, and whether Pike had no other choice but to pay it.

Cole was off the couch and out of the house sixteen minutes after Pike hung up. Who needs deodorant when you're the World's Greatest Detective? Who needs to brush your teeth when you're fighting to absolve your friend's guilt?

The morning traffic down from the canyon and westbound through Hollywood sucked. Bumper-to-bumper with garbage trucks, buses, and citizens headed for work, all of them funneled through streets torn up by poorly planned construction and maintenance projects.

Cole was still two miles from the freeway when

his phone rang. He thought it would be Pike, but didn't recognize the number.

"Elvis Cole."

"This is Steve Brown in London, returning your call."

Brown spoke firmly, as if he was used to being in meetings and getting things done. Cole did a quick calculation. Eight hours ahead made it five P.M. in London.

"Thanks for getting back, Mr. Brown. I'm trying to locate Wilson Smith and Dru Rayne. I was hoping you might know how to reach them."

"Why would I know that?"

Cole thought that was an odd response, considering the people were living in the man's house.

"I understand they're house-sitting for you."

"Uh-huh. And you understand this how?"

Now Brown sounded suspicious, which maybe went with getting a cold call from a total stranger six thousand miles away.

"Your neighbor. Lily Palmer. She told me about the house-sitting, and suggested I call."

"Uh-huh. Okay. What's this about?"

Cole had expected Brown to have questions, and had decided to limit his answers.

"Wilson's shop was damaged. I've been trying to find him so I can tell him what happened, but it looks like they've gone away for a few days. I was hoping you would know how to reach them."

"Uh-huh."

Brown fell silent.

"Mr. Brown?"

"Let me ask you a question. These people are living in my house, Dru and this guy?"

Brown sounded angry, and Cole didn't like where the conversation was going.

"Are they there without your knowledge?"

"I told Dru she could use the place. That's it. I don't know any Wilson Smith. I never heard of him, and I'm fucking pissed off if she's shacking with some guy in my house."

"He's her uncle."

"I don't give a shit if he's her twin brother, though I have my doubts. This wasn't the deal. I didn't want anyone else in the house, and she was cool with it. That's why I let her use the place."

Cole felt a soft chill, and liked the conversation even less. Cole had believed Smith arranged for the house, and invited Dru to stay with him when she came to L.A. to help with his business. Now that was upended.

"Dru works for him. Mr. Smith has a restaurant up by the boardwalk."

"Maybe so, but she wasn't working for anybody when I gave her the keys. She was living off alimony. She never said anything about an uncle, and she sure as hell didn't tell me he was going to move in."

Cole wet his lips, and hated the question he had to ask.

"Why did you let her move in?"

"I was fucking her, why do you think? She wanted out of the dump she was living in, and I was coming back here, so it was a good deal for both of us. Saved me the hassle of vetting a house sitter."

Cole felt hollow.

"All right. Listen, thanks for getting back to me."

"Hold on. How long is she going to be away?"

"I don't know."

"I called her when I got your message, but she hasn't called back."

"We haven't been able to reach either one of them."

"What are we talking about? A few days? A couple of weeks? Has she abandoned the place?"

"I don't know."

"Goddamnit, as of right now, you are telling me my house is empty? Is that correct? She's gone, and no one is taking care of my house?"

"No, sir. Not now."

"Son of a BITCH. That fucking whore."

Brown hung up cursing, and the line went dead.

Cole drove on with a confusion that left him feeling blindsided, and realized he had missed an obvious question. He opened the incoming call list and called Brown back.

"Me again. Sorry. Have you spoken with Dru since you've been away?"

"Hell, yes. I call her every couple of weeks, make sure everything's okay, check on the house."

"She never mentioned Mr. Smith?"

"This is the first I've heard of him, and I don't like it. If this guy's been living there all this time and she hasn't told me, she's been lying to me, and I don't like liars. If you find her, you tell her she better call me, and I mean yesterday. I want that sonofabitch out of my house."

Cole finished the call feeling even worse than before. The picture he now had of Dru Rayne was very different from the woman Joe described. This left him with even more questions, but Cole forced himself to focus on the fact she was missing. He had to mine Wilson Smith's neighbors before the police sealed the mine.

Cole reached the canals a few minutes later and once more walked in. Mendoza and his partner had passed these same houses going to and coming from the Smith house, which was when Jared saw them, and now Cole wanted to see if anyone else had seen them, but he targeted the houses with security cameras first.

Almost out of habit, he checked Jared's window as he moved down the alley, but Jared was missing. Amazing.

The day before, Cole noted three homes with cameras. No one answered at the first house, so he slipped a business card under the door with a note asking them to call. A middle-aged woman answered at the second home, and asked if he was with the police she spoke to the day before. This told Cole that Button and his partner had made the rounds after speaking with Jared. Cole told her he was, and dropped Button's name to fortify the lie. Cole asked if Button checked her surveillance recordings, but Button had not asked, and it would not have mattered if he had—her cameras displayed real-time images but were not hooked to a recorder. The first house had potential, but the second house was a bust.

Cole had better luck at the third house. A housekeeper told him she didn't know much about the security system, but believed the cameras made a recording. She explained her employer was at work, but thought he would be happy to speak with Cole as he was very interested when she told him the police questioned her yesterday. Cole left another card, then reconsidered his plan.

Knowing that Button made the rounds after speaking with Jared, Cole decided there was no point in covering the same ground again. The available witness list was currently limited to Jared.

Cole returned to Smith's house, and found Jared back in his window, straggly black hair, shirtless, wires dripping from his ears. Jared was watching him.

Cole made a little wave. Jared waved back. Cole motioned for Jared to come down, and Jared turned from the window.

Cole was waiting outside his house when the door opened and Jared came out.

"Hey, dude, whassup? You with the police or the big dude?"

"The big dude."

"Dude's all right. I like that cat. I already told him about those banger dudes I saw. Him, and the police. They were here yesterday."

Jared had seen a lot of action in the past two days. He was comfortable with it.

"I'm not here about the banger dudes. I was hoping you could tell me how long Dru's been living next door."

"Dude. I'm so bad with time."

Cole waited, letting the silence press Jared for an answer.

Jared finally shrugged.

"Gotta be three months. Steve hooked it back to London three months ago. That dude has cash. He's always in Europe."

"She moved in the day he left?"

"That's the way it works. Steve brought her over, introduced her to my mom, this is my house-sitter, all of that stuff."

"When did her uncle move in?"

Jared glanced across the street and made a sly smile. Cole wondered at both the hesitation and the smile.

Jared said, "The next day."

Jared glanced across the street again, and Cole sensed Jared wanted to say something so badly he could not maintain eye contact.

Cole said, "What?"

"I see things, dude. Dru has a hot body. She lays out a lot. I'm up in that window for a reason."

"Tell me, Jared."

"I don't think Uncle Wilson is Uncle Wilson. They don't always act like relatives, if you're catching my subtext here."

Cole stared at Jared for a long time. He felt cold inside, but his mouth was dry and the morning sun was hot on his skin. A knot of anger blossomed in his chest like cherry-red fire.

"Do not say this if it's bullshit."

"Dude. I have a dead-on view of their yard. I can see in their windows, and she doesn't pull the shades. I've seen them fucking. I think she digs it that I watch."

The cold grew until Cole felt numb. He stared at Steve Brown's house, and wondered who these people were and if everything the woman told Pike was lies.

Cole looked back at Jared, but didn't know what to say. The best he managed was a nod.

Cole did not try to hide what he did next. Jared might have gone back into his house, but Cole didn't notice because Cole didn't care.

Cole found the key in its place by the gatepost, opened the gate, and let himself into the house. He knew what he wanted and what he would do with it.

He pulled on the vinyl gloves as he went to the kitchen. During his earlier search, he had seen folded paper grocery bags wedged into the gap between the refrigerator and the counter. He pulled out several bags, shook one open, then placed it on the counter. He selected three glass tumblers from the dishes left on the counter, put each in a separate bag, and placed the three bags carefully into the open bag. He collected two empty Diet Coke cans and a water bottle from the family room, bagged them the same way, then went up to the master for the metal box with Wilson's papers. He brought it down to the kitchen.

Cole stopped in the downstairs guest bedroom on his way out. A few of her things were there, but now he wondered if she really used the room or if it was just for show. An empty stick of Dry Idea antiperspirant deodorant was on the dresser. He added it to the bag, then locked the house and gate as he left.

Cole returned to his car, but did not start the engine. He called a friend named John Chen, who was a criminalist with the LAPD's Scientific Investigations Division.

"John? I need you to check some prints. I need it done fast."

"Dude. I'm at a drive-by in Hawaiian Gardens. I've been here all frakkin' night."

"I need this, John. It's for Joe."

Chen hesitated, which told Cole he would agree.

"Okay. Okay, for sure."

"I can bring the samples to you. Where in Hawaiian Gardens?"

"Uh-uh, bro, way too many witnesses here. Meet me downtown in an hour. Make it an hour ten. Outside CCB."

Cole closed his phone and headed for downtown Los Angeles.

24

ELVIS COLE

As an employee of the Los Angeles Police Department, John Chen, like the department's sworn officers, was forbidden to perform unauthorized case work, use city resources for personal gain, or help civilian private investigators off the books. These were good and valid rules to preserve the integrity of case evidence, enforce a professional code of conduct, and discourage employee corruption.

John Chen was corrupt.

A paranoid with low self-esteem, Chen lived for the headline, and this was normally Cole's ace. Cole often gave Chen information that allowed him to make breakthroughs on cases he would not have made otherwise. These breakthroughs led to a media profile few other criminalists enjoyed, Chen having been quoted more than a dozen times in the *Los Angeles Times*, interviewed by various local TV news anchors, and hired as a technical consultant on motion pictures based on two of his cases. Chen, whose obsessions in life revolved around women and money, currently drove a Porsche Boxster. The women had so far eluded him.

Cole worked his way onto the I-10 Freeway for the fifteen-mile trek across the Los Angeles Basin. He was approaching the Mid-City area less than halfway across when his phone rang, and he saw it was Pike. Cole had been struggling with what to tell Pike, but now the call forced his hand. If Wilson and Dru were still alive, he would say nothing until he knew more.

"Was it them?"

"Mendoza and Gomer. They're dead."

Cole felt a kick of surprise. Mendoza and Gomer were the predators. They weren't supposed to be dead. If the predators were dead, where were the victims?

"What about Wilson and Dru?"

"Nothing. Mendoza was in the canal by Washington. Gomer was in a car up at the north end. If the cops found something in Gomer's car, they haven't told me."

Pike quickly described how they were killed, which left Cole even more unsettled.

"When did it happen?"

"Fill you in later. I'm being questioned."

"You're a suspect?"

"It won't be a problem. They're covering the bases."

"There's a third player, Joe. The person who jimmied the kitchen window."

"I know. I've been thinking about it."

Pike hung up and Cole drove on, letting the flow of traffic carry him through increasingly darker thoughts.

When the Los Angeles Police Department relocated their headquarters from a decayed and crumbling Parker Center to the new Police Administration Building two blocks away, they forgot to take the Scientific Investigation Division with them. This wasn't factually the case, but was one of many jokes the criminalists liked to tell. The reality was that until a suitable site was found, SID would remain the last man standing in LAPD's past.

Cole didn't drive to the old Parker Center location. He waited for Chen outside the Criminal Courts Building six blocks away, arriving early and waiting an extra twenty minutes until John arrived.

Chen slipped into the passenger seat of Cole's car so fast it was as if he fell from the sky. He wore oversized dark sunglasses, a Dodgers cap pulled low on his face, and a windbreaker with the collar turned up even though it would reach almost ninety degrees later that day. His grapefruit head was tucked into the collar like a turtle into its shell. Hiding.

"I don't think anyone saw me, but we'd better drive. They might have followed."

Chen's paranoia.

Cole pulled into traffic, determined to make this a short drive. The news about Mendoza and Gomer had left him feeling even more concerned about Smith and Dru Rayne.

Cole reached behind the seat for his bag, and put it

on Chen's lap. There wasn't much room. Chen was tall, skinny, and looked like a praying mantis folded into the front passenger compartment.

"It's breakable, so be careful."

"What's in here?"

"Glasses. A couple of soda cans. Things like that. I also have a metal box you can have when you get out of the car.

Chen took off the sunglasses and put on his regular glasses. The lenses looked like they had been cut from the bottoms of Coke bottles.

Chen peered inside.

"Shit, this is a lot. I have a caseload, man. I have so many cases my backlog has a backlog."

"I know it's a lot, but don't get ahead of yourself. The prints should belong to two individuals—a male and a female who live at the residence. The woman's prints should be on the deodorant stick. The male's prints are probably on the file box. Run the stick first, then the box. If you pull something clean, you won't have to clock anything else."

Chen didn't look any happier.

"I didn't say I couldn't do it. I just gotta figure out how. I'll have to work this stuff into the landing pattern, and that could take days."

The Latent Prints Unit was staffed twenty-four hours a day, seven days a week. The backlog of prints waiting to be analyzed was so large the unit employed almost eighty specialists around the clock to hold back the tide. With so many cases in line to be analyzed, a first-come-first-served waiting list was maintained to reserve the equipment needed for the work. This list was known as the landing pattern.

Cole said, "Days is too long. I need this."

Chen looked over, sour but thoughtful.

"For Joe?"

Cole nodded.

"What's up?"

"I'm hoping you can tell me. If these people are in the system, Joe needs to know why. I need to know why, too."

Chen shifted, maybe trying to get comfortable, but maybe because he was nervous. He was so tall his knees were above the dash and his head touched the roof.

Chen peeked into the bag again, then peered at Cole with enormous owl eyes.

"You know who I am?"

The question caught him by surprise, but then Cole sensed Chen wasn't talking to him—Chen was talking to himself. Cole shook his head.

"Sure you do, bro. All you have to do is look at me. I'm the guy defense attorneys make out to be the bumbling geek, so juries laugh. I hear cops making cracks when I'm at a scene. Every time I look in a mirror, I know why the girls laugh."

"John, you don't have to—"

Chen held up a finger, stopping him.

"When I first met you guys, I was freakin' terrified of Joe. He was everything that scares me shitless. Here's this guy, and no one would have the balls to make a crack or laugh. Here he is, a fucking street monster, but of all the people I deal with, he treats me with more respect than anyone else."

Chen lifted the bag.

"So I will find a way to do this. Pull over. I'll go get started."

"I'll take you back."

"I'd rather walk. It'll give me time to think."

Cole pulled over, and Chen got out with the bag.

"John."

"What?"

"Take the box."

Chen took the bag containing the box.

"If you speak with Joe, don't mention this."

Chen stared at Cole a long time, then abruptly walked away.

25

ELVIS COLE

When Cole reached his office he got down to business. The night before, he had asked a friend on the Hollywood Station homicide table for sheets on Mendoza and Gomer. These he would have used to identify known associates and relatives, but they were no longer necessary. He called her to cancel the request, but she had already printed the information and was pissed she had taken the risk for nothing. He then spread the contents of Wilson Smith's file box over his desk. With Mendoza and Gomer out of the picture, Cole focused on Wilson and Dru.

He quickly determined that most of the files related to Smith's business, with the individual folders containing invoices, bills, equipment warranties, and rental agreements. Smith purchased fresh seafood from a purveyor in San Pedro, sandwich rolls and breads from a bakery in Boyle Heights, and had signed a one-year lease agreement with Lodestar Properties for the storefront that now housed his kitchen. Cole checked through the bills and invoices for a prior address, but everything that had been mailed was sent to Smith's shop. Cole made a list of names and numbers from the various letterheads in case he wanted to phone them, then pushed the business files aside.

He tackled the money files next. There were two folders, one for checking and one for savings, with both accounts drawn on the Venice branch of Golden State Bank & Trust. The statements went back eight months, showing both accounts were opened on the same day. The savings account was opened with a $9600 deposit, from which $2000 was used to open the checking account. Two weeks after opening the savings account, an additional $6500 was deposited. The first statement had been mailed to Smith at a P.O. box in Venice, but the following seven, including the most recent, were mailed to Wilson's Takeout Foods. Cole copied the P.O. box address, then examined the statements. Deposits, withdrawals, and checking activity all seemed reasonable, with most of the drafts made out to pay for rent, utilities, and supplies. The canceled checks were in the file. Smith was obviously a man who didn't believe in online banking. He was also a man who didn't believe in credit cards.

The contents of Wilson Smith's metal file box contained nothing showing a date prior to the accounts that were opened eight months ago, nothing of a personal nature, and nothing to connect Wilson Smith with Louisiana or anyplace else. It was as if the man had been born eight months ago with a $9600 deposit.

Nothing in the file box named or was related to Dru Rayne. It was as if she didn't exist at all.

Among the utilities was a monthly phone bill. Pike had given Cole the cell phone numbers for Wilson and Dru, but this number was different. Cole dialed the number, and reached a voice message informing him Wilson's Takeout Foods was currently closed but was open during the following business hours. The voice was a woman's, and Cole thought it must be Dru. She had a nice voice.

Cole hung up, staring at nothing. He told himself they were house sitters, which was a temporary arrangement, so most of their possessions were probably in storage or packed in a friend's garage, but Cole told himself this was bogus even as he formed the thoughts.

Everything about Dru Rayne and Wilson Smith was wrong.

Cole leaned back and stared out the French doors. The French doors opened to a small balcony and, twelve miles beyond, the sea. Cole could see the ocean on a clear day, but today a wall of haze obscured his view. He felt depressed, and wondered how Pike was doing with the police. He did not like knowing this thing about Dru Rayne that Pike did not know. He did not like the expression he had seen on Pike's face when Pike was shouldering the guilt for whatever trouble the woman was in. Cole had seen that same expression in the mirror too many times.

Cole dialed the takeout shop again to hear her voice. Pleasant, friendly, medium timbre with a hint of a Southern accent. A familiar voice that inspired an ache in his chest. Cole had loved a woman from Louisiana. They had gotten in so deep Lucy moved out with her eight-year-old son. It was a gamble for all of them that didn't work out, so Lucy and her son returned to Louisiana. This had been Lucy's call, not Cole's. Cole would have gone all the way.

When Cole realized he was thinking more about Lucy Chenier than Dru Rayne, he checked the time. Louisiana was two hours ahead. Lucy would be at her office or in court. She was an attorney in private practice with a successful firm in Baton Rouge, and it occurred to Cole she might be able to help. It also occurred to him this was simply an excuse to hear her voice.

A professional voice answered when he called.

"Ms. Chenier's office."

"Guess who?"

Loretta Bean's professional voice melted into warm, Southern comfort. Loretta was Lucy's assistant.

"You dog. You don't call here often enough, and I miss your smart mouth."

"I was falling in lust with you, Loretta. I had to stop calling before I embarrassed myself."

"The terrible things you say, you *should* be embarrassed, but I love every minute of it. Would you like Ms. Chenier?"

"In more ways than you know."

"You awful dog. Hold on and I'll get her."

Cole was placed on hold and found himself listening to canned music. Harry Connick, Jr., on the piano. He was on hold so long Harry transitioned to Branford Marsalis before she came on the line.

"Hey, you. Sorry I took so long. I was on with a client."

Hearing her voice, warmth spread through him despite the twinge of discomfort he felt these days when he called. He tried not to phone her as often as he once did, but that was more for her than him. He didn't want to push. He didn't want her to cringe when he called.

"No worries. I bill by the hour."

She laughed.

"Then I'm happy to help. We here at Rotolo, Fourrier, Day, and Chenier want you to make lots of money."

"Got a few minutes? I could call back later if now isn't good."

The joking in her voice was replaced by a warm contralto that always made him feel they were the only two people in a remote mountain cabin.

"Sure, hon. Hang on—"

She told Loretta not to put anyone through, then returned to their conversation.

"Everything good?"

"I'm looking for background on a woman named Dru Rayne and a man named Wilson Smith, both of whom claim to be from New Orleans."

"Uh-huh. And why does the word 'claim' draw my attention?"

"Joe knows the woman, and I'm not convinced she's been honest with him about their circumstances or even about who they are."

"When you say involved, you mean like boyfriend-girlfriend?"

Cole described how Pike saved Wilson Smith from the beating, and subsequently met Dru Rayne. He left out the parts about Latin gangs, abductions, and bodies cut so badly their heads were almost severed. The violence he encountered as part of his job was what drove Lucy away.

When he finished, Lucy shifted into lawyer mode.

"All right, first, are we talking about a potential crime here? Is Joe giving them money?"

Cole hesitated, realizing he would have to describe parts of the situation he had hoped to avoid.

"No, it isn't like that. They've disappeared. They might be in trouble, so we're trying to find them."

Lucy was quiet for a moment, and Cole hoped he wouldn't have to tell her Pike was being questioned about the murders of two Venice gangbangers.

"When you say disappeared, are you speaking of a voluntary disappearance or a forced disappearance?"

"Could be either."

"Damnit, Elvis, you should be speaking with the police, not me."

"The police are doing their thing and we're doing ours."

"Why isn't that a surprise?"

"My concern now is Joe. He's all in, and I'm just trying to make sure he's in for the right reason. I'm also trying to figure out what kind of trouble these people are in."

"Hang on—*I'll call him back. No more calls now, Loretta, I am out of the office*—all right, hon, I'm back. Tell me what I can do."

Cole smiled, and loved the way she said it without hesitation. Tell me what I can do.

"If I can locate someone who knows them, maybe I can get a line on what's happening. Getting a line is the problem. All I have are their names. No former addresses, no social security numbers, no last known addresses, nothing. I don't even have a picture of these people."

"I understand. I'm thinking—"

She fell silent, and Cole let her think.

"They left with the storm?"

"That's what I'm told. I don't know if it's true."

"He owned a restaurant in New Orleans?"

"Owned or worked in, I don't know which, and I don't even know if it's true. He's a cook."

"Okay, pretending it's true, do you have a name for the place?"

"Sorry, Luce."

She fell silent again.

"The storm was so many years ago. There were sites and services for refugees to reconnect with missing family, but I don't know if those things still exist. Did you meet Terry when you were here?"

Terry Babinette was the investigator used by Lucy's firm. He was a retired Baton Rouge Police detective.

"Shook his hand."

"Let me talk it over with him to see if he has any ideas."

"That would be terrific, Lucille. Thank you."

"Why aren't you convinced?"

Cole didn't understand.

"About what?"

"Earlier, you said you weren't convinced they were honest with Joe. Why aren't you convinced?"

Cole propped his foot on the edge of his desk, feeling bad all over again with the deep-in-the-gut fear you might lose something precious.

"I have reason to believe their relationship is not as they've described it."

"Joe and Dru?"

"Dru and her uncle."

Elvis described his conversation with Steve Brown, then repeated the things Jared Palmer told him.

Lucy sounded hollow when she spoke.

"Oh my God."

"Uh-huh."

"Do you believe this kid?"

"He's been spot-on about everything else. And Brown was furious. Smith's been living there without his knowledge, and he's been talking to the woman every couple of weeks. That makes her a liar. She told Joe she moved in with Wilson, not the other way around, so that makes her a liar twice. So she could be lying about their relationship, too."

"What does Joe think?"

Cole hesitated, because this had been eating at him since he spoke with Jared.

"Joe doesn't know. I haven't told him."

"Oh, man, this is so hard."

"I'd like to have more than Jared's word before I lay this on him."

Neither of them said anything for a very long time.

"I miss you, Luce."

"I know, baby. I miss you, too. What are you going to do?"

"Talk to you. I guess that's why I called."

She sighed. A long, slow breath into the phone that he wanted to feel on his skin.

"Do you believe this boy?"

"Yeah. I can't prove it. I have nothing but his word for it, but after what Brown said, I believe him. I believe he was telling the truth."

"Tell him."

Cole nodded to himself, but found nothing to say.

"The longer you wait, the worse it will be. Do you understand that?"

"Yeah."

"Joe's built to save people. That's how he sees himself, and that's who he is. He's trying to save her, so whatever he feels for her, it will get deeper."

"I know."

"I know you know. That's you, too. That's why you two found each other, and why you're joined at the hip. It's why you do what you do."

Cole rubbed his left eye. His throat felt thick.

"Is that why I lost you?"

"You didn't lose me, baby. Here we are. If he wants to save her, fine, but he deserves to know who he's saving."

"Being a friend is hard."

"If it was easy, anyone could do it."

"I love smart women."

"Smart women love you."

"I'd better go."

"Call me later."

Cole put down the phone. It was still early, but he had plenty to do, and Lucy had given him a good idea. He scanned the list of food purveyors and suppliers Smith had dealt with. All were people in the food and restaurant business who probably swapped stories about cooks, cooking, and the good and bad restaurants where they worked. It was possible Smith mentioned a New Orleans restaurant where he had worked, or maybe a chef he had worked with, and one of the people on the list might remember. Having a place to start would make Lucy's job easier.

Cole opened a fresh bottle of water, pulled the phone close, and got back to work.

26

ELVIS COLE

Cole was still at his office later that day when Pike phoned, saying he was coming over to fill Cole in about the bodies. Cole suggested they meet at his house, saying he would make dinner while they talked, and they could have a few beers. Cole did not mention Dru or Wilson, or the sick feeling he had from the ugly news he was about to share with his friend.

The twilight sun melted into a magenta haze as Cole crept up the hill toward home. The traffic on Laurel Canyon was brutal, so Cole took a neighborhood bypass, winding between the trees and gated homes up Outpost Drive to Mulholland. Cole drove a yellow 1966 Stingray Convertible, and liked it a lot. It ran well and was fun to drive, but Cole didn't wash it often, so it was dirty. Pike washed his Jeep every day. Its immaculate red skin was so slick with polish, Cole joked that dirt probably blew off with the wind. Thinking about Pike's gleaming

Jeep left Cole feeling sad. It would have been a lovely drive home, any other night, with the Stingray's top down and the cool canyon air scented with eucalyptus and wild fennel. Any other night, it would have been fine.

Home was a redwood A-frame on a narrow street off Woodrow Wilson Drive at the top of a canyon. The little house was a two-bedroom, two-bath fixer Cole bought during a flush year before prices went crazy. If he wanted to buy it today, he couldn't. There was no yard to speak of, what with being perched on a drop-away slope, but a deck across the back of the house gave Cole a great view of the canyon and glimpse of the city.

Cole pulled into the carport, and let himself in through the kitchen. A black cat was on the counter. It looked at its bowl when Cole walked in, and made a soft *mrp*.

"Okay. Let's get you squared away."

Cole put out fresh food and water, then helped himself to a beer. Negro Modelo. The cat looked up from the food.

"Mrp."

"Okay, but not too much."

Cole poured a little beer into a saucer.

The cat had come with the house, and had been part of Cole's life longer than any living thing except Joe Pike. It was a mean animal, and given to attacking people. Cole did not know why. Once, a heating and air-conditioning repairman was working on the forced-air unit in Cole's hall closet. The repairman

217

was kneeling in the door with his back to the hall when the cat climbed his back and bit him on the neck four times. Cole's insurance company settled the claim, but Cole had to do a personal job off the books for his broker to get a new policy.

"It's going to be a tough night, bud."

The cat bumped his hand with surprising gentleness, then went back to eating.

The house was warm from being closed all day, so Cole opened the big deck doors. He took a small skirt steak from the freezer to thaw, then rinsed a large can of white beans and put them aside to drain. The first Modelo was gone by then, so he helped himself to a second, drinking it while he sliced zucchini, Japanese eggplant, and two large tomatoes for the grill. The joy of cooking was oblivion. Slicing and seasoning made it easier not to think. The Modelo went a long way toward helping that, too.

When the vegetables were good to go, Cole went upstairs, changed into a T-shirt, then returned to the deck to fire up his Weber. The sky was a beautiful sangria by then, and inspired him to have another beer.

When Cole went in, Joe Pike was in the kitchen. Unannounced and silent as a ghost. The cat was twined between his ankles, purring. Pike was the only person besides Cole the cat would abide.

Cole tipped his empty toward the vegetables.

"White bean salad with grilled veggies we can share. Maybe a little couscous. Carne asada for me. Sound good?"

"Good."

Sure.

Notice how the loyal friend prepares his subject for the evening's festivities.

"I'm having a beer. Get one, then you can fill me in while I'm prepping the coals."

Pike took a beer from the fridge. Cole grabbed a third, and followed him out. The cat trailed behind them. He liked to watch the slope for field mice and gophers.

Cole pushed at the coals, which was a completely unnecessary act. Notice the immaculate technique as the World's Greatest Best Friend stalls the moment of truth.

"You go first, then I'll go. What happened with Mendoza and Gomer?"

Pike related what he knew about Mendoza, then moved on to Gomer. At first Cole only pretended to listen, but the graphic nature of their murders drew him in. Gomer's body was found behind the wheel of a car parked near the north end of Grand Canal. The blood in the vehicle suggested Gomer was killed at the scene. The first cut was likely a downward stab wound on the left side of the neck that sliced through the carotid artery, the esophagus, most of the surrounding musculature down to visible bone, and into the upper thorax. The second cut was drawn from the right ear across the throat to the base of the left ear, also exposing visible bone.

Pike said, "They didn't have a good time-of-death

on Mendoza, but Gomer probably died between eleven P.M. and one A.M. this morning. When the cops cut me free, I checked the spot where they found him. He had a head-on view of Wilson's house. Mendoza was probably set up on the other side."

When Cole realized what Pike was saying, he held up a hand.

"Waitaminute. Are you telling me these guys were watching the house?"

"Yes."

"But that doesn't make sense. If they grabbed Wilson and Dru this morning, why go back to the house? What did they want?"

"Maybe someone Wilson and Dru told them about, but that's only a guess. It was probably the man who killed them. The light I saw in the upstairs bedroom when I called you this morning, that was probably the killer. The same man who jimmied the kitchen window."

Cole didn't like it, or what it might mean.

"Mendoza and Gomer came back for this guy, but he was already there. He saw them first, and took them out?"

Pike cocked his head the other way, and the tangerine sunset gleamed on his glasses.

"Yes. I think he was still watching the house when I was there this morning. I could feel him."

Cole prodded the coals, and watched firefly embers swirl in the heat. Everything had changed in the space of a day. A neighborhood shakedown had become an illusion. Vandalism and assault were a sleight-of-hand trick to hide something worse, and now Cole knew the magicians were liars. None of it was real, and probably never had been.

Pike's voice came from the embers.

"Now you."

Cole looked at his friend.

"I spoke with Steve Brown today, the man who owns Smith's house, and I had another talk with Jared. I have to tell you some things, and you're not going to like it. I don't think Dru has been honest with you."

Cole paused for Pike to react, but Pike gave him no more reaction than a department store mannequin. The cat left the edge of the deck, twined once through Pike's legs, then sat, its eyes narrow and watchful.

Cole put his bottle on the rail.

"Brown has never met Wilson Smith or heard of him. He let Dru use the house because they had a relationship. She was supposed to be there alone, and Brown was furious when he found out someone was living with her. He knew nothing about her uncle, or Dru working at Wilson's food place, or any of it. He believed she was living on alimony. Until we spoke this morning, he expected to resume their relationship when he returns."

Pike remained motionless, floating at the edge of the deck. Cole wished he could see behind the black glasses, but that view was hidden.

"After I spoke with Brown, I talked to Jared. Jared told me things that put the lie to everything this woman told you about herself. It's not good, Joe. It's pretty damned bad."

"What?"

The cat crouched at Pike's feet. Its tail snapped and twitched as Cole repeated Jared's story. Cole kept it brief, but left nothing out.

"If you want to talk to him again, I'll go with you, but I believe Jared is telling the truth. When I left him, I took some things from their house that should have their prints, and gave them to John Chen. I don't know that these people are in the system, but they might be, and the prints might help us figure this out. Also, I spoke with Lucy. Until we hear back from Chen, all I could give her were their names, but her investigator is going to see what he can find in New Orleans. That's it. That's been my day."

Pike seemed to sway, as if pushed by a breeze, only the air was still.

"I'm sorry, man. If you want me to call off Chen and Lucy, I will."

Pike turned toward the canyon and placed his hands on the rail. Cole wondered if he needed the rail to stop swaying.

"No. Don't call them off."

"All right. You want another beer?"

Pike shook his head.

Cole said, "What do you want to do?"

"About what?"

"We're in this because you want to help this woman. I'm fine with that, but now, well, maybe things have changed."

"She still needs help."

"Okay. If that's what you want."

"That's what I want."

The cat whipped and twitched its tail at a furious rate, and its eyes were dangerous slits.

Cole said, "I'm sorry, man."

His phone rang. Cole wasn't going to answer, but decided to give Pike some time. He covered the grill then went inside for the phone. He scooped up the handset a second after the message machine, and spoke over the recording.

"Hey, I'm here. Don't hang up—it'll stop."

"Mr. Cole?"

Cole didn't recognize the man's voice.

"That's right. Who's this?"

"My name is Charles Laine. You were at my home today on the canal. You spoke with my housekeeper about my surveillance system."

Cole glanced outside to signal Pike, but Pike had left the rail.

"Yes, sir. Thanks for getting back to me."

"Not a problem. Is this about the police investigation? The police came by yesterday."

"Yes, sir, same thing, but I am not a police officer. I'm a licensed investigator working in private employ."

"I know. I have your card here. Irma says you asked if we record the camera feed."

Cole looked at the opposite end of the deck, but still did not see Pike.

"Yes, sir. We're looking to identify two men who might have passed by your house yesterday morning."

"I might be able to help. The system I have here records, but I'm not sure if you'll see enough of the street. I know you can see some of it, but the camera is set up to show people who come to the gate."

"I understand. Could I take a look at whatever you have?"

"Sure. I'll try to burn a copy tonight. I've never done it before, but I have an instruction booklet somewhere around here. If it works, I'll get it over to you tomorrow. If not, maybe you could come here."

"That would be great, Mr. Laine. Thank you."

When Cole put down the phone, he went back to the deck. He wanted to share the one piece of good news he had gotten that day, but when he stepped outside, Joe Pike was gone.

"Joe?"

The cat was gone, too.

"Joseph?"

The canyon swallowed his voice.

Cole went to the rail. Down below, the first few flickering lights twinkled in the shadows. Darkness pooled in the deeper cuts like purple mist, and would climb as the sun died until it consumed him. But not now, and not yet.

"It's going to be okay, buddy. It only hurts for a while."

His voice a whisper meant only for himself.

Then the cat growled, somewhere to his right and below on the slope. It started low, and spiraled louder like a terrible war cry until it filled the canyon with an anguished wail as if the cat was in pain. Cole thought it was the cat. He was pretty sure it was the cat.

Cole leaned over the rail, trying to see. He stretched as far into space as he could, trying to find the cat by listening to its scream, but saw nothing. The cat was there, but so well hidden he could not be found.

Sometimes you want to help them, but can't.

27

THE AIR FELT CLEAN when it cooled in the evening. Pike opened the Jeep's windows, letting the air chill his skin. Oncoming headlights, flaring brake lights, and neon signs scribed molten arcs on the Jeep's gleaming hood. As he neared the ocean, streetlights cast halos in the mist, each halo brighter than the last. Pike drove back to the canals.

Gomer had been murdered in an empty lot on the west side of Grand Canal where a home had recently been razed. Pike had visited the site earlier when the police cut him free, but Gomer had been killed at night, so Pike wanted to see this place in the darkness as Gomer and his killer had seen it. He had no place else to go.

Pike parked on the street, and walked past an abandoned trailer across bare ground to the canal. Earlier, the area had been filled with officers, but now it was deserted. Not long after the project was started, a new foundation had been poured and the trailer was brought in for the construction manager, but somewhere along the way the money dried up and the project had been abandoned. Gomer had driven up onto the construction site and parked facing the canal.

Smith's house was several houses to Pike's right on the opposite bank not far beyond the mouth of an adjoining canal. The location offered a good view of Smith's backyard, half the ground-floor windows, and the second floor, but Pike thought Gomer was an idiot for having parked where he was openly visible. Pike could see families in the houses across the canal and people crossing the footbridge that spanned the adjoining canal, and knew any of them could see him just as they could have seen Gomer. One of the people who'd seen Gomer that night had left him soaking in blood.

Pike studied the houses and the shadows beneath the pedestrian bridge and the play of light on the water. He felt he understood everything that had happened until Mendoza and Gomer returned to the canals to be murdered. He did not understand why they had returned, why they were killed, or who had killed them, and now this business about Dru and Wilson made him rethink himself, and them, and everything he had believed was true. Maybe that was good. He believed the answers were here in this place, so his task was to recognize the signs. If he found them, he could re-create the events, and then he would know what happened. The same as reading the words in a book. Reading each word and adding it to the next to build a sentence, then connecting the sentences to learn the story. The task was to find enough words.

Pike slipped out his cell phone and called John Chen, who answered in his typical paranoid whisper.

"Yes? Who is this?"

"Pike. Two bodies were bagged on the Venice Canals this morning. You know about them?"

Chen didn't answer.

"John?"

"Sorry. I thought you were asking about something else."

"Their names were Mendoza and Gomer."

"That's Sandy Lancaster. I'm not on it, but she's here in the next cube. What do you need?"

Pike asked if either showed signs of defensive wounds or ligature marks, and whether the police had located the place of Mendoza's murder. Chen told him to hang on, and Pike could hear murmurs as Chen spoke with the criminalist in the next cube. A few moments later, Chen was back on the line.

"Nah, man. Nothing defensive and negative on the ligatures. These guys didn't see it coming, if that's what you're after."

"What about Mendoza?"

"They think so, but they can't confirm until the blood work comes back. She said they found a good-sized splatter on one of the pedestrian bridges they have down there. I don't know which one."

"That's okay, John. I can figure it out."

Pike was staring at the pedestrian bridge that joined the north end of Smith's street. There would be another bridge at the south end. With Gomer watching the north side, Mendoza would have been watching the south. Each fact was a word to build the story.

Pike started to end the call, but his eyes found Dru's house again.

"Did you find any prints on the things Elvis gave you?"

Chen's voice grew wary.

"What things?"

"The things Elvis gave you today."

"I didn't see Elvis today."

"I just left him, John. He told me about it."

Chen hesitated even longer than before.

"You're not mad, are you? He told me not to say."

"I'm fine. Did you get anything?"

"I haven't even had time to piss. I'm sorry, man, I'll get to it before I leave. Promise."

"That's okay. Just asking."

"I know it's important, her being your girlfriend and all."

Pike was sorry he brought it up.

"She wasn't my girlfriend."

"All women are rotten, bro. Nobody knows that better than me. I can't even get a bitch to break my heart."

Pike closed his phone, then forced himself to think about Mendoza and Gomer, imagining them set up to watch Wilson's house. It occurred to Pike that Azzara might have had them killed. Maybe he found out they murdered Wilson and Dru, and was angry they did it against his orders. He could have ordered them to the canals for a phony reason, then sent a crew to kill them. Pike was considering this when he remembered the upstairs light and jimmied window. A crew sent by Azzara to murder Mendoza and Gomer would have had no reason to enter the house. The window had been jimmied by someone else, and Pike now suspected this was their killer.

Pike reset the image of Gomer and Mendoza watching the house. The killer was good. Neither man had fought back or tried to defend himself. He had taken them by surprise, and killed them cleanly and efficiently with overwhelming speed. This suggested a professional, or someone with professional training. If the killer had jimmied the window, then he was probably already in place when they arrived, which meant he had not come for Mendoza and Gomer—he had come for Wilson and Dru.

Pike felt the pieces begin to fall into place. The words began to feel like a story.

The killer had come to the house early as evidenced by the time of his entry, did not find what he was looking for, so he had set up to wait. This meant he was somehow connected to Wilson and Dru. Pike had assumed Mendoza and Gomer abducted Wilson and Dru, but maybe their first attempt failed, so they returned for another chance. The killer had probably watched them take their positions, and either knew they were waiting for Wilson or concluded they were by their actions. He might have watched them for hours. Then he killed them, and probably continued waiting for Wilson and Dru.

Each new thought was a word, and the more Pike tested the words the better he liked the story. The signs were here. He just had to read them correctly and in the right order. There were still holes and questions, but he saw it unfolding and liked the way it felt.

I am here.

A new player had entered the scene, but maybe he had been in the game longer than anyone thought.

Pike turned from the water, and drove the few short blocks to Wilson Smith's shop.

28

PIKE PARKED AT THE curb in front of Wilson's store. A café and the coffee shop on the next block were still open, along with the Mobil station and the tattoo shop across the street. Pike waited for a strolling couple to pass, then went to the new glass window with his flashlight and shined the light inside. The heads and entrails were gone, and the interior had been cleaned. The city might have sent a hazmat team, or maybe Betsy Harmon and her son had cleaned it themselves. None of it mattered now, not to Pike or anyone else.

The light flashed on the wall where the message had been scribed in blood.

I am here.

Pike and the police both assumed Mendoza and Gomer had trashed the shop, just as they assumed Mendoza and Gomer had committed the abduction, but the nature of the message had always bothered Pike, and now he realized why. *I am here* was an announcement, and felt like an awkward message for Gomer or Mendoza to leave, but maybe not so awkward for the man who had killed them if that man had been searching for Wilson and Dru.

I am here. I. Singular.

I have arrived.

Fear me.

Pike decided the new man had hung the heads, spread the blood, and did so to announce his arrival.

The story was clear.

He had not written *I am back*, so he had not started here, gone away, and returned. *I am here* implied he had started his search elsewhere but had now arrived, which suggested a passage of time. He had been searching for them, and now had found them and wanted them to know, which also suggested they knew or knew of him. Pike was suspicious of these last conclusions because they went against his instincts. You didn't warn your target you were coming. Wilson had seen the message, understood, and immediately disappeared. Pike now felt Wilson's intention to flee had nothing to do with Mendoza and Gomer and everything to do with the new man's arrival.

Pike snapped off his light, turned away from the window, and considered the shops across the street as he thought through the contradiction. Wilson had seen the message, panicked, and run. Maybe that was the point—maybe the man warned them because he wanted them to flee, like a hunter flushing game from cover. He had probably been watching Wilson's shop when Wilson arrived that morning. He probably followed Wilson back to the house, but Mendoza and Gomer interrupted his play.

Pike returned to his Jeep for Jack Straw's phone number. Straw answered on the third ring, sounding relaxed and hazy like a DJ on an FM jazz station.

Pike said, "Did you have people watching Smith's shop the past few days?"

"Yeah. On and off. Why?"

"They might have seen the man who killed Mendoza and Gomer."

"Hang on."

Pike heard sounds like Straw was cupping his phone. The noises continued for almost a minute before Straw returned to the line.

"Look across the street."

Pike glanced across, and knew they were watching him. Straw immediately spoke again.

"See the tattoo parlor?"

"Yes."

"See the office above it?"

Upstairs, black windows with a FOR LEASE sign taped to the glass. Of course.

"Come through the tattoo place, and go out the back. You'll see a stair. The man at the counter says anything, tell'm you're with the band."

Pike crossed between cars and went through the tattoo shop. A bald man with tattoos on his scalp and cheeks and a large metal ring through his nose was reading a James Ellroy novel behind the counter. He glanced up when Pike entered, but went back to reading when Pike pointed at the ceiling.

Pike passed walls lined with thousands of tattoo designs, then through a narrow back door and up a flight of metal stairs. Straw was waiting at the top, wearing jeans and a loose V-neck T-shirt that needed a wash. He showed Pike into a tiny two-room office suite without furniture. The only light came from a single lamp burning in the back room. The front room overlooking the street caught a wedge of light through the partially open door, but the windows overlooking the street were covered with black cloth spotted with small rectangular cutouts for viewing the street. The man in the orange shirt was cross-legged on the floor with his back against the wall. He stared at Pike with indifference and made no move to offer his hand.

It was a bare-bones hide, smelling of pizza, cigarettes, and body odor. Suitcases piled with rumpled clothes were in the corners near air mattresses mounded with sleeping bags. Empty soda cans and Starbucks cups spilled from a garbage bag. Straw's team had come in light, and hadn't planned on staying as long as they had.

Straw smiled as he gestured to the room.

"I'd say pull up a chair, but we don't have chairs."

"Mendoza and Gomer didn't trash Smith's shop. The man who killed them did it, and your guys might have seen him."

Straw and the orange man stared for a moment, then the orange man tipped forward, interested.

"What does he look like?"

His voice was higher than Pike expected, and hoarse at the edges, as if he was getting over a cold.

"What's your name?"

Straw answered for him.

"This is Kenny. Let's leave it at first names."

Kenny was watching Pike now, his eyes intense.

"Can you describe the guy?"

"Haven't seen him."

Kenny smirked as he slumped against the wall, his interest gone.

"Oh."

"He wanted to know when people came and left, when the shop was empty, what kind of alarms there might be. That means he was here."

"Yeah? So how do you know what he wants?"

Pike stared at Kenny, then looked at Straw.

"Because that's what I would want. He's hunting Wilson and Dru. He blooded the shop to flush them, and probably followed Wilson back to his house, but Mendoza and Gomer got in the way. This isn't about a couple of bangers shaking down a cook. This is bigger."

Straw and Kenny glanced at each other again as if they were having a silent conversation, then Straw shrugged at Pike.

"I don't get it. Why all that business with the blood and the heads if he wanted to kill them? Why not just kill them?"

"I don't know. Maybe to see where they'd go."

Kenny grinned, bugging his eyes like Pike was an idiot.

"Maybe he's crazy. If, you know, he's real."

Straw frowned at Kenny for a moment, thinking.

"Okay. I'm listening. What do you know?"

Pike walked them through his reasoning about the message left in Wilson's shop and the conclusions he drew from the way in which Gomer and Mendoza were murdered. If Straw wondered how Pike knew so much about their bodies, he did not ask.

"Okay, I'm not saying I buy this, but if you're right, and we saw the guy, how would we know?"

Kenny mumbled to himself.

"Wore a shirt, said KILLER. Don't you remember?"

Then Kenny laughed to himself, but Pike was focused on Straw.

"You would have seen him more than once. After three or four passes, you realized you kept seeing him. A fifth pass, and maybe you wondered who he was and why he was interested in Smith's shop."

Kenny glanced at Straw.

"I don't remember anyone like that. You?"

"Only the people who work in the other shops around here, but I'll ask the guys. Maybe one of them saw something."

Kenny crossed his arms and closed his eyes.

"Sure. You ask."

A long-lens camera and a night vision spotting scope were on ballistic carry bags beneath the windows. A video camera hooked by a cable to a nearby laptop computer was part of the jumble. Pike had seen them when he entered, and now pointed them out.

"What about your vid?"

Straw shook his head, and was already moving to show Pike out.

"We tracked Azzara's guys. We never turned the

thing on unless we saw one of his bangers. That's all we got."

Pike glanced at the little rectangles cut in the fabric, backlit by the lights below. He wondered how many hours they spent seeing the world through the narrow patchwork windows.

"Check the vid. You never know."

Kenny mumbled again, not opening his eyes.

"That's right. You never know."

Straw told Pike he would call if one of his people had seen something, then showed him out as if Pike had wasted enough of their time. Kenny didn't open his eyes.

After Pike left, he drove back to the canals. It was later now, but not yet as late as when Gomer was murdered.

Pike did not return to the construction site. He parked on Venice Boulevard near Smith's house, then approached on foot. Smith's house. Steve Brown's house. Pike thought of it as Dru's house, and it was now the only dark house on the short, narrow alley. Jared's light was on, but Jared was missing. Probably downstairs with his mother. Rocking the big screen.

Pike used the hidden key to unlock the gate, then went past the house to the fence at the edge of the canal. The smell of the water was strong. He quickly picked out the construction site where Gomer had been murdered. He was not trying to hide. He wanted to be seen.

Pike wondered if the killer used night vision gear. Pike had the equipment, but had decided not to use

238

it. If the killer was here, Pike wanted him to feel like he had the upper hand. Pike noted the cuts and shadows along the banks and between the houses where a spotter could hide, and hoped the man was watching. His presence would mean he had not yet found Dru and Wilson, and they would still be alive. If the killer was watching, he might grow curious why Pike was in their yard, and decide to take a closer look. The killer might decide to kill him, which would be even better. The killer would need to move in close to use his knife, and Pike was fine with close. Pike wanted to learn what he knew.

Light danced on the water. Traffic noise from the surrounding streets was loud, as was the music and voices that bounced along the canals, but all of these living sounds would fade as the night grew deeper.

Pike waited alone in the dark, wondering where Dru and Wilson were, and how the man with the knife knew them, and whether or not they were living or dead. He wondered where they had come from, why they were here, and why he decided to put air in his tires on that particular morning at that particular gas station at that particular time.

None of it mattered, there in the darkness. He had told her he would take care of it. Told her they wouldn't bother her again.

Pike whispered.

"I am here."

Whoever and whatever she was did not matter. If she needed him, he would be there.

Pike whispered again.

Part Four
The Prince of Solitude

29

PIKE CHANGED LOCATIONS SEVERAL times during the night, drifting from Dru's house to positions where he had a view of likely areas where someone watching the house might hide. Pike found no one, and as the eastern sky lightened, he grew convinced the killer no longer watched Dru's house. This meant the killer had what he wanted or had tracked Wilson and Dru to another location. Either was bad, and left Pike hungry for a new trail.

At twenty minutes after nine that morning, Pike was crossing the Dell Avenue Bridge when Elvis Cole called.

"Laine came through. He messengered over a disk."

Charles Laine. Dru's neighbor with the surveillance system.

"Show anything?"

"It just arrived, but I need you here to look at it. I've never seen these people. I don't know what they look like."

Pike studied Dru's house across the water with a lack of enthusiasm. Cole was right, but Mendoza and Gomer were dead, so even if they lucked into a glimpse of the abduction, leaving to view a recording of questionable value now felt like a waste of time. Then another possibility occurred to him that left him more interested.

"How many hours of camera time do we have?"

"Seven days from whenever he burned the disk, which was sometime last night. Why?"

Pike told Cole about his conversation with Straw and explained his belief in the killer's professionalism. He had probably reconnoitered Dru's house as well as the takeout shop, and was likely the person who jimmied the kitchen window. This meant it was possible the killer had moved past the camera.

"Okay, get here, and let's see if this stuff is even usable. Laine told me we'll be able to see a little of the street, but we won't know what that means until we see it. We might see nothing but shadows."

The trip through the city took forty minutes, but shortly Pike pulled up outside Cole's A-frame and let himself into the kitchen.

Pike poured himself a cup of black coffee, grabbed a raisin bagel from Cole's stock, and followed his friend to a desk in the living room. They pulled over chairs from the dining table with Cole sitting in front of his Mac. Cole slipped in the disk, and the drive spun up with a soft whine. Neither of them spoke while they waited, as if their expectation wrapped each man in silence.

A few moments later, a disk player appeared showing four screen-capture images. They were from each of the four cameras monitoring Laine's home, one on either side of his house, one in the rear, and the front entry camera. Pike saw Cole relax when the images appeared.

"Here we go. The cameras record concurrently on different tracks. Laine said we can watch each track separately, and move back and forth like watching a DVD."

Cole clicked on the entry image, which expanded to fill the screen. The picture was a ghostly wash of grays and blacks with a time code at the bottom showing the image had been recorded at PM11:13:42 the night before. Cole glanced over.

"Not bad. We can see a little of the street here in the background, and the clarity is pretty good."

It didn't look so good to Pike. The camera was parallel to the street to focus on visitors who were in a small alcove at Laine's front door. This left its field of view limited. The right third of the screen was the steel door. The center third was the alcove wall directly opposite the camera where a visitor would stand when they pressed the bell. The left third of the screen showed a narrow wedge of street in the camera's peripheral background. If they were going to see anything useful, it would be in this narrow wedge.

Pike said, "Murky. It's hard to see anything past the wall."

"Think positive. This was shot at about eleven-fifteen last night with infrared light. The background will brighten up during the day."

Cole crossed his arms and glanced over again.

"You want to look for the killer?"

"Yes."

"Okay, think about it. Seven days means we have one hundred sixty-eight hours here. Fast-forward runs about eight times the real-time speed, so it will take us twenty-four hours to watch what's here if we go back to the beginning. You really want to spend that much time looking for a guy we won't recognize?"

Pike thought he could narrow the time.

"We can start smaller. The day they went missing, I checked their house around ten and you were there about one. Whoever jimmied the window did it during those three hours. Three hours isn't so bad."

Cole nodded, but it was a slow nod, and Pike knew he was thinking. Cole thinking was a good thing because he came up with good ideas.

"Tell you what, let's start earlier that morning. If you're right about the killer casing their place, he might have made two or three passes before he entered the property. He also might have followed Wilson home from his shop, so we might catch him on the follow. You see?"

Pike nodded. Good ideas.

"Also, if we get a glimpse of the abduction, we might see what kind of vehicles were involved and get an idea what condition Dru and Wilson were in when they were taken. This might help us find them even though Mendoza and Gomer are dead."

"Start whenever you want."

Pike wanted to get on with it.

Cole used the skip-reverse button to jump back through the recording in one-hour increments until the morning of the abduction. As the still images moved backward in time from night into day, Pike was relieved to see the images gained clarity, depth, and color.

When the time counter showed AM05:13:42 on the morning of the abduction, Cole clicked the play button, then increased the playback speed. Though dim in the early-morning light, the real-time image now grew sharper. The landscape remained frozen, but the ambient light changed and colors grew richer as the time counter advanced.

They saw the first sign of life at 5:36. A figure zipped past on the far left side of the screen, and vanished before Cole hit the pause button.

Cole said, "Jogger."

He reversed the recording, then replayed it in real time. A female jogger appeared out of the left edge of the screen with her back to the camera. Because the camera was parallel to the street, she looked as if she was coming from behind the left side of the camera on a slight left-to-right path, and was visible for only four seconds.

A second jogger appeared at 5:54, this time a young man with ropy Rasta hair who ran toward them on a path past the camera. Cole froze the image to study him.

Pike said, "Can you print his picture?"

"Sure. Think it's him?"

"We'll see."

Pike had no feeling about the man either way. He wanted pictures of all likely males who passed the house.

They saw no one else until 6:22 A.M. when the silver Tercel raced past at fast-forward speed.

Pike said, "That's them."

Cole reversed the recording, then brought it forward frame by frame until they had the best possible view of the driver. The frozen image was grainy, but Wilson Smith's face and features were clear enough. He was alone in the car.

"Wilson. This is when he's on his way to the shop."

Cole printed the image, then resumed play at the faster speed.

The activity on the alley grew with the morning hour. They stopped the image every time a figure sped by, then rewound and advanced in real time. The silver Tercel reappeared at 6:55, emerging from the left edge of the screen as Wilson returned home. The angle made it impossible to see Wilson behind the wheel, but no one else appeared to be in the car.

Between 7:00 A.M. and 8:00 A.M., they stopped the recording eighteen times and printed seven photographs, but none of the twenty-two people they saw appeared to be more than ordinary people out for a walk or a jog. Two cars passed the field of view as residents left their homes between 7:20 and

7:45. Neither was the silver Tercel, but Pike and Cole were encouraged in both cases because the outbound drivers were clearly visible.

Pike watched with a dull hope Cole was right, and he would see them leave before Mendoza arrived, but Jared came past the wall at 8:07 A.M. He quickly grew larger until he disappeared past the camera.

Pike said, "Okay. Sometime between now and when Jared returns is when Mendoza and Gomer arrive."

Cole nodded without looking away from the screen.

Two women with small dogs walked past, then another man jogged. At 8:42, another figure passed quickly from left to right, and Cole stopped the image.

"That's Jared. He's back."

Jared was carrying a plastic grocery bag. The moo.

Cole glanced at Pike, then shook his head.

"Real time, Mendoza and Gomer are at their house right now. This is when Jared saw them."

"They used the pedestrian bridge."

"Yeah. And if your killer used the bridge and stayed at the end of the alley, we're not going to see him, either."

"Play it out."

Cole let the image advance in real time, and, at 8:53, the Tercel crept into view. Pike leaned forward when it appeared even as Cole paused the image, rolled it back, and brought it forward one frame at a time.

As the image grew, Pike saw three people in the car. Wilson was driving. Dru was in the passenger seat, and another figure was in the back. This confirmed the bad guys had used the footbridge to enter, and forced the victims to drive them out. It was a good plan considering the narrow dead-end street with so many potential witnesses.

Pike said, "Mendoza is in back, but I only see three people."

"Could have left by the bridge, the way he came. Is that Dru in front?"

"Yes."

Cole printed her picture, then walked the frames forward.

Six frames later, the angle had changed enough to reveal a fourth person in the vehicle.

Cole said, "Here we go."

The second man sat directly behind Wilson, though he was still difficult to see. Cole advanced the image two more frames, and the second man's face emerged from behind Wilson's head.

Pike studied the blurry face, then leaned closer to the screen.

"Bring it one more."

Cole advanced the image.

"One more."

Pike felt a spike of surprise, then the surprise melted into the calm he felt when he steadied the crosshairs on a target. Cole was watching when Pike looked up.

"What's wrong?"

"This isn't Gomer. It's Miguel Azzara."

"I thought he didn't know anything about this."

"He lied."

Cole glanced at Azzara.

"Two people are dead, two more are missing, and here's *El Jefe* in on the abduction. This is bigger than a couple of bangers being pissed off because they got arrested. You think these guys found out about Straw's investigation?"

"Don't know."

"Maybe Azzara was worried Wilson could hurt him. Maybe Mendoza and Gomer were killed because he thought they were cooperating with the Feds."

Pike didn't know, but it was no longer important. Azzara gave him a target, and if Pike could see his target he could hit it.

Cole was printing Azzara's picture when his phone rang, and he told Pike the caller was Lucy Chenier. Cole took the phone outside onto his deck for the call, and Pike resumed watching the recording.

Pike watched at high speed, but the image still moved in slow motion because he thought about Azzara, and how he could find him. More joggers came and went, but most were female and the few men didn't appear to be likely candidates for experienced knife killers. Pike saw himself arrive, and leave, but no one else appeared on the street. Pike had skimmed through one hour and twenty minutes of the three-hour window when Cole returned from the deck, looking unhappy.

Pike paused the recording.

"What?"

"That was Lucy's investigator. The guy I told you about, Terry Babinette."

Pike waited, knowing from Cole's expression the news wasn't good.

"After the storm, the city put up websites so people could post the names of friends and family members who evacuated or were missing. All Terry had to work with were their names, so this isn't definitive, okay?"

"Say it."

"The names Drusilla Rayne and Wilson Smith are on a list of the dead. Drusilla Rayne was a forty-two-year-old Caucasian who died indigent at Charity Hospital three days before the storm. Wilson Smith was a seventy-six-year-old African-American male who died of a heart attack while being evacuated to Natchez, Mississippi. No known relatives for either. That's it."

Pike felt achy and numb. The man and the woman he knew as Wilson Smith and Dru Rayne had taken their names from the dead, and probably used the deceaseds' social security numbers to assume their identities.

Pike didn't know what to say, and now Cole looked uncomfortable.

"You want to look at more video?"

"No point."

"What do you want to do?"

Pike glanced at the frozen screen, then stood.

"Azzara has them. I'm going to take a shower, then I'm going to find Azzara."

Pike left Cole at the computer and walked back to the guest room.

30

DANIEL

Daniel said, "If our intel on the Mexican is accurate, I'll know their location before noon."

The Bolivian sounded more excited than Daniel had ever heard the man, which meant *all* the Bolivians were excited. Daniel pictured them sitting around in their compounds, strokin' their stiffies, thinkin' they were finally gonna get their revenge. Nothing those nasty little fuckers liked better than vengeance, and now they would have it. Thanks to Daniel.

"Stand by, sir—"

Daniel waited for the thunder of a departing Hawker business jet to fade before he continued. Those Hawkers were nice.

"Sorry, sir, I'm at the airport. Were we able to confirm the flight departed this morning?"

Yammer yammer.

"All right, yes, that's perfect. Do we have the aircraft registration number or its make and model?"

Yammer.

Cleo said, "Yammer."

Tobey said, "Yammer."

Daniel shushed them.

"Shh."

Daniel listened carefully while the Bolivian rattled out the latest intel from Mexico. The crush of information from Mexico and New Orleans during the past two days had been invaluable, but there would have been no information without Daniel, and the Bolivians knew it. Daniel had finally found the fuckers, and the dumb fucks had tried to cut a deal instead of running, and now their deal was killing them.

"Yes, sir, I will keep you advised—absolutely."

Daniel wanted to get off the phone, but the Bolivian kept going, saying how pleased they all were with Daniel, his loyalty, his determination, yadayadayada.

"Thank you, sir. No, really—I appreciate your faith in me. Thank you."

Daniel killed the link.

"Asshole."

Cleo snickered. "What an assfart."

Tobey laughed. "Big gapin' assclown, clown."

Daniel squinted across the runway at the control tower, then up into a hazy white sky. He leaned back until he looked straight up, enjoying the morning sky, and this place, and this moment. Daniel had assassinated people at airports like this all over South and Central America. He had also kidnapped people, blown up airplanes, stolen cargo, and pretty much every other damn thing a person could do.

"Been a long hunt, boys."

Tobey said, "Way too long."

Cleo said, "Too damn long."

Santa Monica Airport was a single runway lined by hangars and businesses, along with a very nice viewing area where Daniel now sat. He would be able to see the jet land, and still have plenty of time to get into position. Daniel already knew where the inbound jet would park. A stretch limo, a candy-gold SS396, and a chopped-down Monte Carlo were waiting directly across the tarmac. A moron's idea of a welcoming committee, for sure, but the limo was a fat black roach that would lead him to the promised land.

Daniel checked his watch. If the Bolivian was right, the Mexican would touch down in less than an hour, then be on his way to their meeting.

"You guys ready to kill some people?"

Tobey said, "Fuck yeah."

Cleo said, "Kill'm real good, good."

Daniel chuckled.

"Me, too, boys."

"Kill'm and eat'm?"

"Eat'm?"

"You boys are insane."

"'Sane?"

"'Sane?"

Daniel enjoyed the sun on his face and the pleasant company of their echoing voices.

31

Cole watched Pike drive away, then returned to his desk for the pictures of Dru and Wilson, who weren't really Dru Rayne or Wilson Smith. People change their names to hide, but hide from what, and who? Cole had been an investigator long enough to know people sometimes had good reasons to hide, but most of the time their reasons were bad. Cole had a bad feeling about these people, and the more he learned the worse his feeling grew.

The woman's picture was best. She was turned to her left as if she was speaking with Mendoza or Azzara, so she was facing the camera. Wilson was peering over the steering wheel, which gave a three-quarter view with part of his face blocked by the side view mirror.

Something about their expressions bothered him, but Cole couldn't decide why. After a few minutes, he put the pictures aside, and called Bree Sloan at the phone company to follow up on the cell numbers.

Sometimes they called back right away. Sometimes he had to nag.

She said, "Are you a mind reader? I was just about to call."

"Good news?"

"No, you're going to hate it, but I still get the tickets, right?"

"Of course."

Cole got premium Dodgers tickets from a former client, and shared them with people who helped him. Especially people like Bree, who was a regional manager at a midsized local telecommunications provider. Seats in the exclusive Dodgers Dugout Club worked better than search warrants.

"You at your computer?"

"Staring at it. It isn't as sexy as you."

Bree laughed. She had an excellent laugh.

"Man, you're something."

"Amazing, aren't I?"

"Okay, now stop that and listen. These three numbers you gave me—8272, 3563, and 3502?"

Cole glanced at his notes. These were the last four digits on the numbers for Wilson's shop, Wilson's cell phone, and Dru's cell.

"Uh-huh. I'm with you."

"8272 is a landline with ATT billed to Wilson's Takeout Foods. I'm going to send you the inbound and outbound records for the past forty-five days, okay? That's all they have."

"I understand."

Phone service providers usually kept call histories

for only forty-five days, though they kept billing information longer. Cole had expected this when he examined the bills he found in Smith's file box.

"Now the bad news. 3563 and 3502 are prepaids out of a small provider based in Phoenix. You owe me big-time for these two—the guy I talked to over there was a monumental jackass."

"These are the cell numbers?"

"Yeah. The provider is a company called Electrotelepathy. They rent antenna space from the larger companies like we do, but on a way smaller scale. They specialize in prepaid options. Keeps their infrastructure down."

"Did you get the histories?"

"I'm sending them in the email, but this is the part you aren't going to like. The numbers were activated only twelve days ago. There isn't much in the way of history."

Cole tipped back in the chair. Wilson and Dru used throwaways, which probably meant they changed numbers often. Fake names. Untraceable numbers. How much more perfect could it get?

"Was there a text history?"

"Electrotelepathy doesn't keep texts or emails. That isn't unusual. Some of the big companies don't, either. And before you ask—because I'm a mind reader, too, and I know you're going to ask me—these phones are not GPS-enabled. Electrotelepathy is a low-end company, so they sell a low-end product."

"How recent are the histories?"

"Through this morning. That's when I spoke with him. For the *third* time."

"Okay, pal, thanks. I appreciate it."

"A Giants game, right?"

"The Giants."

Bree was a Dodgers fan, but her life partner, Estelle, was a Giants fan from San Francisco. Theirs was a mixed marriage.

"You're my hero, Elvis. Estelle will love it."

"Tell her she's the luckiest woman alive."

"I do. Every night."

"Go Blue."

"Go Blue."

Cole laughed as they hung up.

When Bree's email appeared, Cole opened it and found three attached documents, one for each of the three phone numbers. The two cell histories were short, just as Bree warned. Cole didn't know which was Dru's and which was Wilson's until he skimmed them and found Pike's cell number on the 3502 log. 3502 would be Dru's phone. Her last call was made to Pike's number almost three days earlier at 11:32 P.M. Cole decided this was the missed call Pike had told him about. She had made no calls on the phone since that time. Cole checked 3563, and found no entries since earlier that same day, which meant Wilson had made no calls in the past three days, either. This coincided with the abduction, but Cole knew Wilson phoned Detective Button after seeing the carnage at his shop. No such call was listed on the call list. Cole checked to see if the call had been made from Wilson's shop phone, but found that no calls had been made from the shop that morning, either. This left Cole puzzled and suspicious. If the call to Button did not show on any of the three records, how many phones did Wilson Smith have?

Cole printed all three documents, then found himself staring at the two pictures again. It was as if the pictures were trying to tell him something that he couldn't quite hear.

Frustrated, he put them aside, poured himself another cup of coffee, then went through the call histories looking for recurring numbers. He was making a list of the most frequently called numbers when his phone rang.

John Chen said, "Can you talk?"

"Yeah. Where are you?"

"On my way to Los Feliz. Some idiot lost a game of Russian roulette. This is the only time I get any privacy, man, driving to a crime scene. I've been waiting all morning to call."

"You get some prints?"

"Am I not the Chen? Eleven distinct samples, and I'm pretty sure some belong to a female. That's based on size, so I'm only guessing, but whoever it is isn't in the system. You don't have to worry about her. The other guy is a different story."

"You got a hit on the man?"

"Kinda."

"What's *kinda*, John? C'mon. What's his name?"

"I don't know. That's why I said kinda. I got a

sealed file. All you get is a file number and a directive telling you who to contact."

"What does that mean?"

"Could mean anything. The guy could be a cop, a federal agent, maybe in witness protection, something like that. We see these with military personnel, too, like when it's a Delta guy or a SEAL or one of those top-secret things."

"Are you telling me this guy is a spook?"

"I was just giving examples. I'm guessing the guy is a criminal or a cop."

"Why?"

"The directive. It says to contact the FBI or the Louisiana Department of Justice for information. That kinda rules out him being a spook."

"Did you?"

"Hell, no! They'd know I'm involved. It's bad enough they're gonna ping our computer for submitting the print. They might come snooping around to see why we had his prints."

Cole felt a stab of concern.

"Are you going to get jammed up because of this?"

"Nah. I used Harriet's password when I logged on. It can't get back to me."

Harriet was John's boss.

Chen said, "Sorry I couldn't get the information, bro, but this is as far as I can take it. I really wanted to help. Tell Joe, okay?"

"You helped, John. You really did. What's that file number?"

Cole copied the file number, then immediately

phoned Lucy Chenier. She was in a meeting, but had left instructions to be interrupted. When she came on the line, Cole explained what he needed.

"Does Terry have a contact in the Louisiana Department of Justice?"

"Probably more than one. Why?"

Cole told her about the sealed file with its directive to contact the Louisiana DOJ.

"The DOJ and the FBI. I don't like these things we're learning."

"Me, neither. Can I give you the file number?"

Cole read it off, waited as she copied, then listened as she read it back to make sure she had the correct number.

"Okay. I'll see how Terry wants to handle it."

"Thanks, Luce."

"One thing—"

He waited.

"These sealed files can mean anything, but one thing they always mean is that it's important to someone that this individual's identity is protected. Once Terry makes the inquiry—even through one of his sources—we can't put the genie back in the bottle. The people who are hiding this man might turn out to be a very pissed-off genie."

"I understand."

"Are you sure you want to go forward?"

"Yes."

"We'll get back to you when we can."

Cole put down the phone with an uneasy sense that his legs had been swept from beneath him by a furious river of unknown events and unknowable people, and the river was carrying him with it. He stretched until his shoulders cracked, then remembered the pictures, and realized what had been bothering him.

He placed the pictures of Wilson Smith and Dru Rayne on his keyboard, and studied their faces again. Their eyes didn't show the anxious tension of people with a gun at their backs. They didn't look scared. Cole wondered why.

32

PIKE ROLLED HARD DOWN the canyon from Elvis Cole's house until he was free of the high ridges. He called Arturo Alvarez as he entered the flats. The phone rang so many times Pike thought no one would answer, but finally a young woman picked up, her voice so subdued Pike wasn't sure if she was the same young woman he'd met at the Angel Eyes house.

"Hello."

"Marisol?"

"Yes. May I help you?"

"This is Joe Pike. Can I speak with Artie?"

The line was so quiet Pike wondered if she put him on hold.

Pike said, "Hello?"

"Go to hell."

She hung up without saying more, and Pike knew by her anger, something ugly had happened to Art.

The freshly painted stucco house was as subdued as Marisol's voice when Pike arrived. The crowd of kids Pike had seen on his last visit was gone, and the yard was deserted except for a shirtless male counselor on the roof, replacing a tile shingle in the late-morning sun.

The front door was open for air, so Pike did not knock. He stepped inside, and found the living room empty.

"Anyone here?"

Pike heard a voice in the rear, then Marisol appeared in the hall, her arms crossed tightly over her breasts, her eyes angry black gunsights.

"Get out of here."

"Where's Art?"

"You brought them here. Go."

Pike called into the house.

"Art?"

A low mumble he recognized as Art's voice came from the back rooms, but Marisol spoke over him.

"We don't want you here. Go away."

Pike pushed past her and found Father Art in a small bedroom across from his office, one of the tiny rooms a kid used when they had no place else to go. Already hot, but the windows were up and a small electric fan stirred the air. Art was propped on a single bed with couch cushions for support. His left eye was swollen to a slit, and both were purpled and black. Contusions like the Verdugo Mountains crossed his forehead. His nose was twice its normal size and bent to the right, pointing at his split upper lip and a discolored mouse on his cheek. A loose white T-shirt made him look thin.

Pike said, "Azzara."

Not a question. A statement.

Marisol came up behind him, and punched him in the back.

"He don't want to see you. Get out of here."

She punched him again.

"You listenin' to me, motherfucker?"

Art lifted his hand and spoke through the split.

"Marisol. Not like that."

Pike ignored her, staring at Art's good eye.

"Let's get you to a hospital."

"Won't happen, brother. No hospital."

Pike moved closer, Art's good eye following him.

"Because of me?"

Behind him, Marisol answered again.

"What you think? They blamed him for whatever shit you did at that body shop. They brought it back on Art. He never should've helped you."

Pike lifted Art's shirt. His chest and abdomen were blotchy with purple and green bruises from haymakers and kicks. They had beaten Art so hard the kicks and punches flowed out of Art into Pike until Art pulled his shirt back to cover the marks.

"This is what I teach these kids. You see how violence spreads? You let me down, man."

"Are your ribs broken?"

"I'm fine."

"Let me take you to a doctor."

"It's over. Forget it."

Pike glanced at Marisol.

"You should have called me."

"I was, but he wouldn't let me, not you, the police, nobody."

Art's hand came up again.

"It was done. Now I have to rebuild the trust that was lost."

Marisol said something in Spanish Pike did not understand, but it was harsh and angry, and Pike knew it was directed at Art.

"Where can I find him, Artie? Tell me where he lives."

"So you will kill him? No."

Pike took out the picture of Azzara and Mendoza in the car behind Wilson and Dru.

"So I can save these people or find their bodies. Azzara lied to me. He told me he would stop Mendoza. He told me he didn't know what happened to them, but here he is with them and Mendoza. Miguel is going to tell me where they are, Art. He knows."

"No, no more. If I can't make it here, who is going to help these kids? Who will reach out? Go away, Joe—get out."

Pike studied Arturo Alvarez, and knew there was no more to say. Artie was old-school hard despite the college degrees. In his world, toughness wasn't judged by how well you could give a beating, but by how well you took a beating.

"Let me get you to the hospital."

Art turned toward the window.

Pike glanced at Marisol, then walked away. She followed behind him like an angry guard dog, but Pike stopped in the living room and lowered his voice.

"Does he have a fever?"

"I don't know. Why?"

"Check. If he has a fever or starts running hot, call me."

"You're a doctor now?"

"See if there's blood in his urine."

"He's been pissing blood for two days. I see it when I help him to the bathroom."

"Bright red or pink?"

She glanced toward Art's room, worried.

"Pink, I think. It was red, but now not so much. Is that good?"

"Better than red, but not good. Whatever they broke is healing, but he's still in the weeds."

She crossed her arms again, and her eyes hardened.

"I wish I had been here. I found him the next morning, when it was too late."

"They would have hurt you, too."

The black eyes met his.

"You think? Maybe I would have shot them to death."

The eyes moved back to the hall, but lost none of their heat.

"I would have called the police, but he wouldn't let me. Not even the ambulance. Stupid fool, worried about their trust."

"Talk to him, Marisol."

"About what?"

"I want Miguel."

"What do you think, they send Christmas cards? Art doesn't know where he lives. Maybe where

269

he grew up, but Miguel left us years ago. He is an executive now. He's better than us."

Pike sensed something beyond the disdain in her voice, and noticed a discoloration at the corner of her eye. He looked more closely, and saw the skin on her neck mottled from a trip to the laser, not unlike the fading he had seen on Miguel Azzara.

Pike heard the counselor on the roof. Chipping the tile.

"Were you *Malevos*?"

She stood taller, a neighborhood girl who grew up in the gangs.

"A different set, but *Trece*. Myself and my brother. He was killed."

Maybe I would have taken a gun and shot them to death.

"Do you know Miguel?"

She glanced away, back down the hall toward Artie.

"Once. Not anymore."

"Do you know where he lives?"

"Once."

"I need to find him. For my friends, and for Art."

She nodded, but it took her a while to speak.

"Maybe. I know girls who know him. They've been to his fancy new house."

She glanced away, and Pike wondered if one of those girls was her.

Marisol made a call, and a few minutes later Pike had an address. He stopped at the door as he was leaving.

"Watch his temperature. If his temperature climbs, I'll bring a doctor whether he wants one or not."

"He doesn't want to pay. He won't say that, but I know. His money pays for Angel Eyes, and there is never enough. He's always behind."

"Don't worry about the money. I'll pay."

"He won't let you."

"He doesn't have to know."

She crossed her arms again, but it was not as angry as before. Pike listened to the counselor on the roof, chipping the tile, trying to make the roof stronger.

33

PIKE DECIDED MIGUEL AZZARA enjoyed looking at himself. He probably struck poses in front of a mirror, thinking he was way hotter than the male models in *GQ* or all the young actors playing vampires and werewolves. Had to be, because Mikie Azzara had sunk his teeth so deep into Hollywood glam he moved to the Sunset Strip, about as far from his Ghost Town roots as a homeboy could get. Pike wondered what the *veteranos* thought when they found out, battle-scarred old men who ran *La Eme* from prison, living and dying the old way in the same neighborhoods for generations. They probably didn't like it much at first, but decided to go along, figuring college-educated young studs like Miguel were the future.

Problem was, when Mikie left Ghost Town, he left the homegirls who had given themselves to his charisma and movie-star looks, and replaced them with UCLA coeds, aspiring actresses, and the razor-thin girls who cruised the Strip's clubs. This left more than a few resentful homegirls behind, including Marisol's cousin and best friend, Annabel Reynoso, who had visited the house several times before Miguel cut her off.

Azzara rented a small single-story contemporary home on a cross street south of Sunset behind a stretch of clubs, bars, restaurants, and apartment buildings. Azzara's house was the first house south of an alley that paralleled Sunset Boulevard, on the south side of a cinder-block wall that separated the alley from the home owners who lived beside it. The wall was matted with trumpet vines, and overhung by a spare row of dying ficus trees that lined Azzara's property behind it.

Azzara's street—like all the other residential streets within walking distance of Sunset—was thick with parked cars and sluggish with drivers who blocked traffic as they maneuvered in and out of parking spots. Pike did not want to risk being jammed up and spotted in front of Azzara's house, so he parked on Sunset two blocks away and approached Azzara's street on foot.

When Pike reached the corner and turned toward the house, he saw two guards, so he casually turned back to the corner. Azzara's house was hidden by the wall, but the Monte Carlo was parked at the curb, and Hector was in the Monte Carlo. A second man loitered in the alley's mouth, leaning against the wall. Dru's silver Tercel was behind the Monte Carlo.

Pike crossed the street with a crowd of pedestrians when the light changed, and walked along Sunset to the next street. He figured to approach Azzara's from the rear, but when he turned toward the alley, he stopped again. Two men sat in a Chevy pickup, parked to face the alley. More guards, covering the back of the house.

Pike returned to the first corner, and studied Azzara's street from a position behind a cigar shop. Pike felt a dull but steady ping as if he was about to be hit by an incoming missile, but neither guard acted as if they had seen him.

The wall killed his view of Azzara's house, and he saw no good way to approach without being recognized. Pike knew he could work closer once it got dark, but he didn't want to wait. The Tercel promised that Dru and Wilson were inside and alive. Pike didn't want to risk losing them.

Pike studied the buildings along Sunset, and noticed that the building immediately above Azzara's house was an older, two-story commercial space with a huge Regency billboard on the roof. The billboard faced Sunset so oncoming drivers saw its ad, but the back of the billboard cast a shadow over Azzara's home.

Sixteen minutes later, Pike climbed a service stair and crawled to the edge of the roof overlooking the alley. The far side of Azzara's roof was visible through the ficus trees, but nothing more.

Pike backed away, and considered the billboard again. Its back was a frame of steel I-beams supported by three enormous legs made of heavy steel pipe. A caged ladder climbed the center leg to a catwalk that extended from one end of the billboard to the other and wrapped around to the front.

Pike climbed to the frame, then edged along the catwalk. He used the billboard for cover until he found the best view, then wedged himself between the I-beams. Pike now saw most of the backyard and the rear of the house, but the yard was all he needed.

Floor-to-ceiling glass doors along the back of the house looked out at the clean lines of a rectangular swimming pool and patio. Dru Rayne lay on a chaise longue facing the pool, with oversized sunglasses masking her face. A few feet behind her, Wilson Smith stood with Azzara and three other Latin men, one of whom was the cowboy Pike had seen at the body shop. All five men were laughing. Another cowboy was seated by himself on a deck chair on the other side of the patio, and another was inside on a couch in the living room.

Ping.

Pike stiffened with the feeling, but none of the men shouted or ran.

Ping.

He checked the roof below the billboard, but saw no one. He checked what he could see of the alley and the street in front of Azzara's, but the guards had not seen him.

Pike forced himself to relax. A burly man with a face like a pineapple and hard-time ink came out of the house with a bottle of beer, and Azzara immediately left the circle to make room for the man. Azzara's deference was obvious. He went into the house, and soon returned with three brown bottles. He gave one to an older, squat cowboy, one to Smith, and took the third to Dru. She gave him a very nice smile when she thanked him, and Azzara returned to the others. The congenial host.

No one looked abducted.

Pike felt hollow, like a bubble floating on water. He drifted like the bubble would drift; an emptiness confined by a delicate skin, having no weight or substance. Pike concentrated on the bubble. He forced it to grow smaller until it was gone. The emptiness remained, but could not be seen without its skin. Without the bubble, there was only nothingness, and now Pike felt nothing.

Ping.

The burly man with the ink shook the squat cowboy's hand. They smiled at each other, and laughed again, and related to each other as equals. Pike decided the burly man was a *La Eme veterano* of high station, but he wondered about the cowboys.

It was obvious that Dru and Wilson were where they wanted to be and in no immediate danger. Pike considered calling Straw, Button, and Elvis, but he decided to see what developed.

Twenty-two minutes later, a black stretch limo turned into Azzara's drive. Wilson, the squat cowboy, and the burly man followed Azzara into the house, but Dru and the cowboy who sat by himself remained outside. Pike now had to decide whether to stay with the house or follow the limo, and he had to decide before he knew what Wilson and Dru would do. Reaching his Jeep would take several minutes, so if he was going to follow, he had to leave now. If he waited to see them leave, he would never reach his Jeep until after the limo was gone.

Pike decided to follow.

He spidered back through the girders, and ran hard along Sunset to his Jeep, thinking the limo might already be gone, but when he nosed up to Azzara's street, the tail of the limo was still in Azzara's drive. Pike backed away, parking in a red zone in front of the cigar shop. Five minutes later, the limo backed out and rolled uphill toward him. Pike lowered the visor and slumped down behind the wheel. The limo stopped directly in front of him. Pike could make out the dim shape of the driver, but the dark rear windows hid whoever was in back. When a hole appeared in the traffic, the limo turned. Pike let two cars pass, then pulled out behind them.

The limo dropped through the city on La Cienega Boulevard, cruising slow and steady the way limos do. Pike followed them down to the I-10 Freeway, then west toward Santa Monica. When they crossed the 405, Pike thought they were heading to Venice, but they dropped off at Bundy and turned onto Ocean Park. Three minutes later, they pulled into the north side of Santa Monica Airport, and Pike was forced to drop farther behind. The limo drove to a gate that rolled aside to let them enter the hangar area, then stopped alongside a white Citation business jet. The jet's door was open, its stair down and waiting.

Pike pulled over to watch.

The limo driver popped out to open the doors, but the people inside didn't wait. Wilson, Miguel Azzara, the burly man, and the squat cowboy climbed out of the stretch. Dru had stayed at the house.

The four men gathered near the jet, and once more shook hands. The cowboy clapped Wilson on the shoulder like they were the best friends in the world, then climbed aboard. He pulled the steps up himself and closed the door as if he had done it a hundred times while the rest of them returned to the limo.

Pike noted the tail number. XB-CCL. The XB prefix meant the plane was registered in Mexico.

Azzara, the burly man, and Wilson stood by the limo as the jet spooled up its engines. Pike could see the pilot and co-pilot reaching for switches as they went through the start-up procedure. It took several minutes, but Azzara, the burly man, and Wilson waited. When the jet finally taxied away, they waved like flunkies, telling Pike the squat cowboy was a very important man.

Once the jet was gone, the burly man threw his arm around Azzara's shoulders and hugged him as if he had done a good thing. Azzara beamed his movie-star smile, then held the door as the burly man got into the limo.

Pike had seen enough. He made a slow U-turn as he drove away, and phoned Elvis Cole.

34

DANIEL

Daniel glanced at the turd in the Monte Carlo as he walked past the house, dumb fuck so stupid he was falling asleep. Daniel loved fuckin' amateurs, them being so easy to kill, but the bangers had so many people around the house, they were cramping his style.

He continued downhill to the next street, then climbed into his van. Sign on the van was for something called Hero-Rooter—CALL A HERO TO SAVE THE DAY! DRAINS CLEANED AROUND THE CLOCK! Daniel had picked the van because there were no windows in the side panels and the vehicle would blend in anywhere. He had left the driver in a Dumpster behind a Nigerian restaurant in Long Beach.

Tobey was irritated.

"Why're we wastin' time?"

Cleo was annoyed.

"Fuckin' around, around?"

Daniel said, "Shut up. I'm tryin' to think."

Daniel had followed the Mexican and his dumb-ass banger entourage from the airport, so he knew the Mexican was inside with the cook and the waitress. The Bolivians had come through big-time with their tip about the Mexican, but reaching his targets had turned out to be a problem.

Daniel circled the block up to Sunset, planning to cruise through the alley beside Azzara's house, but that's when he saw the tall dude sliding out of a red Jeep Cherokee.

Tobey, suspicious.

"Lookit those arrows."

Cleo, alarmed.

"Dude on the bridge, bridge."

This made twice, and twice was bad. Daniel had seen him at the canal, and now here he was again, a block from the cook and the waitress.

Daniel let the van slow to catch the light. The man reached Azzara's street, rounded the corner, then did a fast one-eighty to blend in with a crowd of pedestrians.

"He must be a cop. Gang unit, maybe. How else would he know?"

Tobey whispered, "Looks like a cop."

Cleo hissed, "Smells like a cop, cop."

When the light changed, the arrow dude crossed with the crowd, walking along Sunset like he was normal. Daniel clocked the dude as he passed. Big guy, hard, but he moved as if he was floating. Nasty hands, though, with big, coarse knuckles and veins wrapped under his skin like vines.

Daniel turned at the first cross street, then powered around the block back to Sunset, looking for the Jeep. He found it quickly, copied the tag number, then maneuvered into a parking lot to call the Bolivian.

First thing the Bolivian asked was whether he had bagged the targets.

"No, sir, not yet, but I have them located. The Mexican led me right to them."

Cursing, screaming, the usual Bolivian bullshit. Daniel rolled his eyes.

"Sir, the situation is under control, but I do need your help with a matter. We have a man on the scene who may be a police officer or a federal agent."

More blah blah yadda yadda.

"No, sir, it won't affect the outcome, but I would like to know who he is. I have his license plate here."

Daniel read off the tag, then hung up before the sonofabitch could go on with more bullshit. Daniel was now officially concerned about the arrow dude, and didn't like not knowing where he was and what he was doing. The arrow dude was a wild card and wild cards could bite you on the ass. Daniel decided he would kill the fucker if he saw him again, even if he was a cop, so long as it wouldn't fuck up his shot at grabbing the cook and the waitress. Daniel didn't want to kill them. He needed to take them alive, and save the killing for later.

Tobey said, "Kill'm."

Cleo said, "Cut off their heads, heads."

That was the plan. Cut off their heads, and ship'm to the Bolivians. The Bolivians liked creepy shit.

Daniel circled back to Azzara's street and parked below the house, looking north toward Sunset so he could keep an eye on things. Daniel studied the surrounding houses and the traffic up on Sunset. The guards ignored his van. Stupid. Daniel checked the pedestrians crossing on Sunset, thinking he might spot the arrow dude again. He wondered where the big fucker was, and whether he was watching Azzara's, or if the whole thing was just a coincidence and the dude was up there on Sunset getting another tattoo. Daniel stared at the billboard for a long time. Much of it was hidden by trees, but Daniel had considered using it earlier, and now he thought about using it again.

Daniel was watching the idiot in the Monte Carlo when a black limo passed and eased into Azzara's drive. Daniel remembered the tag. The same car had brought the Mexican from the airport, which meant it was now going to take him back.

Daniel thought, "Adios, muchacho."

Daniel was watching the limo when he caught a movement on the billboard through the trees. Someone was climbing down, and Daniel knew it was the dude with the arrows.

"MotherFUCK! He was watching the house!"

"Fuck, -uck, -uck."

Thirty seconds later, the tall dude ran across the street at the light, heading toward his Jeep. He must have seen the limo, too, and now he was going to follow.

Tobey boomed, "Kill'm, kill'm."

Cleo shrieked, "Get'm, get'm."

"We can't! We gotta stay on the house!"

Daniel smelled blood in the water, and knew he was close.

The Mexican, Azzara, a fat banger, and the cook came out and got into the limo. Daniel sat higher in the seat, and clenched the wheel until he thought his bones would pop through his skin. The cook and the waitress were separating, the cook going with the Mexican, the waitress staying at the house. Daniel was FUCKED!

Tobey murmured, "Mellow out, Daniel."

Cleo cooed, "Easy, dude, easy."

The limo backed out of the drive, then rolled up to Sunset.

"Easy, my ass! What about the cop? What if he bags the limo?"

Tobey said, "Let'm. He's after the Mexican."

Cleo said, "Take the waitress, Daniel. We'll figure it out, out."

Daniel felt as if his arms and legs were being yanked off at the joints, the cook ripping him in one direction, the waitress ripping him in another, but the voices were soothing. The voices helped him think.

Tobey whispered, "The waitress is here, get the waitress."

Cleo hissed, "The waitress will give you the cook."

Daniel knew they were right. He watched the limo disappear as it turned onto Sunset.

First he would take the waitress, then he would get the cook, and then he would have everything.

35

ELVIS COLE

Cole wedged his phone under his ear, trying to reconcile what Pike was telling him. It felt as if Pike was describing one reality while Cole had been working to understand another.

"What you're telling me is these people are not being treated like prisoners."

"Four guards were outside the house, and at least two more were inside. You put guards on the outside, you're not keeping someone in, you're keeping someone out."

"I don't get it. How did a *Trece* crew go from shaking down Smith to being his host in three days?"

Pike didn't respond.

Cole said, "Feel free not to answer."

"The way they were shaking hands tells me it's business. The private jet tells me it's big business."

"You get the tail number?"

Cole copied the number as Pike recited it.

"Okay. I'll try to find out who owns it. Where are you going?"

"Back to Azzara's."

"Come here first. I want to go with you."

Cole thought for a moment, trying to sort out the new facts.

"Someone is hunting these people. We know that for sure. We thought it was Mendoza and Gomer, but it wasn't, and now Miguel Azzara is their best friend."

"Yes."

"Protecting them?"

"You go into business with people, you take care of them."

"I can't help wondering why a *Trece* street gang and Mexican cowboys with their own jet need to be in business with a man who fries oysters."

"I'll be there soon. We'll find out."

Cole spent the next ten minutes trying to identify the owners of Citation Jet XB-CCL, but had no luck. He was still on hold with the FAA when his call waiting told him Lucy Chenier was calling. He dropped the FAA and took Lucy's call.

Her voice was in full-on professional mode.

"Can you talk?"

"Absolutely. What did you find out?"

"I'm going to put you on speaker. Terry's here."

The sound quality went from crisp to hollow when she put him on speaker.

"Hey, Terry. Thanks for helping on this."

"Hey, man, no problem. You hear me okay?"

"Hear you fine."

Terry had a mellow voice with a woodsy Louisiana

accent. He'd grown up in a family of police officers, and had been an officer himself before retiring to work as an investigator for Lucy's firm.

Lucy said, "So you know, we're in my office and we're alone. No one can hear what we say except you, me, and Terry."

"Okay."

"Are you by yourself?"

"Yeah. It's just us."

"Joe isn't there?"

"Not yet. He's on his way."

Cole wondered why she was being so legal.

"Okay. I'm emailing two pictures. Are you at your computer?"

"Will be. I'm going there now."

"Tell me if they're the people you know as Dru Rayne and Wilson Smith."

Her email was waiting when Cole reached his computer.

"Hang on. I'm opening it."

Cole wasn't surprised when the picture of Wilson Smith turned out to be a booking photo, but still felt a vague disappointment. The picture of Dru Rayne was a snapshot, showing her behind a bar, with her hair up, a crooked smile, and rainbows of cheap bracelets on her wrists. She was wearing a tight black T-shirt that read: *Tip the Waitress or She'll Spit in Your Drink.*

"Yeah. This is them."

Terry came back sounding pleased.

"Damn, boy."

Lucy said, "What we're about to tell you comes from a senior investigator with the Louisiana DOJ. Remember what I said about not being able to put the genie back in the bottle?"

"Are they going to call me?"

Terry spoke up again.

"He pressed me, buddy. I didn't give him your name or location, but five will get you six he's on the phone with the FBI. They're tracking a string of murders tied to this case, and the number is growing."

Cole felt a leaden I-knew-this-would-get-worse feeling as he stared at Smith's mug shot.

"Smith's a murderer?"

"Yeah, he probably is, but I'm not talking about him. At least eight and possibly nine murders have been committed by a person or persons trying to find the man you know as Wilson Smith."

Cole felt a cold tingle in the center of his chest. Pike was right—something way more dangerous than street-corner bangers had been in the Venice Canals.

"He found them. He's here."

Lucy and Terry spoke over each other, garbling each other's words before Lucy won out.

"How do you know he's found them?"

Cole told them about Mendoza and Gomer.

"We're not sure why they were watching the house, but they were found murdered the next morning. Joe believes they were murdered by someone who's looking for Wilson and Dru."

Terry's low voice was directed to Lucy.

"This isn't good. If this is the guy, we need to put our folks down here on his trail while it's hot."

"Elvis and I understand that, Terry. Tell him about Rainey."

Cole thought he heard Terry take a breath, almost as if he was trying to regain composure before he could get back to the business at hand.

"Smith's real name is William Allan Rainey. He smuggled cash out of the country for some boys down here hooked up with a Bolivian cartel. My guy says, all told, he probably transported six or seven hundred million dollars before he was done."

"Drug money?"

"Where else you gonna see that kind of cash?"

Drugs were a cash business, and the problem for foreign drug suppliers was getting their cash out of the country. Experienced cops had told him it was far easier for suppliers to get their drugs in than to get their cash out. They couldn't deposit it in banks or transfer it in meaningful amounts because banks were watched by the government, and transferring a few thousand here and there was useless to an organization that generated hundreds of millions in cash.

Cole said, "Smuggling cash doesn't rate a sealed file."

"That was the DEA. They broke him, then cut a deal with him for info about the cartel's business."

"He was an informant."

"Yeah, for a couple of years, and maybe that's why he did what he did. Rainey and the woman disappeared two weeks before Katrina with twelve million dollars of Bolivian money. They've been on the run ever since."

Cole leaned back.

"Twelve million. Get out."

Lucy said, "Cash."

"The cartel boys put a million dollar reward on Rainey's head and sent up a specialist to find him."

"Specialist as in a killer?"

"Specialist as in finding people the Bolivians want found, and doing whatever it is they want done. Over at the DOJ, they called him the executioner. That's who you have runnin' around out there."

Cole felt a second chill, and listened as Terry continued.

According to Terry's contact, William Allan Rainey had spent his life jumping between small-time criminal activity and questionable business ventures. Rainey opened several restaurants and bars that failed, but eventually created a stable business for himself as a wholesale seafood supplier, buying shrimp and fish from local fishermen to sell to other people's restaurants. The fishermen Rainey dealt with were one-boat operators who fished the Gulf from pinprick towns in the bayous along the Louisiana coast. Investigators believed it was during this period that Rainey became involved with people who were in business with the Bolivian cartel, and Rainey, who had always been attracted to easy money, saw a way to cut himself in on the partnership. The Bolivians needed a way to sneak their cash out of the country, and Rainey provided the method. His daily contact with fishermen allowed him to recruit people who were open to carrying questionable cargo. Especially if they were behind on their rent and needed the money.

Cole stopped him.

"Did these people know what they were carrying?"

"The deal was, no questions asked, but Rainey told at least two fishermen they were carrying pot on its way to Miami. That's the way it was packaged, in black, waterproof bales. How it worked was, Rainey and a couple of guards would hand off the bales to a fisherman on his way out, along with waypoint coordinates to meet up with a vessel out past the rigs. All they had to do was hand over the bales, then get on with their fishing."

"Rainey was telling the DEA about this?"

Terry laughed.

"Uh-uh. He fed them an occasional inbound shipment or dropped the dime on small-time players. Just enough to keep the DEA off his back. They didn't know he was smuggling cash until everything blew up."

"What happened?"

Lucy said, "The woman. Dru Rayne's true name is Rose Marie Platt. Rainey met her when she worked at a restaurant down in the Quarter for a man named Tolliver James. She and James were living together."

Terry jumped in again.

"James bought fish and shrimp from Rainey, so the speculation is this was how Rainey and Platt met. Couple of months later, she broke up with James and moved in with Rainey. Couple of months after that, which puts us two weeks before the storm, Rainey and Platt disappeared with the Bolivians' money. On or about that same day, a shrimper named Mike Fourchet went fishing, but didn't come back. Mike and his boat were found at a landing on Quarantine Bay. Fourchet had been shot in the back of the head."

"Was Fourchet one of Rainey's fishermen?"

"That's how the DEA made the connection. They found Fourchet's name in Rainey's business records. Then they really got stoked when they found out the woman's ex-boyfriend, Tolliver James, was murdered during the storm."

"Did Rainey do it?"

"Not even close. The DEA believes he was killed by your specialist. He was beaten to death—beat real bad, too, like he was tortured. The bones in his legs were broken so bad they were nothing but splinters down in the meat."

Terry paused as if he realized he was being too graphic with Lucy in the room.

"Sorry, Ms. Chenier."

"Terry, please."

"Anyway, all this stuff I'm telling you, it took the Feds and the DOJ two or three years to figure out. You know how investigations come together—you build'm a piece at a time."

"You said Rainey was good for a murder."

"Fourchet. The case dicks learned Rainey delivered the twelve mil to Fourchet the morning he went

292

out. They believe Rainey went back later without the guards, or maybe told Fourchet to meet up with him on his way out, but either way, Fourchet ended up dead, and Rainey and Platt split with the money."

"So Rainey and Platt murdered Fourchet?"

"Everyone down here thinks so, including the Bolivians. That's why they put out the reward and sent their man up here. This guy's been after them for years."

"Do you know who he is?"

"All I know is what I've told you. He's their go-to executioner."

"Executioner."

"That's how my guy described him before he shut down. An executioner. What else you gonna call an animal who racks up nine killings?"

Terry corrected himself.

"Eleven."

Nobody spoke for a moment, then Terry remembered something.

"Wait, I guess there is something else. All these people he's killed have been connected to Rainey or Platt—someone in the family, someone they worked with, someone who might know how to find them. He's been eating his way through their friends and family. Like with Tolliver James."

A silence settled between the three of them that no one seemed anxious to fill.

Finally, Cole said, "If the FBI comes back to you, give them my name."

Lucy said, "Are you sure? We can delay this or stall it. I don't want you in jeopardy."

Cole smiled, and for the first time during the call felt a flush of comfort.

"You're the best, Lucille."

"Sometimes."

"Yes, you are, but give them my name. Terry, I appreciate this, man, but if they call, put them on me. We'll have to bring in the locals here anyway. They need to know this."

Cole told Lucy he would call later, then printed the new pictures of Wilson and Dru. Cole corrected himself. William Rainey and Rose Platt.

Cole said, "It just keeps getting better."

He heard Pike pull up outside as the second picture emerged from the printer, and met him in the kitchen. Cole thought Pike looked tired, his gaunt face hollow and lined behind the gleaming dark glasses. Pike drank an entire bottle of water before he came up for air.

Cole said, "How long have you been awake?"

"I'm good."

Cole figured he was going on forty-eight hours.

"Grab something to eat."

"I'm good to go."

"Okay, we finally have something. Lucy found out who they are. It isn't good news."

Pike leaned against the counter as Cole went through it, arms crossed, as still as a hardwood statue. Pike only moved once as Cole related the information.

He said, "The names."

Cole didn't understand, and asked what Pike meant.

"Rainey. Rayne. You think she picked her name because it was so close to his? Maybe he picked it for her."

Cole stared at Pike, but quickly pushed on to soothe his own aching heart.

"What do you want to do?"

"Call the police."

"Good. I think that's the right call. You have Button's number?"

Pike reached into his pocket for his phone, but it buzzed with an incoming call before he got it out. The phone buzzed again as Pike studied the Caller ID, and Cole wondered why Pike was staring. Pike looked up on the third buzz.

"It's Dru."

Pike opened the phone and answered.

Part Five
The Sentry

sentry   n; a soldier standing guard at a point of passage.

—*Webster's Ninth New Collegiate Dictionary*

36

SHE HAD NOT USED her phone in three days, but there was her name, DRU, in the phone's tiny window. That was how he had stored her number in the memory.

Pike opened the phone with delicate care, and answered the same way, thinking it might be Smith or Azzara or one of Azzara's thugs playing around. He stared at Cole as he answered.

"Yes?"

"*Willieyouhavetogivehimthemoneypleasegiveit-tohimhehasmeandhe's—*"

The words exploded out of her, but then she was gone, as if her call had been chopped by a headsman's ax.

Cole moved closer.

"Was it her?"

Pike wondered if this was real or another incomprehensible lie.

"Talk to me, Joseph. What did she say?"

"I don't know."

Pike held up a finger, saying wait as he dialed her back, but his call went straight to her voice mail.

"What did she say?"

"She called me Willie. Like she was talking to Rainey. She begged Rainey to give him the money. She said he has her. That's it."

"Who has her, the executioner?"

"That's how it sounded."

Pike replayed her call in his head, her voice as tight as breaking wire. She sounded authentic, but she could have made the call from Azzara's pool, surrounded by cowboy spectators who cheered her acting ability.

Cole said, "Let's call Button. We have to call him anyway."

Pike was already on his way out.

"Dru doesn't know we found them. Let's see if she's still at Azzara's."

"Rose."

Pike stopped at the door, not understanding.

Cole said, "It's Rose. Not Dru."

"If her call was real, then he has her—let's check Azzara's. We can call Button when we know."

Cole didn't look confident, but they went in Pike's Jeep, pushing hard down Laurel Canyon to Sunset, then west to Azzara's. Pike described the layout of the house and the position of the guards as they drove. He nailed a parking spot a block from the Regency billboard, then led Cole to the corner to scan Azzara's street.

"There was a guard in the alley. Another guard was in the Monte Carlo. You see it?"

"The car, yeah. I don't see any guards."

"They're gone."

The Monte Carlo and the Tercel were still in front of Azzara's, but the alley and the car appeared empty.

Cole said, "These guys don't know me. Wait here, and I'll take a closer look."

Cole strolled down the sidewalk as if he were just another pedestrian.

Pike watched the surrounding cars and the alley for movement, but no one appeared as Cole reached the house. He stopped on the sidewalk beside the Monte Carlo, stared at the car for a moment, then motioned Pike closer.

Pike trotted down, knowing something was wrong by Cole's flat expression.

"Look."

Pike saw the body, then moved to the car for a closer look. A man was curled on his side across the front seat as if he were sleeping on a red satin pillow. Hector.

Pike immediately turned for the house.

"Side gates. You right, me left. The back of the house is glass."

They moved without another word, Cole racing across the tiny front yard as Pike headed up the drive. Pike let himself through the side gate and ran to the rear, pulling his .357 from under his sweatshirt. Cole emerged at the far side of the patio as Pike stepped from the side of the house.

The pool was empty. Dru's beer bottle, still almost full, stood on the concrete deck by the chaise.

The cowboy who had been seated by himself was sprawled on the patio, his immaculate cream-colored hat upside down three feet away. The big glass sliders were as they had been—pushed open wide so Pike and Cole had an unobstructed view of the carnage inside the house.

Cole made a soft whisper.

"This is bad."

The cowboy from the body shop was seated on a couch, still wearing his hat, but his head was all the way back as if he were staring at the ceiling. A younger man with banger tats was piled up on the floor beside a large square coffee table, eyes open but sightless.

Cole entered the house through the left side of the opening, and Pike went in through the right. A second banger was dead beside the kitchen island and another cowboy lay crumpled outside the powder room door. The cowboy's pants were unbuckled and a black Heckler & Koch pistol was on the floor near his body. His bowels had let go, leaving a smell that burned Pike's eyes.

Cole whispered again.

"None of these people got off a shot. No wonder they call him the executioner."

Pike moved past Cole into a hall.

"I'll get the bedrooms, you check the garage. Azzara drives a black Prius."

Pike pushed along a short hall to a bedroom where he found clothes for Rainey and Dru. The next bedroom was set up for the guards, with futons and duffels filling the floor. The last bedroom was Azzara's. Pike swept through the rooms fast, then pounded back to the great room. Cole looked up from the cowboy sprawled on the couch.

"Anyone else?"

"No. The garage?"

"Empty. If Azzara was here, he's gone, but look at this—"

Cole held up the cowboy's wallet, showing a blue-and-gold star and picture ID. The ID card read POLICIA FEDERAL MEXICO.

"Mexican Federal Police. The *Federales*. What do you think these guys are doing here?"

Pike studied the card.

"You think they're fakes?"

"I don't know. The guy outside and the man by the toilet have badges, too, and they're all packing HKs. *Federales* carry Hecklers."

Pike shook his head, thinking it didn't matter to him who they were or why they were here or how many of them were dead. The only person who mattered was Dru.

"The limo probably dropped off Azzara and Rainey and the *veterano*. They found this mess and split. The Tercel's still here, so Rainey went with Azzara."

Cole didn't seem convinced.

"We don't know anything, Joe. Maybe they never came back. Maybe they're having lunch at the beach. Maybe Rainey went with the *veterano*."

Pike knew Cole was right, but his last best chance was Azzara. Azzara knew what happened here, and

Azzara might know how to find Dru.

Cole turned away from the body.

"What do you want to do?"

"Call the police. We'll find Azzara faster with the police."

They called Button from the house. Cole sketched out the bare bones about William Allan Rainey and Rose Marie Platt, and told Button they would give him the rest when he arrived. Button took it pretty well except for one brief exchange.

Cole said, "Because we only found this out an hour ago, Button. Stop wasting time, and come see for yourself."

Pike said, "Hang up."

They waited at Pike's Jeep for the police to arrive. They did not want to be in the house when the first uniforms got bug-eyed by the blood and the bodies.

The passing time felt like ants marching through Pike's veins. Cole spoke once or twice during the time they were waiting, but Pike did not answer. He was thinking about Dru, and why she had called him for help.

37

DANIEL

Daniel took the woman's phone, rolled her onto her belly, and taped her hands behind her back. Great thing about stealing a rooter-dude van, it was filled with usable stuff. Duct tape, rope, wire. Plenty of things that cut.

The woman did not speak to him or look at him, which was fine by Daniel. When her wrists were secure, he flipped her over and taped her mouth, a big silver rectangle that made her look like a robot. He liked her better that way.

They were on Wilshire Boulevard, in a parking lot across from the La Brea Tar Pits. Daniel liked the dying mammoth. There was this huge statue of a mammoth stuck in the tar like it was being sucked down to its death. Daniel enjoyed thinking about the big sonofabitch drownin' in tar. He wondered if the heat killed it first, maybe boilin' it to death before it drowned. That would be even better.

The satellite phone rang as he climbed into the

front seat. The Bolivian. Daniel answered in his most professional, ass-slurping voice.

"This is Daniel. Do we have anything on the tag?"

Instead of answering Daniel's question, the fuckin' Bolivian launched into meaningless shit that ended with the inevitable question.

"I have Ms. Platt now. Yes, sir, she is in my possession. She is three feet away from me. No, sir, I do not have Mr. Rainey. He is with his Mexican friend, but I'll have him in a few minutes, and we'll have what we have."

Blah blah, rant. Blah blah, rant. Jesus, the man could go on.

Tobey said, "Fuck'm."

Cleo said, "Hang up, up."

Daniel was getting pissed off.

"Sir, were you able to pull anything off the tag? I'd like to know who I'm dealing with."

Fucker still didn't answer. Instead, he wanted to know why Daniel asked about the plate and how the man drivin' the Jeep was involved. Daniel felt put on the spot.

"I don't know how he's involved, sir. He was at Rainey's house at least once, and I saw him today at Azzara's. He clearly knows who these people are, and that means he's a problem."

More Bolivian ass gas. The guy had an endless supply.

"No, sir. I believe he followed the Mexican and Mr. Rainey back to the airport, but I can't know that for sure. I chose to take Ms. Platt."

Fuckin' Bolivian blew like a ripe pimple, screaming that the Mexican might have brought the fishmonger down to Mexico. This is why Daniel hated talking to the fuckers, all the screaming hysterics.

"Sir, Mr. Rainey is still in Los Angeles. Ms. Platt just spoke with him. Can we please get back to whatever you've learned? I have to move quickly."

The Bolivian puked up a wad of information about the dude with the arrows. Dude's name was Pike. A Force Recon Marine who became a police officer. Daniel heard that, he worried the guy was a Fed, but the Bolivian then said something interesting.

"Excuse me, sir, I want to be clear on this. He is no longer in law enforcement?"

Blah blah, blah blah.

"He's a mercenary? We know this for a fact?"

Daniel listened more carefully. The arrow dude shit-canned off the cops, then became a gun for hire, and had worked for the top Private Military Corporations out of London and Washington in conflicts all over the world, including Central America. Daniel thought, cool, and wondered if they had ever crossed paths. The cartels hired mercs from time to time, and so did the governments who fought the cartels. Daniel never met one of those boys he couldn't kill.

"Do we know who he's working for?"

The Bolivian didn't have a whole lot to say. They were asking around, still trying to find out, blah blah blah. Daniel wondered if the man was being evasive.

"I have to go, sir. The next time we speak, I'll have more good news. That's a promise."

More overblown, effusive praise for Daniel's efforts.

"Thank you, sir. Really. You're too kind."

Dickweed.

Daniel killed the link.

Tobey's giggle echoed in his ear.

"You're too kind, that's a good one."

Cleo joined in.

"Too kind, what an ass potato."

They sounded like chipmunks.

"Would you two shut up?"

"Up—"

"—up."

Daniel stared at the mammoth stuck in the sludge, head back, tusks high, like it was begging God to pluck it from the muck. He wondered if the Bolivian was lying about the arrow dude. If the guy was a merc, then maybe the Bolivians had hired the sonofabitch to find Rainey and Platt just like they hired Daniel. Maybe they fed him all the same information, and had given him all the shit they learned from Daniel. These things were possible and made Daniel's head hurt. Made it hurt bad.

Tobey's calm voice soothed him.

"Stop it, Daniel."

Cleo's gentle echo comforted him.

"Make it stop, stop."

Daniel concentrated on the mammoth, trying to imagine what it felt like to be boiled in hot tar. Probably not so hot.

Tobey's laugh boomed like faraway gunshots.

"That's a good one, Daniel!"

Cleo laughed, too. Like revved-up chainsaws.

"You're killin' me, killin' me!"

Daniel pushed the paranoia aside. Either the Bolivians were fuckin' him or they weren't, and they probably weren't. Even the Bolivians weren't stupid enough to fuck with a werewolf.

The dude with the arrows had probably heard about the reward, and was working for himself. Daniel was fine with it. Being a mercenary meant the guy was in it for the money, which meant he could always be bought if it came to that, but for all Daniel knew, the dumb asswipe lost Rainey and stopped off for a hamburger. Daniel might never see the tattooed, sunglasses-wearing asscheese again.

Tobey gently chided him.

"Let's not be stupid."

"Stupid, stupid."

The boys were right. If the Bolivians hadn't fed the arrow dude information, then the guy was fuckin' good. Way he showed up at the canal, way he popped up on the billboard—this guy was dangerous good.

Daniel picked up the woman's phone, and looked at her. She was lying back there like she was dead. Daniel liked'm that way.

"Your fuckin' boyfriend better call soon. I'm gettin' anxious."

She didn't move. Not even a twitch. Just stared at him with these narrow, watchful eyes. Like she was thinking.

Daniel jiggled the phone, and smiled at her.

The deader the better.

38

BOTH ENDS OF AZZARA'S street were blocked by black-and-white radio cars when Button and Futardo arrived. By then, LAPD barriers and yellow crime-scene tape ran from the house to the street, and Hector's Monte Carlo was hidden by a collapsible screen. Hollywood Station owned the crime scene, but the *Malevos Pacificos* and Venice *Trece* belonged to Button.

Button hammered Pike and Cole with questions as they walked through the scene, but Pike wanted him focused on Azzara.

"We believe he returned here from the airport because his car is missing. He drives a black Prius. Get his tag, and put it out to patrol."

"Did Azzara kill these people?"

Cole said, "We told you who killed them. Azzara probably has Rainey, and one or both of them can probably help find Rose Platt."

Cole showed them William Rainey's booking photo.

"I wrote Rainey's file number on the back. Call the Louisiana Department of Justice. They'll back up what we're saying."

Button's jaw worked as he stared at the photo, but he handed it to Futardo.

"Call down there and see if you can find someone who knows about this."

Futardo started away, but Button stopped her.

"Hang on—before you call, pull Azzara's DMV and give it to the patrol commander. Tell him Azzara is a suspect in a multiple homicide. Tell him I'll call him as soon as I can."

She started away again, but he stopped her again.

"Futardo. They give you any shit down in Louisiana, bring me the phone."

This time he let her go, and turned back to Pike.

"Twelve fucking million dollars, and this guy is making sandwiches in Venice?"

"Po'boys."

As Futardo left, a Pacific Station gang detective named Eduardo Valenti waved them over to the banger by the coffee table.

"I know this one, too. Bobby Ruiz, aka Lil Rok."

"One of Azzara's people?"

"You bet. Born and bred *Malevos* over by Ghost Town."

Valenti had already identified the banger by the kitchen island as a *Malevos* lifer named Trejo Hermanos, who was known as Crazy T.

Pike didn't care who they were. The entire Los Angeles patrol division would now be looking for

Azzara's Prius, which was what Pike wanted, so now Pike wanted to continue the search himself. If Azzara had Rainey, then finding Azzara would give him Rainey, and Pike wanted Rainey.

Pike left Cole with Button and Valenti, and stepped outside to call Marisol.

"How's Artie?"

"Hold on—"

She was probably with Artie, and had to change rooms to speak freely. She came back on the line a few seconds later, her voice soft so Artie wouldn't hear.

"He's better, I think. I checked his temperature like you said. It's okay."

"What about the blood in his urine?"

"Kinda pink, but not as much. I've been giving him cranberry juice. You think that's okay, the cranberry juice?"

"Yeah. Sounds good."

Pike waited while a Coroner Investigator went by on his way to a dead *Federale*. While Pike waited, he saw Straw enter the great room. Straw badged a uniformed officer, who pointed him toward Button. Then the CI was gone, and Pike continued with Marisol.

"I'm at Azzara's house. That was a good address you gave me. It helped."

"You are with Miguel?"

"No. Azzara isn't here, but six people were murdered. Three of them are *Malevos*. It will probably be on the news, so I wanted you to hear about it from me, first."

"I understand. Thank you."

"Azzara took off with one of my friends when he found the bodies—a man from Louisiana. I need to find him."

"I don't know what to tell you."

"People run home when they're scared, and Miguel will be scared. If you hear something, will you call me?"

"May I ask you something?"

"Yes."

"Did you kill them?"

"No."

"Did Miguel?"

"No. A man who wants to kill my friends killed them. That's why I have to find them first. Will you call?"

"Yes. Of course, I will call."

"Stay with Artie. Watch his temperature."

"You are a strange man."

Pike closed his phone, then went to the chaise longue where Dru Rayne had lain in the sun. He sat where she sat, and stared at her bottle. It was still on the deck. Dos Equis. Pike took out his phone and called her. Voice mail. He put away his phone, and thought over his options as he watched Cole, Button, Straw, and Valenti talking. Straw saw him and raised a hand, but Pike did not respond.

The call from Dru told him the killer would keep her alive until he had Rainey. By letting her make the call, he was using her as bait, but this didn't mean he would kick back until Rainey showed up. He was a predator, so he would hunt. He was probably searching for Rainey even as Pike sat in the sun on Azzara's chaise longue. Pike felt confident he understood what the killer would do, but he was less certain about Rainey.

Pike wondered if Rainey would deal with the killer or run. Dru's call suggested Rainey had the money, so Pike thought Rainey would probably run. Even if he wanted to stay, Azzara might not give him the choice. Whatever business Rainey had with Azzara and the Mexicans might force him onto a private jet.

Button came outside while Pike was thinking, and called him over.

"Stop sunning yourself and c'mere! Valenti has a question."

When Pike went inside, Valenti said, "The guy who looked like a *veterano*, you said he had a ghost on his arm? Was it Casper the Friendly Ghost? You know that cartoon?"

"Yes. It was Casper."

Valenti turned to Button.

"José Eschuara had a Casper. They called him the ghost because he'd sneak up behind people to shoot them—his vics never saw him."

Cole said, "Creative."

"Eschuara's a big deal—a senior member in *La Eme*'s command structure in California. If Eschuara was here with the *Federales*—if these cowboys are really *Federales*—this was a high-level meeting. Way over Azzara's pay grade."

Button said, "Thanks, Eddie. Get us a picture of him. We'll have Pike take a look."

As Valenti walked away, Straw examined the dead cowboy on the couch.

"The person who did this is the same person who killed Mendoza and Gomer?"

"That's how it tracks. Cole says he's a Bolivian hitter. Rainey used to be in business with a Bolivian cartel."

Straw frowned at Pike.

"These people are Rainey and who?"

"Rainey and Platt."

Straw glanced from Pike to Cole as if he didn't believe it.

"You're sure about this?"

Cole said, "Positive. We had a vision."

Button laughed, but Straw seemed annoyed.

"Did your vision show you where Mr. Rainey is?"

Button weighed in like he was tired of Straw's questions.

"That's what we're doing here, Straw. We're trying to find these people. This is all late-breaking news. We'll know more when we talk to the Louisiana FBI office. They have the case."

Straw arched his eyebrows.

"Louisiana? Okay. I'll give them a call. They'll move faster for a fellow agent."

"Thanks. We can handle it."

Cole received a call on his cell, and moved away to talk. Straw watched him leave.

"I'll talk to them anyway. They might like to hear about Cole's vision. They also might have an ID on the lunatic who did this."

Pike said, "Did you ask your men if they remembered anyone?"

"I did. They didn't."

Button frowned, suspicious that they'd had a conversation he knew nothing about.

"What are you talking about?"

"A picture of the killer. If he cased the sandwich shop, Straw might have him on video."

"I'll have my guys check, but I told you, we only set up on the bangers. Unless this guy cruised the shop when Azzara's people were there, we won't have him. And I don't see how we'll recognize him even if we have him."

Pike had been thinking about it, and thought he knew how.

"Elvis has a security video from one of Rainey's neighbors. Look at both of them. If the same person shows up on both recordings, he's our guy."

Button said, "That's a pretty good idea, Straw. Makes sense."

Straw turned away to call his guys, and Pike went over to Cole.

"I'm going to look for Dru."

Cole nodded, telling whoever was on the phone to hold on.

"Where?"

"Venice. I'll start at the body shop."

"Okay. I'll call you if I get anything."

Pike turned away, then stopped.

"Thanks for not telling me her name is Rose."

Pike left before Cole could answer.

39

PIKE DID NOT THINK Azzara would go to the body shop, but it was his last best place to start looking. *La Eme* gangs were families. If Azzara wanted a different car or help getting out of the country, he would go to someone he trusted.

Pike spent thirty-five minutes driving to Venice, and was still five minutes from the body shop when Elvis Cole called.

"Where are you?"

Pike told him where he was going and why.

"Don't bother. Azzara and Eschuara are dead."

Pike took his foot off the gas and steered toward the side of the street.

"Rainey?"

"No sign of Rainey. They were found five minutes from here on a side street off Doheny. Shot."

"The Bolivian?"

"I'm heading there now to take a look, but it sounds like Rainey killed them. They were shot with a large caliber—at least a nine millimeter.

The vics at Azzara's were shot with a twenty-two. Hang on—"

Pike heard a voice in the background that was probably Button, then Cole came back on the phone.

"I guess Rainey and the bangers couldn't agree on a plan. Looks like he shot them, pushed them out of the car, and took off. There's no sign of the Prius."

Pike thought for a moment, trying to decide what to do.

"Did Button get through to the investigators in Louisiana?"

"Yeah. They're going to email some things."

"Do they have the executioner's picture?"

"Uh-uh. They're sending what they have, but there isn't a picture."

"Keep me advised."

Pike closed his phone. It had been reasonable to think someone at the body shop would hear from Azzara, but now Azzara was dead, so Pike focused on Rainey. With twelve million dollars, Rainey could have homes, apartments, and cars stashed all over the city. He might even be sailing out of the marina as Pike sat on the side of the street.

Pike thought about how Dru called him, but had been pretending to call Rainey. If she had never reached Rainey, he might not know the Bolivian had her.

Pike dug out Rainey's cell number and gave it a try. The phone rang once, then immediately went to voice mail. Pike closed his phone, then had a follow-up thought, and dialed Rainey's number again.

This time when the voice mail answered, Pike left a message.

"He has her."

Pike left his number, then phoned Cole.

"Is Straw still at Azzara's?"

"He left before us. He's going to check their video and compare it to the disk we got from Laine. That was a good idea."

"He's doing that now?"

"Yeah. It's going to take a long time. He wanted to get started."

Pike decided to offer his help. He drove directly to Straw's stakeout across from Rainey's shop. The shop was now busy with police, but Pike ignored them. He went through the tattoo parlor as he had before, and once again climbed the rear stairs.

No one answered when Pike knocked. He knocked harder, then tried the knob and found it unlocked.

The two-room office suite was empty. The bedding and trash bags and gear were gone. Even the black sheet with its rectangular cuts was missing. The shakedown crew had moved on, and taken their video with them.

Pike ran back to his Jeep for Straw's number, and called.

"Jack Straw."

"Where are you?"

"Who is—Pike, is that you?"

"What's going on with the video?"

"I have a man going through it right now."

"Straw, I'm at your stakeout. It's empty."

"You need to relax, Pike. We closed that place down. The shakedown op is history. Most of my crew is already on their way home."

"Louisiana doesn't have a picture of the Bolivian."

Straw was silent for a moment, and when he spoke again, his voice was measured.

"I know they don't. I spoke with an agent down there twenty minutes ago. So I've got Kenny looking at the recordings right now. If he sees anyone who looks suspicious—anyone who even remotely might be our guy—he will let me know. You better settle down, man. You sound like you're losing it."

Straw hung up.

Kenny. One man to look at hundreds of hours of video.

Pike settled back, and scanned the surrounding buildings and the gawkers on the sidewalks outside Rainey's shop. Rainey probably wouldn't return, but you never knew—Rainey had been running for years, but this time he hadn't. Rainey had broken his pattern, and people never changed without a very good reason. Instead of running again, Rainey and Dru had moved in with Azzara, but left several things at Brown's house, suggesting they felt the move would be temporary and they planned to return. Maybe Rainey left something at the house he needed before he would leave.

Pike drove to the house. The police had blocked the surrounding streets, so Pike left his Jeep on the boulevard and tried to cross the pedestrian bridge. The police had blocked the footbridges at both ends of the alley, so Pike found himself with three neighborhood women and six children at the construction site where Gomer had been murdered. They watched the activity as uniformed and plainclothes officers searched Brown's house.

Pike spent little time looking at the police. Gawkers had gathered at the bridges and bike paths, and residents with a view of the scene were in their backyards. Pike searched the faces for Rainey, but knew the Bolivian killer might also be among them. If the killer was still hunting for Rainey, he might return to the house for the same reasons as Pike.

Pike found Lily Palmer's card in his wallet, and called.

Jared answered, his voice low and dull.

"Hullo."

"It's Pike. Remember?"

Jared perked up.

"Oh, man, you should see this place. The cops are everywhere."

"I know. I'm across the canal."

"No shit? Man, did you know? Wilson and Dru are criminals. Did you know that?"

Jared came out to the edge of their pool and waved when he saw Pike.

"Hey, dude, there you are! I see you!"

Pike said, "Has anyone been next door?"

"At Steve's place?"

"Yes."

"Dude, look at it. The place looks like a cop convention."

"Not now. Before the police."

"Right, yeah, the cops asked that, too. No, uh-uh, I didn't see anyone."

"Not just today. What about yesterday and last night?"

"Nada, man."

"Did you hear anything?"

"No, dude. And you know me—all eyes all the time. No evil shall escape my sight."

"Get something to write with. I'm going to give you my number."

"Sure, dude. Hang on."

Jared jogged into his house, and reappeared a few moments later.

"Okey-doke, we are ready to copy, Houston."

Pike recited his cell.

"If you see anyone next door after the police leave, I want you to call me. Will you do that?"

"Sure, dude. We're supposed to call the cops, too."

"That's fine. Call them, but call me, too."

"You got it, bro. No problemo."

"And Jared—do you have alarms on your house?"

"Yeah."

"Lock up tonight. Don't leave any windows or doors open. Lock it and arm up."

"Dude, you are freakin' me out. Wilson's cool with me. We joke around."

Pike wasn't thinking about Rainey.

"Lock up, Jared. If you see someone or hear something, call 911, then me. Tell your mother. Give her my number."

The excitement left Jared's voice.

"Yes, sir. I'll tell her."

Pike closed his phone.

Jared stared at him for a moment, then waved again and walked slowly back into his house.

Pike studied the near bridges and surrounding houses. If Rainey showed up because he wanted to enter the house, he would leave, but return later when the police were gone. Pike had nothing else, so he settled in to wait.

Forty minutes later, Pike's attention was drawn when two men stepped from the crowd at the head of the pedestrian bridge. Special Agents Straw and Kenny showed their badges to the officer blocking the bridge, who immediately let them pass. They disappeared when they reached the end of the bridge, but Kenny reappeared a few minutes later in Rainey's backyard. Pike wondered why he was here with Straw instead of checking the video.

Kenny walked to the fence, then turned toward the house. A few seconds later, Straw joined him. They spoke for a moment, then Straw went to the kayak hanging on the dock. He rocked it absently back and forth, then spoke to Kenny, who only shook his head in answer. They stared at the house as if trying to solve an unsolvable puzzle, and neither appeared ready to leave.

Pike wondered if Kenny had finished checking the video or if Straw had simply lied.

Pike called Straw on his cell. He listened to Straw's phone ring, and watched as Straw checked the incoming call window, then returned the phone to his pocket without answering.

Pike said, "Mm."

Pike dialed again, and again watched as Straw checked the incoming call without answering. This time he said something to Kenny, who shook his head as he walked away.

Pike immediately dialed again, and this time Straw broke. He answered his phone.

"Hello?"

"It's Pike. How's it coming with the video?"

"You're becoming a pain in the ass, you know that? We're getting there."

"I'll pitch in. Maybe Kenny needs some help."

"He's doing fine without you."

"He find anything yet?"

"No, Pike, I told you I'd call you, but here you are calling me, and it's slowing us down. Don't call again."

Pike watched as Straw lowered his phone. He said something to Kenny, which made Kenny laugh.

Pike jogged back to his Jeep and drove along Venice Boulevard until he found the green Malibu. If Straw wasn't going to check the video, Pike would check it himself.

Pike didn't know what he would find or if he would find anything, but the Malibu's back seat was filled with their duffels and sleeping bags. Pike checked to make sure no one was watching, then used a jiggler key to open the car.

Pike wanted the camera case, but did not see it, so

he searched through the duffels. The top duffel was jumbled with clothes and toiletry bags. He quickly checked for the camera, zipped the bag, and shoved it aside. Pike was working fast, but when he opened the second bag, he spotted a thick manila envelope with *Rainey* written in longhand on the cover.

Rainey's name stopped him.

Pike could tell by the envelope's worn condition and faded ink that nothing about it was new. It looked old, and used, and as soon as Pike saw it he knew something about Jack Straw was wrong.

The envelope contained photocopies of what appeared to be reports and documents about William Allan Rainey written on Drug Enforcement Agency letterhead and field forms. The documents appeared official, and contained blurry, black-and-white photocopies of surveillance pictures. Like the envelope, the documents showed their wear with torn edges, coffee rings, and handwritten notes in the margins. Pike was fingering through the pages without reading them when he found a smudged picture of Rose Marie Platt with a banner for Jazz Fest behind her in the background. The picture quality was so poor she was almost unrecognizable, but Pike knew it was her.

Pike pushed the pages back into the envelope, and continued looking for the camera. He found it a few seconds later, closed the duffel, and left the bags on the back seat as he had found them.

Pike hadn't been looking for files and documents, but now he wanted to see what Straw had. He took the camera and envelope, and drove to a quiet residential street three blocks away.

Pike checked the video first. He spent a few minutes figuring out how to work the camera, then watched several seconds of Straw's recording. He fast-forwarded, then skipped between tracks to watch more. A hard knot between his shoulder blades grew larger with each scene he watched, and soon it spread down his back.

Straw's surveillance team had not recorded Azzara or the members of Azzara's gang. They had recorded Rainey and Dru. Entering and leaving the shop. Entering and leaving the house on the canal. Dru in the backyard. Rainey in the kayak. Driving their Tercel.

The video confirmed what Pike suspected the moment he saw the worn envelope bearing Wilson Smith's true name.

Special Agent Jack Straw had lied. Straw and his team never cared about Miguel Azzara. They had known who Wilson and Dru were since the beginning. They were chasing Rainey and Platt.

40

PIKE PUT THE CAMERA ASIDE, then skimmed the reports. Most of the documents were case notes recounting meetings or conversations with Rainey by a DEA agent named Norman Lister, who appeared to be Rainey's handler. Most of the reports were written while Rainey was still functioning as an informant, though many were dated when the agents were investigating his disappearance. Pike skipped these parts as he did not care about Rainey. He wanted to read about Dru.

He searched the pages until he found the picture of Rose Marie Platt, and discovered a collection of documents stapled together. The first was a compilation of Lister's notes condensing statements made by Rainey's associates, describing how they knew Rose Platt, and what they knew, if anything, about her relationship to Rainey. Their names were highlighted in yellow, and their addresses were handwritten in the margins.

Most of those interviewed were identified as

co-workers, and most knew nothing incriminating. One of those interviewed was Rose Platt's mother and two were identified as her brothers. These condensations were as short as the others, and contained no information useful to Lister's investigation. The brothers claimed they had not seen their sister for six years, and the mother complained she had not seen nor heard from Rose in almost ten years. Rose was alternately described as rebellious, fucked up, selfish, and a tramp.

Pike flipped past the remaining statements, but paused again when he found a copy of the warrant issued for Rose Marie Platt's arrest. The warrant contained an information sheet with a second picture of Dru, her physical description, and background information that might prove useful to investigators. The names of friends and relatives, prior addresses, schools attended, and past employers were all neatly typed into the appropriate boxes.

Pike read this sheet carefully. A tiny box at the top of the page was checked to show she had no arrest record. Another box showed her fingerprints were not on file.

According to the investigators, Rose Marie Platt was born in Biloxi, Mississippi. She had been married three times, the first when she was seventeen years old, the second when she was nineteen, and a third time when she was twenty-two. The first two marriages occurred in Biloxi; the last in Slidell, Louisiana. The names and last known addresses of the three men were listed, along with the brief descriptives: DVR, NO CHLDRN. Divorced, no children.

Pike thought about the young girl in the snapshot Dru showed him. He could picture the little girl clearly. Amy. A pretty kid with a happy smile standing beside a couch. *The love of my life.*

The form listed parents and siblings. Pike studied it. Dru's mother and father were named, but a box by the father's name was checked. Deceased. The names of her two brothers were typed beneath her parents. Beneath the names of the two brothers was another checked box and a single descriptive: SISTERS—none.

Pike stared at this line the longest. Sisters— none.

Dru had told him Amy was staying with her sister.

Pike stared out the window at nothing, aware but not caring about passing cars or the light that dappled through tortured elms. Pike could see the scene perfectly and recall every nuance of her expression. The awkward uncertainty as she took out her billfold. How she shrugged when she showed him the picture, as if expecting him to reject her. How her smile flashed like summer lightning when he asked her out anyway.

But no sister meant there was no Amy, which meant none of it was true.

Pike tamped the pages together and slid them back into the envelope. He thought for a moment, then started the Jeep and turned toward Pacific Station. It was only five minutes away. He took out his phone as he drove and called Jerry Button. Button had returned to his office.

Pike said, "Who is Straw and what is he doing?"

"What do you mean, who is he?"

"Were you in on it with him?"

"Pike, I'm busy. What the fuck are you talking about?"

Pike decided Button's annoyance was real, which meant Straw had lied to Button, too.

"Straw didn't come here to bust Azzara. They were watching Rainey. They've known Wilson was Rainey since the beginning."

Button came back sounding uncertain.

"Did he tell you that?"

Pike described the DEA reports and Straw's video but Button didn't want to believe it.

"This better not be bullshit."

"Meet me outside in five minutes. You can have the camera and the reports. I'll give them to you."

Button fell silent, and Pike knew why. Button was embarrassed.

"I'm on my way now, Jerry. You should have checked him out."

"That fuckin' Feeb. Those arrogant pricks *always* pull underhanded shit like this."

"If you had done your due diligence, we would have known what we were dealing with. We could have stopped the Bolivian."

Button cleared his throat, anxious to change the subject.

"I hooked up with the New Orleans agents. Did Cole tell you?"

"Yes. They don't have a picture?"

"No, but they're pretty sure he's an American named Gregg Daniel Vincent. He's not a Bolivian."

"What do they know?"

"Not much, and most of it they can't confirm. Made his bones guarding dope farms in Honduras from government raids. Made his rep killing snitches and cops the Bolivians want out of the way. Tortures them to death. The Bolivians have this whole rap about him escaping from some kinda nuthouse for psychopaths, but that's probably bullshit. They use him to scare people."

Pike didn't care about any of that, and wasn't impressed.

"Is there a description?"

"They know he's a white guy, but that's it. They don't have a description or a photograph."

Pike pulled to the curb by the flagpole outside Pacific Station. He put the Jeep in park, but did not turn off the engine.

"I'm here, Button. By the flag out front. Come get Straw's stuff."

Button sounded sick.

"You really have it?"

"Come get it. I'm leaving it on the curb."

Pike closed his phone, got out with the envelope and the camera, and left them on the sidewalk. Less than one minute later, he was driving away when his phone rang. He thought it was Button, calling him back, but it wasn't.

"Pike? Is this Joe Pike?"

Pike recognized the voice.

"This is Bill Rainey. You know me as Wilson Smith."

41

DETECTIVE-SERGEANT JERRY BUTTON
Los Angeles Police Department
Pacific Station
Button's hands were shaking when he returned
to his desk with the camera and the files. He tried
to make them stop, but had to wedge them under
his hams. He glanced at Futardo, who was typing in
her cubicle across the room by the door. The new
guy always got the desk by the door. Button had the
prime desk in the rear, right outside the LT's office.
The distance between the two desks was a lot longer
than it looked.

Button felt angry, humiliated, and scared. Straw—
the arrogant Feeb prick—had pulled a typical,
underhanded FBI move by lying about his case. Like
all Quantico pricks, he thought city police were
incompetent losers, to be used, abused, and kept in
the dark.

And Button had proved him right.

Hello, Jerry Button, you are now the Pacific

Station Jackass of the Year.

Button flipped through the DEA documents, then watched a few minutes of the camera's video to make sure Pike hadn't been fucking with him. But Pike, of course, had never fucked around and wasn't fucking around now.

Button felt even more sick when he put down the camera. He picked up his phone to call Straw, then reconsidered. He was definitely going to confront the sonofabitch, that was for sure, but he wanted to have all the facts straight before he did. Button intended to file an official complaint.

Button called Dale Springer in the FBI's New Orleans office. Springer was the agent Button had spoken with about the Rainey case less than an hour ago.

"Special Agent Springer."

Button even hated how these condescending pricks answered their phones.

"Jerry Button in L.A. again. I stepped into something out here I need to ask about."

"Sure. What's up?"

Button noticed Futardo looking at him, which made his stomach clench. He would have to tell her about his fuckup as soon as he got off the phone.

"You know an agent named Jack Straw?"

"Sure. Jack's a good friend."

"Uh-huh. Well, who's his supervisor down there?"

"What do you mean?"

"I'd like to speak with his supervisor. Your Mr. Straw misrepresented himself to the Los Angeles

Police Department and is acting like an underhanded prick. I'd like to get this straightened out."

Springer cleared his throat.

"Hang on, Sergeant. I'll get him for you."

A few seconds later, a different male voice came on the line.

"This is Jack Straw. Who is this, please?"

Button felt a stillness settle into his belly.

"Jerry Button with the Los Angeles Police Department. Your name is Jack Straw?"

"That's right. Have we met?"

"You're working the William Rainey case?"

"I'm one of the original case agents, Detective. Can I ask what this is about?"

"Ah, listen, is there another Jack Straw on the case?"

The New Orleans Jack Straw laughed.

"Not the last time I looked. What's going on, Detective?"

"We have a gentleman here identifying himself as an agent named Jack Straw from your office. He has FBI credentials."

"That isn't possible."

"I'll call you right back."

Button leaned back in his chair and checked his hands. Steady as parked cars. He looked at Futardo. She was back on her computer, typing away. She was a good kid. He got up and walked over. She jumped to her feet when she saw him coming, but he motioned her down, and pulled up a nearby chair.

"Sit down, Nancy."

"Did I do something wrong?"

Her eyes were dark as black forest chocolate, but wide as demitasse saucers. She probably thought he was going to chew her out, which he did, often, but now he wanted to teach her.

"No, you didn't do anything wrong. It was me. I fucked up bad. That FBI asshole who came here, Straw? He had the credentials, he knew what to say, but he's a fake. The real Jack Straw is sucking crawfish heads down in New Orleans right now. I should have checked the guy out, but I didn't. That was a stupid, bush-league mistake, and it may have put a woman's life in danger."

Futardo stared at him as if one or both of them might have a stroke.

"You will never make this mistake, Nancy. For the rest of your career and beyond, you will question everything anyone tells you and you will always check out what they say. Is that clear?"

"Yes, sir."

"Promise me."

"Jesus, Jerry, what are we going to do?"

Button didn't answer. He returned to his desk, and got the real Jack Straw back on the line. Button explained the situation and provided a detailed description of the fake Jack Straw to the best of his ability. When the real Jack Straw started telling Button how he wanted Button to handle the imposter, Button hung up. He took one deep breath, let it out, then dialed the number he had for the fake Jack Straw.

"Jack Straw."

"Jerry Button here. We caught a break, man. We're rolling to bag Rainey in five. You wanna go?"

"You found him?"

"A motor cop spotted the Prius. I am rolling in five, brother. You want to go or not?"

"All right. Sure. Where do I meet you?"

"Where are you?"

"Santa Monica."

"Okay, that's close. I'll pick you up on my way."

Button gave a location, then stowed his phone. He checked his pistol, then clipped it to his belt. Not many dicks still carried the old .38 Snubbies, but Button saw no reason to change. It was small, light, and he had never fired it against another human being.

Button slipped on his jacket and headed out. He saw Futardo grab her purse and jump up to intercept him

"What are you going to do?"

"I'm gonna bag the fucker, Nancy. That's my job."

"I want to come. Can I? Please?"

Like a kid. All anxious and eager, and maybe a little afraid.

Button considered letting her come, but finally shook his head.

"Finish your reports."

He left to bag the fake Jack Straw, and did not see when she followed.

* * *

Straw was leaning against his car at the edge of a Ralph's parking lot on Wilshire Boulevard. Button saw the fake prick as he put on his blinker to turn, and gave a little beep. Straw stepped away from his car, all ready to go.

Button wondered what the guy was up to, pretending to be a federal agent, but figured it probably had something to do with Rainey's money.

Button turned into the lot and pulled up by Straw with the passenger door on the far side of the car.

Straw started around to the passenger side, but Button stopped him.

"Hang on a sec. I gotta give you a vest before we split. It's in the trunk."

Straw hesitated as Button climbed out.

"I don't need a vest."

"LAPD rules, man. I know it's stupid."

Button held up his hands to measure Straw's shoulders, and grinned as if he was making a joke.

"It's one size fits all, but it oughta do. I hope it doesn't have too many bullet holes in it."

The business with measuring Straw's shoulders let Button get close. He grabbed Straw's wrist, twisted his arm behind his back, and shoved him against the car.

"Stay there. Stay on the car."

Button cuffed his right wrist, then hooked up the left. When the fake Straw was secure, Button stepped back and checked him for a weapon.

"Stay on the car, fucker. You're under arrest. Do not turn around."

"What is this, Button? What are you doing?"

"Jack Straw, my ass. I know you're not Jack fuckin' Straw. I just spoke to the sonofabitch."

Detective Jerry Button glimpsed movement between two nearby cars, but did not see the man in time even when a blowing horn drew his attention. It sounded like a long, anguished wail.

Something hard punched him twice, so hard he staggered, which was when Kenny shot him again. Button fell to a knee, fumbling for the Snubbie as a tan Crown Victoria banged through oncoming traffic, spraying firefly sparks as it jumped the curb into the parking lot. Button saw Futardo, those black chocolate eyes all big in her head, coming to save him.

Button said, "No, honey—"

Kenny shot her through the windshield, then quickly walked to her window and shot her again.

Button had the Snubbie by then, but the fake Jack Straw was shouting.

"Button! Get Button!"

Button got off one round, then Kenny shot him again, hit him so hard it felt like being speared with a javelin, and the Snubbie fell free.

Straw said, "Get his key. Get me out of these things."

Kenny snatched up his gun and rolled Button onto his back as he searched for the keys.

The sun was so goddamned bright and right in his eyes, but they were over him, Kenny uncuffing Straw.

Button said, "Pieces of shit."

Straw glanced down, letting Button see the fear in his eyes.

"They know, man. We're done."

"Don't panic. We're close."

"We gotta go. We're fucked."

"No, we're not—"

Kenny pointed the gun straight down, blocking the sun, and Button stared into the tight black sphincter of its barrel.

"Fuck you."

Then a gun went off, and Button thought he was dead, but Kenny staggered sideways and fell. His falling gun hit Button on the nose.

Button saw Futardo, face dripping red, leaning out her window as she struggled to fire again.

The fake Jack Straw calmly picked up Kenny's weapon, and shot her twice more through the glass.

Button tried to grab the man's legs, but his arms wouldn't move. He tried to shout for help, but all he managed was a bubbly grunt.

Then the fake Straw looked down at him again, aimed his weapon, and fired.

42

"THIS IS BILL RAINEY. You know me as Wilson Smith."

Pike cranked the Jeep, ready to roll.

"I know who you are. Where is she?"

"I need your help."

"Where is she?"

"You really know who I am?"

"William Allan Rainey. Her name is Rose Platt. Where is she?"

"I dunno."

"Is she alive?"

"Yeah, I guess, but he'll kill her."

Rainey hiccupped, but Pike realized it was a sob. Rainey was crying.

"Don't guess. Do you know if she's alive?"

"Are the police on me?"

"Yes."

"Fuck!"

"Is she alive?"

"Jesus FUCK!"

Pike gave Rainey ten seconds of silence. Rainey

was coming apart, but Pike needed him to calm down and think.

"You want me to call you Bill or Wilson?"

"I don't give a shit. Whatever. He has her."

"What does he look like?"

"I dunno. All these years, and I've never seen him. We've been runnin', man. He killed Rose's old boyfriend. He got my sister, my ex-wife—Jesus, he keeps coming."

"Why me?"

"What?"

"Why did you call me?"

Now Rainey was silent, but the silence was good. The silence meant he was thinking.

"I can't call the police."

"Call them."

"I can't. You see what these Bolivians are like? How long would I last in prison? How long would she? I call the police now, it's killin' both of us later."

Pike gave him more silence, so Rainey filled it.

"You're a mercenary, right? I'll pay you."

"Twelve million dollars?"

Rainey laughed.

"Who told you that, the police? Is that what they think I got?"

"Yes."

"They're full of shit. It was eight-point-two."

"All right. You'll pay me eight-point-two?"

"It's gone. I'll give you everything I have left. Three hundred forty-two thousand and change."

"Don't want it."

"Cash. Tax free. It's yours."

"Don't want it."

Rainey fell into a deeper silence.

"I can't do it myself. I dunno. I had to ask."

"Why'd you kill Azzara and Eschuara?"

"Hell, you *do* know it all."

"I saw you at Azzara's. I followed you to the jet."

"She was right about you."

Pike wondered what he meant, but kept pressing forward.

"Why'd you kill them? They wouldn't help?"

"They wanted me to leave. They were taking me to Mexico or some bullshit like that. I couldn't leave without her. I love her, man."

Pike took a slow breath. Rainey was calm and controlled now, comfortable with the talking, so Pike asked again.

"Do you know for sure that she is alive?"

"She was alive as of, lessee, sixteen minutes ago. That's when she left the last message."

Pike checked the time. It was 4:22 P.M.

"She's leaving messages?"

"I guess he doesn't want me to know what he sounds like. I don't answer the damned phone, man. I'm scared to. This is the only way I can stall him. He doesn't know if I'm getting the messages or not. But I gotta call soon—"

"Why?"

"She said I gotta call at six. He must be gettin' pissed off, not being able to reach me. I don't call at six, she says he'll kill her."

344

One hour, thirty-eight minutes away.

"If you call at six, what will happen?"

"He'll probably tell me what he wants."

Pike went through the call he received when Dru pretended she was talking to Rainey. She had begged Rainey to give up the money.

"He wants the money."

"He'll say he wants it, but that's bullshit. The Bolivians want us dead. That's all they care about."

Pike checked the time. One hour, thirty-seven minutes away.

"How many messages has she left?"

"Three. She's called three times."

"You have them?"

"Yeah."

Pike wanted to hear her voice.

"Where are you?"

"Ah, right now? I'm in Hollywood. I'm behind a restaurant here, what is it, Musso and Frank?"

Pike thought he understood how the killer would play it, and began to develop a plan. He calced the drive time between where he was now and where he wanted to be, then told William Allan Rainey where to meet him at exactly 5:30. This would give Pike time to pick up a few things and call Elvis Cole. When they moved, they would have to move fast. They had to be ready.

Rainey said, "You're gonna help?"

"Yes."

"What are you going to do?"

"Sell you."

43

SIXTY-TWO MINUTES LATER, Pike slid out of his Jeep when Rainey got out of the Prius. They were in the parking lot behind a diner on Sunset Boulevard, trapped between a reinforced hillside and the restaurant, not five minutes from Miguel Azzara's house.

Rainey looked shrunken and feeble, as if his body was collapsing along with his life.

Pike twisted his arm behind his back and shouldered him hard against the Jeep.

"Fingers laced behind your head. Feet out."

Rainey did as he was told and did not resist.

"It's in the car. Under the seat."

"Shut up."

"I hadda shoot them. I told you."

"Like you shot Michael Fourchet?"

Pike found nothing except keys, a wallet, and a phone. He pulled open the Jeep's passenger door, pushed Rainey inside, then went around to the driver's side and climbed in behind the wheel. When

Pike pulled the door, Cole leaned forward from the back seat and patted Rainey's shoulder.

"If Pike won't take the money, I will."

Rainey jumped.

"Who are you?"

"Pike's evil twin."

Pike held up Rainey's phone.

"This the phone she calls?"

"Yeah."

Cole said, "So this is the number she'll answer when we call?"

"I guess. What are we gonna do? What was that shit about selling me?"

Pike gave the phone to Rainey.

"Play her messages. Put it on speaker."

Rainey fumbled with getting the phone's voice mail to play back on speaker. The cheap phone made her difficult to hear, but they finally got it going.

Her first message was almost identical with what she told Pike, Dru saying he had her, and pleading for Rainey to give him the money. Pike didn't listen to Dru so much as he listened for background noises, but he heard nothing useful. The condenser mics built into cell phones were designed to reduce background sounds.

The second message was much the same, but with small differences. Now Dru said he wanted all the money, and added a plea for Rainey to call back. This time she left her number.

Cole stopped Rainey before he played the last message.

"Does she know you only have three hundred left?"

"Hell, yeah, she knows. She helped spend it."

"She's making it sound like you have all eight million."

"She's letting me know she hasn't told him. I told this one—"

He glanced toward Pike.

"—these Bolivians don't want the money. I know, 'cause I tried to pay'm, plus extra."

Pike said, "How can you pay them if you don't have it?"

Cole saw the deal first.

"The *Federales* and *La Eme*. You cut a deal with them."

"You bet your ass I did. Those *Federales*, they work for a cartel down in Baja. They run dope up through your Mexicans here—"

"They're not *my* Mexicans."

"You know what I used to do, right?"

"Yeah. You smuggled cash offshore on fishing boats."

"This oil spill mess created a lot of opportunity. People still can't fish the way they used to. I got to thinkin' about it."

He faced Pike again.

"I talked to the Mexicans here and they talked to the Mexicans in Mexico, 'cause I can bring their shit in and their cash out, just like I was doin' back home. The Mexico Mexicans liked it, and offered the New Orleans crew a deal. The fucking Bolivians pretended to go along, but it was all bullshit, so here we are. Fucked."

Pike glanced at Cole, then studied Rainey. Something about his story didn't add up.

"If you were in business with these people, why did Mendoza and Gomer beat you up?"

"We weren't in business, then. Those assholes were trying to rob me, just like you thought. Then Azzara came around to lean on me, making all these bullshit threats, *La Eme* this, *La Eme* that, and that's when I got the idea."

"Azzara."

"Yeah. I was in business with drug traffickers for years, and all traffickers have the same problems. I laid it out for him. Here's what I can do for you, but here's what you gotta do for me."

"Make the Bolivians back off."

"Yeah."

Rainey took a moment, then shook his head.

"That's how bad they hate me, those fuckers. Now they got a war with this Baja cartel, and they don't even give a shit."

Pike cut him off.

"Play her last message."

Dru's third and final message was more desperate. Her voice showed the mounting stress as she gulped shallow breaths, and Pike could hear her fear.

"Stop it now, Willie, you hear? You must call me at six o'clock. I'm begging you. Please get this done. You know how to get it done. You don't call, he says he'll kill me."

Her call abruptly ended.

None of them spoke for a moment, then Rainey stared at Pike.

"You asked why I called you. When she says, get this done, you know how to get this done. She's telling me to call you. That's when I called."

Pike didn't understand.

Rainey frowned, showing a weakness in his eyes that told Pike he was embarrassed.

"When this started with the bangers and you waded in, she told me you were the kind of guy who could get stuff done. She liked that."

Pike studied him until Rainey looked away, then Pike took the phone. He checked the time. Ten minutes before six. Time was running out.

Pike said, "Does she have a sister?"

"What?"

"Rose. She has two brothers. Does she have a sister?"

Rainey squinted like Pike was speaking in code.

"No. What does that have to do with anything?"

Cole said, "Where's the cash?"

"I got a storage space up in Van Nuys. You want it, it's yours. All three-forty-two."

Cole glanced at Pike.

"This time of day, that's two hours, there and back. No good."

"We don't need it."

Rainey shifted, looking from Cole to Pike.

"What are we going to do?"

"The Bolivian, the one who wants you dead. What's his name?"

"Jesus, it's a cartel. It's a whole bunch of guys."

Cole leaned forward and tapped Rainey's head.

"Think. Who did you rip off? Who's the alpha male?"

"It's gotta be Hugo Joaquin. He was runnin' it. Who gives a shit? What are we going to do?"

Pike checked the time. Three minutes. He had what he needed.

"I'm ready."

Rainey said, "Ready for what?"

Cole tapped Rainey again.

"Get out. We're waiting outside."

"For what? What's he going to do?"

Pike checked the time again. One minute to go.

"This is the part where I sell you."

Cole climbed out, pulled Rainey out the front, then closed the door, leaving Pike alone with the phone.

On the other side of the parking lot, a family got out of an SUV and went into the diner. The father carried a curly-headed little girl on his shoulders. Fifty feet away, cars crept along Sunset Boulevard, jammed up by rush hour. Pike blocked all of it out and called Dru Rayne.

44

SHE ANSWERED ON THE third ring. Pike figured it took one ring for Gregg Daniel Vincent to show her the incoming number, one for her to confirm this was Rainey, and the third for Vincent to punch the answer button and hold the phone to her ear. Her voice sounded tentative.

"Hello?"

"Is he listening?"

Saying it for Vincent.

A full twenty seconds passed before she answered, which was probably Vincent figuring out what to do.

"Yes, he's listening. Where's Willie? Willie was supposed to call."

"Willie can't call. You good?"

"Ah, yeah, I'm okay. He hasn't hurt me."

"Give him the phone."

"He, ah, he doesn't want to talk. If Willie doesn't call, he's going to hurt me."

"No, he won't. I have Rainey and the money, but mostly I have Rainey."

"Ah, he wants to know who you are."

"Tell him."

Pike heard her tell Vincent his name. Vincent said something, but too low for Pike to understand. They were still talking when Pike spoke again.

"What's his name?"

"What?"

"His name?"

Another mumble in the background before she answered.

"Ah, his name is David."

The corner of Pike's mouth twitched.

"You're a liar, Mr. Vincent. Your name is Gregg Daniel Vincent. Knock off the bullshit, and get on the phone. If you don't want Rainey, I'll sell him to the Bolivians."

Thirty seconds of silence this time, edging to forty before a male voice came on the line.

"What's your deal, boy? How do you know my name?"

"A friend told me."

"I'll kill your fuckin' friend, you, your family, any motherfucker you've ever met. Your friend tell you *that*?"

"My friend told me you're the guy the Bolivians send to scare people. I know who you are. None of it matters."

"I have friends, too. You work Nicaragua or Honduras? You work Ecuador or Colombia? You think maybe we faced off before?"

The corner of Pike's mouth twitched. He had not

told Dru where he worked, so she couldn't have told Vincent. His name, yes, and that he had been a military contractor, but no more than that. Vincent had checked him out, which meant he saw Pike as a threat.

"All right. We both have friends. Maybe our friends are the same people."

"What does that mean?"

"I have Rainey and the money. I'll sell him to you."

"Sell'm, my ass. You need to walk, and hope I don't come looking."

"If I walk, I'll sell him to Hugo. They've already offered a million. Maybe I can get more."

The silence felt different this time, and when Vincent spoke, his voice was both thoughtful and wary.

"Yet here you are, talking to me. I must have something you want."

"The girl."

"Ah."

"The girl, plus one half of the remaining money. You get Rainey and the other half."

"Walk away, boy. I'll cut this bitch in half."

"I'll still have Rainey."

Vincent shouted.

"I'll cut you in half, too, you motherfucker, then I'll have'm both."

Pike knew he was winning. The shouting was good, so Pike kept his own voice low and steady.

"Here's where we are. You're only going to get one

of these people for Mr. Joaquin, so which one do you want? Which one does he want most? Rainey ripped him off. Rose was just along for the ride."

Pike let it sit. Outside in the world, Cole and Rainey were watching. The family returned to their SUV, carrying boxes overflowing with hot dogs and fries. The traffic moved like a sluggish pulse.

Vincent said, "You working for the Bolivians?"

Pike was surprised by the question. Vincent was concerned about his position with the Bolivians.

"I never discuss my employers."

Pike let it sit again, knowing that Vincent's insecurity would grow. By playing it vague, Vincent would think Pike's friend was a Bolivian. He also knew that Vincent would be trying to figure out how he could get both Rainey and Rose.

Vincent finally made his decision.

"Okay. How do you want to do this?"

"However you want. Let's meet somewhere. You give me the girl, I'll give you Rainey, all there is to it."

Vincent laughed, as Pike expected. Pike had talked it out with Cole while they were waiting for Rainey. Vincent would never expose himself. He would never walk the girl out to Pike and Rainey, two on two, because this would make him a target.

"No way, dude. C'mon, are you being serious?"

"Have the girl where I can see her. I have to see she's alive. She looks okay, I'll send Rainey with your half of the money. They meet at the halfway point, she comes to me, he goes to you. Sound better?"

"Waitaminute. What if the sonofabitch runs?"

"Shoot him."

It was a stupid scenario filled with holes, but that's what Pike wanted. Vincent would see the holes as opportunities. Pike's only concern was jamming Vincent into showing Dru Rayne. Vincent would not expose himself, but he would stay near the girl, watching from a hidden location with a clean escape route. Pike knew he would want this because this is what Pike would want. Vincent would watch from a hide and try to kill Pike. Pike could almost hear him thinking about it.

Vincent said, "Okay. We're getting somewhere."

"How about Rainey's house, on the canal? It's empty."

"Too tight in there."

Which is why Pike suggested it, pushing Vincent to think of escape routes and a wide field of view.

"Wherever you want, Vincent. You want to think about it, call me back?"

Vincent fell silent again, then mumbled something Pike couldn't quite hear. Pike thought he was talking to Dru, then realized Vincent was talking to himself.

Two minutes later, they had a time, a place, and had worked out the details.

Pike rolled down the Jeep's window and motioned to Cole.

"We're on. Let's roll."

45

DANIEL

Daniel lowered the phone and stared at the waitress. They were back in the van's bay, all four of them.

Daniel said, "You fuckin' that boy?"

Tobey snorted, "Yeah, she's fuckin' him."

Cleo giggled, "Fuckin'm real good."

Her eyes were narrow and smart, like some tough-ass Bogotá hooker planning to grab a wallet. But she also looked scared. Damn well better.

"No, we're not like that."

"Why he wants you, he ain't fuckin' ya?"

She glanced away, then down and up.

"I don't know. I haven't known him very long."

Tobey snickered, "Slut's fuckin' him."

Cleo hissed, "Slut, slut."

Daniel hoped they were right. The arrow dude might be some kinda bad-ass mercenary, but if he had a hard-on for the waitress, he was way past the money stage. Men stayed sharp when it came to money. Men got stupid when it came to women.

Daniel ripped off a fresh piece of silver tape, and pressed it over her mouth.

"You know what you are?"

Tobey said, "Tramp."

Cleo said, "Cooze, cooze."

She shook her head, talking now being beyond her.

"You're a staked goat. These Swahilis in Africa, they stake a goat under a tree as bait for a lion. They cut it, make it bleed, then they wait up in the tree. That lion, all he can smell is the blood. That's a pretty good way to hunt a zombie, too."

Daniel left her in back, and climbed up in front behind the wheel. He reviewed what the Bolivian had told him about Pike, which was pretty impressive by anyone's standards, and thought he had a pretty good idea how Pike would come at him. Daniel had no doubt Pike would try to kill him, and he figured Pike knew Daniel would be trying to kill him, too. It went without saying. Daniel just had to stay ahead of him in the planning department.

Daniel pulled out into traffic, considering the variables for their upcoming meeting. He wanted to get up to the location as quickly as possible, but there were a couple of things he needed to pick up.

Daniel cruised through Hollywood, running different tactical scenarios until he found one he liked.

Three minutes later, he slipped under the overpass at Vine, and spotted an old dude taking it easy on a bus bench, skuzzy gray beard, fading gray hair, none of that talkin' to voices you get with the schizos.

This one, a dedicated drunk on hard times. Even had a little sign: *will work for food.*

Tobey's voice rumbled, all hoarse and hungry.

"Looks good to me."

Cleo rasped, "He'll do."

Daniel pulled up by the bench and called out the passenger window.

"Yo. You mean it, that sign? I got two hours' work."

Dude eyeballed the Hero-Rooter van, then shook his head.

"I ain't no plumber."

"I'm not a plumber, yo. All I need you to do is hold a light for me. My regular guy took sick."

Lazy fuck didn't budge.

"What kinda light?"

"A fuckin' flashlight, yo. I need a helper to hold a flashlight. There's forty bucks in it for you. Two hours' work. You want it or not?"

"Forty dollars?"

"Job's up the hill here. C'mon, man, I'm running late. You want the forty?"

Tobey said, "What is it with this guy?"

Cleo said, "Sheesh, eesh."

Dude finally peeled himself off the bench.

"I want twenty up front."

"No way. Forty when the job's done or I'm moving on. Let's go."

Dude gave him a look like he was doing the world a favor, but finally climbed in, smelling like rotten cabbage. Slammed the door, checked out the van as he settled himself, and clocked the back bay, but by then it was too late.

Daniel pushed him between the seats right on top of the waitress.

Tobey screamed, "Kill him."

Cleo purred, "Kill."

Daniel said, "Later."

46

PIKE CONSIDERED THE VAN in the fading brass light. Hero-Rooter. CALL A HERO TO SAVE THE DAY! DRAINS CLEANED AROUND THE CLOCK! Based on the little he knew about Gregg Daniel Vincent, Pike judged the location as close to perfect. Pike would have picked an identical place.

The Hero-Rooter van was parked in the brush on a flat, undeveloped ridge a hundred yards off Mulholland Drive, overlooking the San Fernando Valley. On the south side of Mulholland, the mountain had been cut away, leaving a steep slope dotted with dying pines and no good place to run. The Valley side was better. Vincent would have an unobstructed view in both directions along Mulholland, and of the houses that filled the canyon below. Mulholland was the only way in or out, but if the police appeared, a man with Vincent's skill could easily slip down through the brush to disappear in the winding streets and houses.

Pike lowered his binoculars and whispered into his cell.

"He's smart. It's a good place to kill."

Cole's voice came back.

"See anyone?"

"Just the van. It's on a ridge where they're clearing the hill. Rainey will see it."

Cole and Rainey were parked in a turnout a quarter-mile to the east, three-quarters of a mile from the van.

"Stand by—"

Pike studied the van again. Dru was probably inside, but Vincent would be on the slope. The setup was easy. When Rainey turned onto the ridge, Dru would get out of the van so Pike could see she was healthy. Rainey would then get out of his car, and advance halfway with the money. Dru would walk out to meet him, check the money, and then Rainey would continue with the money to the van while Dru went to the Prius.

This was the plan Pike and Vincent worked out, but none of it would happen. Pike knew it, and Vincent knew it, too. Vincent would be looking for Pike, just like Pike was looking for Vincent. If Vincent won, he would kill Rose Platt, then torture Rainey until Rainey produced the rest of the money, and then he would kill Rainey. Everything in Vincent's history affirmed this. Vincent liked to torture and kill.

Pike studied the brushy area off Mulholland where Rainey would stop, then a gentle rise behind the van. Vincent would be in one of those two places. When Rainey turned onto the ridge, he would be facing the van. Vincent would be behind him, in a high position where he could see Rainey and also watch for Pike. Pike searched the two areas, but saw nothing, and returned to the phone.

"I'm moving. Give me eight minutes, and go. Ten, and be there."

Pike slid beneath a twisted scrub oak and down the crumbling hill. He carried his Python, a .45 Kimber, and a Remington Model 700 bolt-action rifle he rebuilt himself, along with a pouch for his binoculars and a FLIR thermal imaging camera. The FLIR read infrared heat images. When Pike was closer, the FLIR would let Pike see Vincent in the brush.

Pike moved fast down the steep slope, slipping between and around dry brush at a hard run, then climbed the next finger. He stayed low around the outside shoulder to keep Mulholland and the van above him.

He rounded the shoulder into the next canyon, and paused to take his bearings. The next finger was ahead and above him, with Mulholland to his left. He picked two scrubby oaks as navigation points, dropped down through a sea of gray brush, then up an erosion gulley until he reached the lip of the ridge. He could not yet see the van, but knew he was midway between the van and Mulholland. He checked the time. Nine minutes. Rainey and Cole were rolling.

Pike climbed the last few feet, creeping low in the brush until he crested the ridge. The van was thirty yards away. He broke out the FLIR and scanned the area. The FLIR wouldn't read a human through

363

metal, but Pike wanted to see if Vincent was under the van.

The image in the view screen was a landscape of grays and blacks. The colder something was, the darker its image. The hotter, the lighter. The van was a shimmery gray shape, lighter than the background because of heat it absorbed from the sun. The sky above the horizon was black.

No one was hiding beneath or near the van.

Pike swept the FLIR toward the turnout. Nothing. He expected to find Vincent on the rise above the turnout, but no one was in the weeds.

Pike lifted out his cell, and whispered again.

"Give me three extra."

Pike changed position to try a new angle, but again drew a cold read. No one was in the brush by the road, or along the turnout.

Pike slowly examined the surrounding slope. He checked the ridge from Mulholland to the van, then the uphill rise in the background, and that's where Pike found him. The screen showed the bright gray shape of a man lying under a mound of sage, facing downhill in a prone sniper's position. Pike lowered the FLIR, then checked the sage with his binoculars. The man was invisible in the sage, but Pike soon found the unnaturally straight edge of a rifle barrel sticking out from beneath the branches. A lovely place for an ambush.

Pike lifted his phone again.

"He's on the rise above the van. Rifle."

Cole whispered back.

"How long do you need?"

"Two minutes."

"We're almost there. If we stop, he'll see us, and wonder why we're stopping."

"Two minutes."

Pike dropped back down the slope and crabbed fast along the finger past the van and up the back side of the rise. He glimpsed the Prius turning onto the ridge as he crested the ridge, but slowed to maintain his silence.

The gray mound of sage was now ahead of him. Pike lowered his rifle and pouch, and drew his .357. He eased closer, and finally saw a camouflaged leg beneath the bush.

I am here.

Pike quietly closed the distance until he was directly behind the man, then pushed the Python into Vincent's side.

Pike knew the man was dead by the stillness of the body, and realized in that moment the man was not Vincent.

Pike tensed, his muscles rigid against the bullet he expected, but the shot didn't come.

The corpse was an older man with matted gray hair and a small-caliber bullet hole in his temple. Fresh kill, still warm with life. Bait.

Then Pike heard Dru shout, and William Rainey call her name.

* * *

DANIEL

Daniel studied the distant slope through his rifle scope, whispering to himself.

"I got you, you sonofabitch. C'mon. Lemme see your lame ass."

The van was one hundred sixty-two yards in front of him. Daniel had paced it off. He was wedged between two dying trees on the south side of Mulholland, high on a sharp slope with nothing but rocks at his back and a long, steep slide below. Pike would never set up in a shitty, no-way-out spot like this, so he'd figure Daniel would avoid it, too. Which was why Daniel had picked it.

Daniel knew Pike was somewhere in the brush. Eight minutes earlier, he had caught a flash of gray movement on the next ridge, there and gone in a heartbeat. So now Daniel scoped the brush and the ridge and the area around the dead guy. Daniel wanted Pike to find the dead guy. Pike saw that rifle, he might take a shot, then Daniel would have him. Might try to get in closer, and Daniel would catch the movement. But so far, nothing.

Daniel had left the damned rifle sticking so far out of the bush, a cub scout could have found the stiff by now. Daniel was beginning to think maybe this Joe Pike wasn't as good as he had believed.

Tobey said, "The waitress, Daniel."

Cleo said, "Show him the waitress, waitress."

Tobey and Cleo were a couple of royal-ass pains, but sometimes they had good ideas. If he brought the waitress out early, Pike might change his position. Bang.

Daniel eased out his handi-talkie and called her like he had told her he would.

"You hear me?"

Her voice came back all tinny with static.

"I hear you. Is Willie here?"

"Come out. You're gonna go home."

Tobey said, "Here he comes."

Cleo said, "There he is, is."

Daniel thought they were talking about Pike, but they weren't.

The Prius swung around a curve less than a quarter-mile away. Daniel thought maybe he should tell her to stay in the van, but decided to let her come.

He keyed the talk button again.

"Get outta the damn van, woman. I'm not gonna hurt you."

The back door swung open as Daniel scanned the brush for movement.

ELVIS COLE

Elvis Cole was scrunched so far down in the Prius's back seat he couldn't see anything, not even the back of Bill Rainey's head.

"You see the van?"

"Yeah, we're almost there. Don't worry."

The criminal with a Bolivian cartel after him telling Cole not to worry. Perfect.

"Make sure that gun is hidden. He sees the gun, you're history."

"Relax, for Christ's sake. I'm fine."

They had given Rainey a gun. They had also strapped him into a ballistic vest. They wouldn't put him in Gregg Daniel Vincent's crosshairs with nothing.

Rainey said, "We're here. I'm turning."

They bumped off the pavement onto the ridge. A cloud of dust swirled in through the open windows. The windows were down in case Cole had to shoot.

Then Rainey slammed on the brakes.

"The fuck? She's already out. I was supposed to get out first."

Cole saw Rainey's head popping left and right, as if he thought Vincent would jump from a bush. Cole wanted to look, but knew Vincent would be watching their car.

"Take it easy. What's she doing?"

"Looking at me. She's waving her hands."

"Is anyone in the van?"

"I can't see."

"Check our sides. Look for Vincent."

"Fuck this! She's running! She's trying to get away!"

Rainey suddenly kicked open his door, and pushed out of the car.

"Rose! Ro—"

Cole heard the first shot.

Pike stood when he heard them shouting. Below him, Rose Platt ran toward the Prius as Rainey ran toward her, the two of them separated by almost one hundred yards.

Pike broke hard by a sage, trying to draw Vincent's fire. He cut back through the brush just as a sharp crack broke the twilight silence, rolling across the purple canyons. Pike heard the bullet snap past, then dove into the rocks, rolled, and kept running, breaking left and right down the slope.

Rose Platt and Rainey stopped at the sound of the shot. Then Elvis Cole came out of the Prius, and Rose turned back toward the van.

The second shot cracked into the slope at Pike's feet, but Pike saw the flash, and ran harder as he shouted to Cole.

"Other side. Trees up the slope."

Pike fired three times, long shots at the flash, hoping to flush him. Cole and Rainey turned to look for Vincent. Pike saw another flash, only this time Vincent wasn't shooting at Pike.

The bullet cut Rainey's left leg from under him in a spray of pink mist. He spun with his arms and legs out like a puppet and didn't scream until he was down.

Rose Platt screamed once, then lurched behind the van as another shot slammed into its fender.

Rainey sat up, shouted something Pike did not understand, then fired his pistol into the trees. Vincent flashed back. The bullet punched through Rainey's shoulder with another red cloud, but Cole had the flash now, and popped off five rounds.

Pike caught a flicker between the trees, Vincent moving downhill and gone.

Pike shouted again.

"Moving. Downhill."

Cole sprinted across Mulholland and disappeared down the far slope. Pike turned back for Dru, and saw her kneeling behind the van. He was torn in that moment, to go or to stay, but she was safe, so he ran to help Cole. Pike sprinted past Rainey, then up the steep slope on the far side of Mulholland into the trees.

47

DANIEL

Tobey whispered in Daniel's ear, tickling him with furry lips, pleading and urgent.

"You can do this, boy. You can get'm."

Cleo scurried in a circle, spinning like a dervish.

"You can do this, Daniel-aniel. Just like a zombie, ombie!"

"Open your EYES, EYES, EYES!"

Cleo spun faster.

"Kill, kill."

The rocks and rotten branches cut into Daniel's back. He took a tentative breath, and heard a wet popping in his chest. He coughed, but all that came out was aborted vomit.

Daniel looked at the blood on his hands.

"I been shot."

Tobey said, "Takes more than that to kill a werewolf, my friend, friend, friend."

Daniel touched his chest again, and looked down at the blood. He didn't feel so bad. He didn't even remember getting hit. He knew they were shooting, and the bullets were rainin' in, but he didn't remember getting hit. Maybe there was somethin' to this werewolf business after all.

Tobey said, "Find your gun, Daniel. Get the gun."

"Gun, gun."

Daniel felt around until he found it. The rifle was gone, but the pistol was still in his pocket. He flipped off the safety.

"I think I can still get that bastard, boys."

Tobey said, "Bet your ass you can, can."

Cleo said, "Bet your ass, ass, ass."

Daniel was feeling stronger. He took another breath, and felt pretty damned good. Even if he couldn't get the bastard, he was thinking he could get away. Plenty of houses around. Plenty of cars. All he had to do was get across Mulholland and into the canyon.

Daniel listened. He heard movement on the slope, but it was far away and below. They probably thought he slid farther down than he had.

Daniel pushed himself to his feet, using the tree to pull himself up as much as he pushed.

Then Gregg Daniel Vincent saw the arrow dude watching him. Dude didn't say a word, just stood there, no more than three feet away, gun at his side.

48

PIKE KNEW COLE WAS somewhere on the slope below. He could hear Cole pushing through the brush, and the clatter of sliding rocks as he worked sideways across the hill. Pike had seen Vincent moving downhill, so searching downhill was the smart bet, but Pike decided to lag back in case Vincent doubled back.

Pike let Cole move farther away. The farther Cole moved, the quieter it became, and quiet was good.

Pike listened for almost a minute before he heard a pebble dance through the trees on the slope somewhere in front of him. A soft cough followed the pebble.

Pike eased between the trees, and found Vincent in the rocks behind two dying walnut trees less than twenty yards from the road. Pike thought he was dead, but Vincent moved, then slowly struggled to his feet. Vincent was thin, but built strong, with a lean face and pockmarks and circles under his eyes.

He didn't look crazy, but what kind of person tortures and kills for lunatic drug traffickers?

Pike saw that Vincent was holding a gun, but waited to see what he would do. The man had a chest wound, but it was low and to the side. Pike had seen men fight on and win with their bodies turned inside out.

Then Vincent saw him, and his eyes sharpened like a couple of tacks.

"Look at this, boys. We got him."

Pike wondered who he was talking to.

"You Pike?"

Pike nodded.

"Wasn't you shot me. That other guy. You wanna call me an ambulance?"

"No."

"No? I'm bleedin' here, man. Get me some help."

Pike shook his head.

Vincent stared for a moment. He hadn't wanted the ambulance, and would have left before it arrived. He had hoped to catch Pike reaching for his phone or making the call. He wanted the edge.

Vincent said, "You never answered my question."

"What question was that?"

"Down south. You think we faced off before?"

"No."

"How you know that for sure?"

"You'd be dead."

"That's funny. The boys told me the same thing about you."

Pike said, "Who are you talking about?"

374

Vincent brought up his gun. Vincent was fast, but didn't quite make it.

Pike shot him three times in the chest, a tight little group the size of a clover. Pike walked over, picked up his gun, then shouted for Cole.

"He's down. Higher than you, twenty yards in from the road."

Pike searched the body before putting away his .357.

Cole called from below.

"You good?"

"Good. I'm going to Dru."

Dru. Pike said her real name, quietly and to himself.

"Rose."

Pike jogged back across Mulholland, and found Rose Platt squatting beside Rainey. He tried to understand what he felt about her, but he mostly felt nothing.

Rose stood when she saw him, and Pike slowed to a walk. She still had the eyes. Smart, and complicated, and completely alive. Maybe that's what drew him to her. The life in her eyes.

She said, "He's dead."

"I'm sorry."

Rose picked up Rainey's pistol, stepped over his body, and opened the Prius.

"Rose."

She smiled, the smart eyes glittering.

"You're not going to do anything."

Pike stopped, hoping she wouldn't push it.

"Put down the gun."

"I can't give up that kind of money. I lived like a rat for that money. Don't you see? It's mine."

"Three hundred thousand isn't that much."

She cocked her head, and something played in her eyes that left them angry.

"If only you knew."

She turned back for the car, and Pike started toward her.

"Rose."

Her gun came up, and Pike went for his weapon, but two shots snapped past him even before his gun cleared its holster.

Pike saw the bullets hit her, how her shirt puckered and rippled. He saw her eyes flutter, and her mouth open as if she didn't know what had happened. She reached up to touch something that wasn't there, then fell.

Pike did not go to her. He turned and saw Elvis Cole, still holding his gun. Pike saw the tears spill down Cole's face. Pike watched his friend cry, and neither of them moved.

49

DANIEL

Daniel saw dancing lights, and thought they were Cleo, but the lights raced toward him, right up to his face, then tromboned away fast as a gunshot, then snapped into hyper-sharp focus. Daniel saw branches. Branches, pine needles, twisted gnarled deformed warped scrub oak branches like arthritic fingers with leaves.

Tobey cried, "Daniel?"

Cleo whimpered, "Daniel?"

Daniel felt himself shrinking, like the world was growing larger and he was getting smaller, and Tobey and Cleo were farther away.

Daniel said, "Guys?"

Tobey said, "We're looking, dude, where are you?"

Cleo said, "Daniel, aniel?"

Daniel struggled to get up. He fought like a werewolf with a zombie eating its neck, but the zombie was winning.

"Tobey? Cleo? Where are you, you, you?"

Daniel tried to keep his eyes open, but the light grew so bright it turned black.

Tobey screamed, "Daniel, come back!"

Cleo shrieked, "Where is he, is he, is he?"

Daniel tried to answer, but could not, and knew the boys heard only silence.

Tobey said, "Cleo?"

Cleo said, "Tobey?"

"Going?"

"Gone."

". . ."

". . ."

Daniel no longer felt his body, or the earth beneath him, or the air that kissed his skin. He felt like nothing within nothing, and knew he would miss the guys, Cleo and Tobey, his only true and dear friends.

50

PIKE SAT ON THE Venice Boulevard bridge, looking down Grand Canal at the house. He sat on the concrete base of a light pole with his legs dangling down, which you weren't supposed to do, but Officer Hydeck was leaning on the rail next to him.

She said, "You spend a lot of time here."

Pike nodded.

"I see you here a lot, man. You doing okay?"

"I'm good."

Hydeck adjusted her pistol.

"What do you think happened to the money?"

"Rainey said they spent it."

"Who knows? Remember the North Hollywood bank robbery, those idiots with the machine guns? There's three-quarters of a million dollars those guys stole, nobody knows where it is. It happens. This criminal money? It disappears."

Pike didn't respond. Hydeck was okay, but he wanted her to leave him alone.

"Hey, you know what? I don't know if you've

heard yet. Those assholes who killed Button and Futardo? You hear about them?"

Pike knew Futardo had killed one of the men, but the other was missing.

"What about them?"

"They used to be DEA agents. The one who called himself Straw, his name was Norm Lister. That other cat was named Carbone. They worked the Rainey case way back in day one. Lister, he was fired, and the other resigned. I guess they decided to go for the gold, huh?"

Pike recalled the files he had taken from the Malibu. Most of the reports had been written by Lister.

Pike said, "Too bad about Jerry. Futardo, too."

"She was a nice gal. Posthumous Medal of Valor."

Hydeck finally pushed away from the rail. She settled her gun.

"Okay, bud, I'm history. I'll see you around."

Pike looked at her.

"Thanks for helping out like you did."

"You're not supposed to sit there with your feet hanging over."

Hydeck smiled, and ambled back to her car.

Pike went back to staring at the house.

The federal and state investigators from Louisiana had come and gone. They had interviewed Pike, and shared their information. They denied Rainey's assertion he had stolen only eight-point-two million, and related multiple accounts from arrested participants that Rainey had stolen a minimum of twelve million and as much as eighteen million dollars from the Bolivians. Pike believed them. Rainey's nature was to lie, so Pike had no doubt he continued lying until the end.

Rose Platt convinced him.

Pike swung his legs around, pushed off the wall, and walked to the Sidewalk Cafe. He sat in the outdoor area, two tables away from the one he had shared with Rose Platt.

The young waitress there, the one with the dimples, smiled when she saw him. He was a regular now.

"Green tea?"

Pike nodded.

Pike sipped the tea, and stared through the passing people at the ocean without seeing them or the water or anything else. He thought about nothing except the warmth of the tea and the cool ocean breeze, and how good the sun felt as it melted into the horizon.

When the sky was dark, Pike paid his tab and returned to the canals. He followed the sidewalk along the canal past the Palmers and checked Jared's window. Jared was up there, wearing headphones and swirling to a rhythmic, unknown beat.

Pike moved on, stepping onto the tiny dock at the back of Steve Brown's house, where the kayak hung on twin wooden posts.

Jared told him Steve Brown would return by the end of the week. Jared had also told him other things, like how Rainey would sit on the little dock at night, and how he'd go out in the kayak at night, and how Jared had twice seen Rainey wading in the canal at night.

Always at night.

But it was Rose who convinced him, with the things she said at the end, how she couldn't walk away from that kind of money, how she had lived like a rat for that money. The way she had looked at him when she thought she would lose it. *If only you knew.*

Pike wondered if she had known where it was, or if Rainey told her in the moments before he died. Either way, she seemed to be talking about much more than three hundred forty-two thousand dollars.

Pike ran his hands over the kayak's smooth skin, then lifted it from its hooks. Pike knew the money wasn't in the little boat because he had checked it two days ago, but he enjoyed the feel of its weight.

He set the kayak back on its hooks, then sat on the dock. It was a nice night, cool, and the water would be cold.

Eighty-five concrete stones lined the bank from one side of the property to the other, arranged in five staggered layers of seventeen blocks each. Pike knew this because he had counted them when the water was down. He had returned at night twice, and waded to the center of the canal, where, at its deepest point when the tide was high, the water reached his neck. He had probed the bottom and the plants that grew there in feathery clouds, then began checking the blocks to see if any were loose or movable.

Pike searched the blocks beneath and around the

dock first. It was the obvious choice, but Pike had found nothing. Each block had been firm and secure in its file.

There were more blocks to check.

Pike took off his running shoes and pistol. He pulled off his pants and sweatshirt, wrapped the gun in his pants, then put on his shoes and slipped quietly into the water. His muscles clenched at the first shock of cold, but the shock, like all pain, faded.

Pike resumed where he had left off, checked eleven more blocks, and was wading beneath the salt plants when his leg struck a hard object. He felt it with his foot, and realized he had bumped against a ten-inch pipe. He had seen pipes like it in the canals when the water was out. They were drains for rain and runoff collected from the alleys and yards.

The pipes he had seen were capped with a heavy mesh grid to keep out birds and animals when the water was low, but when Pike pushed his foot against this one, he felt the grid move.

Pike took a breath, pulled himself under, and found four nylon duffel bags stuffed up the pipe, tied together with rope. They did not come easily, but after a while Pike had them free.

Once he had them out of the water, he put on his shirt and pants, clipped the pistol to his belt, and headed back to his Jeep with the bags. As he climbed the narrow pedestrian bridge, an older couple stopped on the far side to let him pass.

Pike said, "Thank you."

The lady said, "Lovely night."

Pike's Jeep was on Venice Boulevard not far from the bridge. He dropped the bags in the shadows at the curb, then opened the rear hatch. When he went back for the bags, former DEA agent Norm Lister was waiting. Holding a gun.

"Good job, Pike. Very good. Excellent."

Lister looked ragged and dirty, like he'd been living in a car. He made a pushing gesture with the gun, as if he expected Pike to step back. *If only you knew.*

"Put the keys there in the bed, and walk away."

Pike didn't move.

"Did you know where the money was?"

"No, man, but I knew Rainey. I'm the guy who flipped him. It had to be close."

Pike thought back to the video. How they had tailed Rainey and Platt, watching their every move. Maybe hoping Rainey would visit the money.

Lister made the push again.

"Go away, Pike. This is your pass."

Pike looked at Lister's trembling gun, then at the man's nervous eyes. He thought about Jerry Button, and poor little Futardo, and Rainey and Dru Rayne who turned out to be Rose Platt.

"Lister. If you knew me as well as you knew Rainey, you wouldn't be here."

Pike shot Norm Lister in the chest, then walked over and shot him in the face exactly as he had shot Jerry Button.

Pike loaded the money aboard, leaving Norm Lister on the curb.

51

PIKE BROUGHT THE BAGS HOME, but did not open them for three days. He put them in his bathtub the first night, figuring they would drain. The next day, he moved them to his bedroom at the foot of his bed.

He brought them downstairs on the third day, and opened them for the first time since they'd been out of the water. He slit the plastic wrappers and stacked the packs of cash on the floor. There were a few packs made up of fifties and twenties, but most of the four-inch-thick packs held only hundreds.

It took Pike four hours and thirty-five minutes to count the money, keeping track of how much was in each stack on a yellow legal pad. When he finished, Pike leaned against his couch and considered the miniature skyscraper city spread across his living room.

William Rainey had lied to the end, telling them he only had three hundred forty-two thousand.

If only you knew.

Pike counted six million, seven hundred, fifty-five thousand dollars.

Pike wondered how much remained hidden in other locations, but didn't much care one way or another. He stared at the money for a while, trying to figure out what to do with it, then turned on ESPN and watched the late-night sports.

Later, Pike turned out the lights and went up to bed. He didn't pick up the money. He left the stacks on his floor like the meaningless paper it was.

52

MARISOL RIVERA
Angel Eyes

Father Art was doing better except for the fever. The color had cleared from his urine, but a low-grade fever remained. Not so bad, only a degree or so, but it hung on like bad debts, leaving him weak. Marisol was worried, so she came early and stayed late, and tried as best she could to keep Angel Eyes open.

That morning when she arrived, well before the counselors or kids, Marisol found a blue nylon bag on the ground beside the front door.

That the bag would be here was odd, but more odd was the card pinned to the bag. It was a simple white index card bearing her name.

She looked around to see if anyone was watching, like maybe someone playing a joke to see what she would do, but she saw no one.

She brought the bag inside and put it on her desk. The bag had a hefty, bulky weight, maybe eight or ten pounds, like it might be filled with chocolate.

Father Art called from the back.

"Is that you?"

"Yes, it's me. Who else?"

"Don't come back here. I'm on the toilet."

"Finish your business. Call when you're ready."

Marisol went behind her desk, studied the bag, then pushed her suspicion aside and opened it. The first thing she saw was another white card. The note on this card was simple.

Someone is watching.

53

ELVIS COLE

Cole saw the red mist. The dream woke him that morning, as it had the night before, and the night before that, and more nights than he remembered. Now, he stood on his deck on a bright empty day, thinking about how close they had come.

Muzzle flashes in a dingy room. A woman's shadow cast on the wall. Dark glasses spinning in space. Joe Pike falling through a terrible red mist.

Cole had not seen or spoken with Joe Pike since they left Mulholland Drive eleven days earlier. Even during the aftermath with the police, Pike had seemed more distant, as if he had withdrawn even more deeply into a secret place only he knew.

Cole had left messages, but Pike had not returned his calls. Cole had gone to Pike's condo, but not found him home. Pike could and would disappear for weeks at a time, but this time was different.

Two red-tailed hawks floated in slow circles over the canyon. Cole watched them, wondering what they were searching for. He had been watching them for hours. His cat sat on the edge of the deck, watching Cole watch the hawks. Bored.

Cole said, "Don't you have anything better to do?"

The cat narrowed its eyes, falling asleep, then suddenly stood and sprinted into the house.

Cole said, "Thank God."

Cole went to the sliders as Joe Pike came through the front door. Pike was framed in the door for a moment, surrounded by light, then he shut the door and came out onto the deck.

They stood face-to-face, neither of them speaking, then Pike pulled him close, and hugged him. Didn't say a word, just hugged him, and went to the rail.

After a while, Cole went to the rail, too, looking out at the canyon spread before them like a hazy green bowl.

"Good to see you."

Pike nodded.

"You want something to drink?"

"I'm good."

Cole held tight to the rail for support.

"We should talk."

"No need."

"She was going to shoot you."

"I know."

"I had to. I didn't want to, but I had to. You understand?"

Pike squeezed Cole's shoulder, then looked at the sky.

"Hawks."

"Been up there all day."

"It's where they belong."

Cole nodded, and felt the tears come. They watched the hawks together. Where they belonged.